YA...

NEW YORK TIMES BESTSELLING AUTHOR

GALENORN

IRON BONES

A WILD HUNT NOVEL

NOVEL

BOOK 3

A Nightqueen Enterprises LLC Publication

Published by Yasmine Galenorn
PO Box 2037, Kirkland WA 98083-2037
IRON BONES
A Wild Hunt Novel
Copyright © 2018 by Yasmine Galenorn
First Electronic Printing: 2018 Nightqueen Enterprises LLC
First Print Edition: 2018 Nightqueen Enterprises
Cover Art & Design: Ravven
Art Copyright: Yasmine Galenorn
Editor: Elizabeth Flynn

This is a work of fiction. Any resemblance to actual persons, living or dead, businesses, or places is entirely coincidental and not to be construed as representative or an endorsement of any living/existing group, person, place, or business.

A Nightqueen Enterprises LLC Publication
Published in the United States of America

Acknowledgments

Welcome to the world of the Wild Hunt. This is one of those series that has been haunting me for a while, and now, it's time to put pen to paper (fingers to keyboard) and let the stories out. And boy, do they want loose. By now, the world has fully taken hold in my subconscious and I'm absolutely loving writing this series.

Thanks to my usual crew: Samwise, my husband, my assistants Andria and Jennifer—without their help, I'd be swamped. To the women who have helped me find my way in indie, you're all great, and to the Wild Hunt, which runs deep in my magick, as well as in my fiction.

Also, my love to my furbles, who keep me happy. And most reverent devotion to Mielikki, Tapio, Ukko, Rauni, and Brighid, my spiritual guardians and guides. And to the spirit of the Wild Hunt, Herne, and Cernunnos, who still rule this world.

If you wish to reach me, you can find me through my website at Galenorn.com and be sure to sign up for my newsletter to keep updated on all my latest releases!

Brightest Blessings,
~The Painted Panther~
~Yasmine Galenorn~

Welcome to Iron Bones

Life isn't easy when you bear the mark of the Silver Stag.

I leaned across the stones and mushrooms to touch the powder and as I did, it felt like I was sliding my hand into a vat of pea soup. As my fingers touched the fine grains, a shock resonated through my body and I shouted, pulling my hand back. The tips of my fingers were blistered, and I stared at the rising welts, a quick burn rushing through my body.

I let out a growl, startled and in pain.

The next moment, something came rushing through the trees, on a direct line toward me. I looked around, frantic to hide. I didn't know what was coming, but whatever it was, my instincts told me I didn't want to be around to meet it. But there was no cover in the meadow. As I started to step over the circle, a shock reverberated through my body equally as unpleasant as when I had touched the powder and I pulled back.

Whatever was on the way was big. So big that the trees were beginning to sway. I rubbed my head as a wave of dizziness washed over me. My face felt flushed and my head hurt. With a moan, I fell to my knees and leaned forward, trying to cushion my head. I couldn't escape. All I could do was huddle on the ground, smelling the pungent soil through the verdant grass.

The creature was nearly on top of me now, the nearest trees were beginning to shake, and I tried to force myself to look but every instinct in me screamed Don't and so I closed my eyes tightly, waiting for the end.

The ground rumbled and I drew in a deep breath, the smell of mold and decay filling my nostrils. Everywhere, the scent of death surrounded me, and I whispered a prayer to Morgana.

Lady, if it's my time, please make it quick.

As if in answer, the world around me began to spin as I hunched low, waiting for the end.

Iron Bones: Book 3 of the Wild Hunt Series

Chapter 1

I STARED AT the stack of papers in front of me, my pen hesitating over the last signatory line. This was it. There was no backing out. I had made the promises, handed over the money, gone through all the documents, and this was the final step. Once I signed my name, the house was mine. I glanced over at Angel, whom I had brought along for support, and she gave me an encouraging nod.

Ember Sabina Kearney.

I wrote it with a flourish. Might as well embellish things a little. After all, this was an event that celebrations were made for. This was also one of the biggest purchases I'd ever make in my life. My condo had felt like a major step, but buying a house eclipsed it. I had already sold the condo, with the stipulation that we had until August 31 to move out. One month from today and it would be history, a part of my past.

"Congratulations! You now own a house. I'll walk this over to records and have this filed within the hour. Everything else has been taken care of." The escrow agent shuffled the pages, glancing through them, then tapped them into a tidy bundle, clipped them together, and slid them into a file folder.

Rachel Madison, my real estate agent, was thrilled. "I have your keys for you. The seller was so relieved she said to give them to you right now, given everything has gone so smoothly."

She slid them across the table, positively glowing. The house had been an albatross around her neck. It had been on the market for over a year by the time Angel and I had stumbled across it. The place had been a murder house, and *nobody* had wanted to buy the lovely upgraded home with two large lots, given its grisly history. Until I decided we could make it work.

I glanced at the escrow agent. "Good to go?"

She nodded. "It's not typical form to give you the keys on signing, but I foresee no problem, and that's the owner's choice. Enjoy your new home!" She swept out of the room, leaving the three of us sitting there.

I stared at Angel. "We did it. We have a house."

Well, actually, *I* had a house. I had bought it, but Angel would pay me rent. Right now, the condo was far too small for the two of us. The house was twice the size, with a massive lot, and we had been spending a lot of time mulling over colors and options for the garden. The house itself didn't need many renovations, but the paint job...well...it might not be the ugly "Bellevue beige" that was so popular around here, but neither did I want every room to be white. And the yard and fence needed major work.

"We have a month, but I'd like to get started right away. Why don't we take over supplies tonight so we can start painting tomorrow after work?" I was excited. I wanted in by mid-month because I really didn't like waiting till the last minute. Plus, we had already packed most of our things and the condo was in total chaos.

"Sounds good," Angel said, grinning. "I can feel the excitement bouncing off you like a frog on steroids." Her smile lit up her face. Angel was one of the few people I knew who could shift the energy of the room without saying a word. She was human, an empath, and she had been my best friend since grade school when she shoved me into a mud puddle. I had dragged her down with me, and after a brief tussle, we had become BFFs. Best friends forever.

"Well, it's not every day I take on a half-million dollars of debt." That wasn't entirely accurate. I had put down thirty thousand dollars on the house, and once I closed on the condo, I'd be filtering most of that money—about three hundred thousand—into the loan. But still, I was going to end up owing over two hundred thousand dollars on the mortgage.

"I suggest we celebrate. Why don't you let me buy dinner?" Angel asked, looping her arm through mine.

On that note, I pocketed the keys to the house, and we headed out for our favorite fast food joint, Anton's Fish Shack.

AN HOUR LATER, full of fish and chips, we stopped at HomeTown Central—a mega store with everything you could hope to find for home repair and renovation—and picked up the paint order I had put in the day before. Angel wanted her room to be an early-morning blue, while I wanted mine in forest green and pale lilac. We had decided on a warm apricot for the kitchen, and a watercress green for the living room. I chose the same sky blue Angel wanted for her bedroom to paint the office. We were starting there, and would tackle the rest of the painting after we finished the primary areas. As we carted all the supplies out to our cars, my personal phone rang.

I glanced at the Caller ID. *Crap*. My grandfather again. I sent the call to voice mail.

"Who is it?" Angel shaded her eyes as she watched me ignore the call.

"Who else? Farthing. My grandfather."

She nodded without comment. None was needed. My paternal grandparents had never once contacted me during the time I was growing up. They hadn't contacted me when my parents had been murdered, nor when I moved in with Angel's family. They hadn't reached out when I took on freelance investigating. Only now, after I went to work for the Wild Hunt Agency, had my grandfather decided to get in touch with me. I wasn't much interested in talking to him and hadn't bothered to answer any of his calls after we spoke the first time.

"I'll meet you at the house." I gave her a wave as I slipped into my car and eased my way out of the parking lot. For better or worse, I owned a house, and it was time to make it my own.

WHEN WE GOT to the house, we had a surprise waiting for us. Herne was there, along with the rest of the Wild Hunt Agency. Talia, Yutani—fresh out of his cast—and Viktor were standing beside him. Viktor was holding a big basket stuffed to the gills with sandwiches, pastries, and a couple six-packs of dark stout.

"We thought we'd help with the painting party," Herne said with a grin. He held out his arms and I slid into them, meeting his lips with my own.

He was a tall man, though the word "man" was misleading. Herne was as much of a human as I was. Meaning *not at all*. He was the son of Cernunnos, Lord of the Forest, and Morgana, Goddess of the Fae and the Sea. And he was my boyfriend. Gorgeous, with wheat-colored hair that hit the back of his shoulder blades, and muscled to just the right degree, Herne and I had been drawn to each other from the start.

"How did you know we were going to be here?" I

asked, resting my head on his shoulder.

"A little bird told me." He glanced over at Angel, who grinned. "I know you planned to wait till tomorrow night to start painting, but we decided to make the job a little easier."

They stood back, lining the path to the door. Angel and I glanced at each other.

"This is it. We own a murder house," I said, a shiver running up my back. I couldn't tell if it was excitement or nerves, or a combination of the two. But I loved the house, and I was determined to make it into a safe haven.

I marched up the sidewalk. The path was broken in places with grass and weeds popping through the cracks. Rhododendron bushes crowded in on both sides, overgrown, and at least eight garden spiders had made a tunnel of webs between the massive plants.

I paused, looking around for a stick. I found a small twig on the ground and used it to bring down the striped arachnids that wove their massive webs between the branches. The orb weavers were fat and all shades of green and brown, and they quickly scuttled off as I broke through the anchor lines of their webs.

"Sorry, guys, but you need to find a new home," I said, watching as they hurried away. They'd be back within the hour, though. The critters were nothing if not tenacious. "I have the feeling we'll need to either keep a spider-stick at either end of the walkway, or cut back the rhododendrons quite a bit. Maybe even take them out." I didn't like removing plants and trees willy-nilly, though.

"You can move the sidewalk to skirt around them," Yutani said. The coyote shifter glanced around the yard. "Although that would look a little odd, with two rows of rhodies sitting smack in the middle of the yard."

I shrugged. "We'll figure it out."

I dashed up the porch. The steps and porch were in good condition, as were spindles of the railing that flanked the sides and front of the porch. I had already ordered a porch swing to be installed. The house was painted a navy blue with white trim, and the paint job was still relatively new. Angel and I both liked the color so we decided to spend our time and money elsewhere.

The roses were in bloom, crowding the porch on either side of the steps. We needed to cut them back, but for now, their heady scent filled the air as the deep burgundy blooms spread wide. Talia stopped to smell one of them.

"I love roses," she said, smiling. "They remind me of someone I knew once. He was a gardener, and he took care of his flowers like most people take care of their children."

As I inserted the key into the lock, Herne gave a quick drum roll on the side of the house, and then, the door was open and we spilled through the entryway. I glanced over at Angel.

"Honey, we're home."

She giggled. "Let's just hope we don't have any squatters of the ghostly kind."

I nodded, my smile fading. Chances were good we'd have something to contend with. The energy of the house was heavy, but we hadn't been able to ascertain whether it was because the house was haunted by actual spirits, or simply by the energy trapped in the walls. The murders had been gruesome. Murder-suicides usually were. A freakshow stalker had barged in and axed his ex-girlfriend and her grandmother in the kitchen, then shot himself. We needed to cleanse the energy of the house, but whether or not we would have to call in a professional, we weren't yet sure. Either way, we had some serious psychic housecleaning to do.

"Where do we start?" Herne asked. "Put us to work."

"Paint first, then we do the psychic cleansing. Why don't you set the food in the kitchen?" I motioned Viktor off to the right. "Bring all the supplies in to the living room."

The others made several trips carrying in the paint and supplies, while Angel and I did a quick run-through of the house to make certain everything was as it should be. I had already called a locksmith, asking him to meet us here, and he showed up as we were carrying in the last of the paint.

"Please, change all the locks in the house," I told him. "Even the internal doors. I don't want the same locks anywhere."

As he went to work, we gathered in the living room to sort out the paint cans. Viktor and Angel carried the various colors into their respective rooms while Herne and I spread out tarps. Talia and Yutani began the laborious process of taping off the windows and taking off the switch plates. As I knelt on the floor, evening out the tarp beneath me, I felt something pass by. I thought it was Herne, but when I glanced up, he was standing across the room, focused on taking down one of the light fixtures. I blinked, deciding it must have been my imagination.

"Hey, we didn't buy any ladders." I realized that we had forgotten to add stepladders to our list of necessary supplies.

"I have two in my truck." Herne stood, dusting his hands on his jeans. "I'll get them." As he headed out of the room, Talia laughed.

"You *really* didn't think that we were going to let you two cope with this on your own? You're part of our family now." Her long silver hair was pulled back in a braid, and this was the first time I had ever seen her in jeans. She was wearing a tank top that showed off her well-defined arms. Talia might look like a woman in her early to mid-sixties, but she was still a harpy under the permanent glamour, even if she didn't have most of her native powers.

I sat cross-legged on the floor. "You know, even though neither one of the Fae Courts will accept me because of my mixed blood, I consider myself lucky. I have had three families in my life. My parents, then Angel and Mama J., and now—you guys."

The sting of being rejected by my own people hurt less and less with each year, which was why the request to meet with my paternal grandparents weighed so heavily on my mind. They were Dark Fae, while my mother had been Light Fae. My parents had been brutally murdered for daring to fall in love. I had come home after school to find my mother and father butchered, the floors soaked in their blood. I *knew* my grandparents were behind it, though I never could prove it. If I had been home that day, I probably would have been killed, too. The Fae weren't squeamish about killing those who crossed their rules. And my very existence was enough reason for them to consider me a rule-breaker.

Talia put down her roll of painters tape and sat down beside me. In a show of affection, she reached out and took my hand. "Seriously, we're glad you and Angel came to work for the agency. You two brought a much-needed spark into the company. And you make Herne happy. He's been a friend of mine for hundreds of years, since long before we brought the Wild Hunt over from the UK. I've never seen him seem so at ease."

She spoke softly, but I noticed Yutani glance over at us. I still hadn't fully forgiven him for the backhanded compliment that he had given me over a month before, when he had implied that he was surprised I was good at my job. But I was trying to let it go. He caught my gaze and nodded, a rare smile crossing his lips. He was altogether too serious, more than was good for him.

"Thanks," I said, looking around the empty room. I suddenly felt exhausted, and I lay down on the tarp, crossing my hands behind my head and bending my knees. I crossed one leg over the other as I stared at the ceiling.

"Feeling a twinge of buyer's remorse?" Yutani asked.

"Maybe. No. I think it's actually weariness. The whole process is tiring and right now, I just want one of those beers that you brought, but I feel too tired to get it." As I spoke, Herne entered the room, carrying both stepladders, one on each shoulder. I stared at him. "Good gods, you're strong. Anybody ever tell you that?"

He snorted as Yutani took one of the ladders from him and leaned it up against the wall.

"All the time, babe. All the time. Hey, the locksmith finished and I paid him. He's gone. I put the receipt on the counter. Now, get up, woman." He strode over to me and reached out for my hand. I gave it to him and he pulled me to my feet. "We're about to paint your living room and you aren't going to lie there and play supervisor."

I laughed, dusting my hands on my jeans. "Fine, then. I'll just be too tired for any nook-nook tonight."

"*Nook-nook*? Is that what we're calling it now?" he asked. He handed me a paint roller. "What color is the ceiling going to be? We need to paint it first." He glanced up at the top of the walls, frowning. "Why didn't you tape it off?"

"Ceiling's the same color as the walls, so it doesn't matter."

"Yes, my love, but you have crown molding, and that does need to be taped off on both sides unless you plan on painting it."

I blushed. "Yeah, I guess you're right."

Viktor and Angel reemerged from the upstairs. Viktor was half-ogre, and he was tall enough to almost reach the ceiling with his arms outstretched.

"I'll do it. Give me a roll of tape." He shouldered one of the stepladders and carried it over to the wall. As we watched, he made quick work of taping off the crown molding, and I stared, open-mouthed, startled by how quickly the half-ogre could move. He was burly, and with his bald head, looked like a rough-and-tumble biker. Or bouncer. Or maybe thug.

Angel motioned for me to join her in the foyer.

"I might be imagining it, but I think I felt something upstairs. Something jostled my elbow, like when you're walking down the street in a crowd. I looked around, but there wasn't anybody close by, but I definitely felt a presence and it wasn't just a cat spirit or anything like that." A worried light shone in her eyes.

"I felt something too," I said. "But I wasn't sure. Did you get a sense of what they wanted? Whoever *they* are?"

She bit her lip, shaking her head. "No, but I did feel a sensation of antagonism. Whoever it is, they aren't happy the house is full."

So we had visitors after all. I had learned over the years to rely on Angel's premonitions and intuition. She was accurate most of the time. I took a deep breath and motioned to the stairs.

"Show me where you felt it."

She led me upstairs to my bedroom.

Just peachy. We had an uninvited visitor and they decided to park themselves in *my* room. I walked over to the window and gazed down at the side yard. We considered our backyard to be the lot next door. I had a master bath, and there was a Jack-and-Jill between Angel's room and the third bedroom, then another half-bath downstairs. We also had a sparsely finished basement, which wasn't included in the square footage but which we could fix up and make livable.

As I leaned against the window frame, looking down at the side yard, which was overgrown with all sorts of bushes and plants, a sharp slap between my shoulders jolted me forward and I managed to catch myself before slamming into the window. I whirled to see Angel's horrified face as she stood across the room.

"What the hell?"

"I saw a blur behind you, and then you went hurtling forward." She held out her hands, closing her eyes. "Whoever did that, knock it off." Her tone shifted from concerned to pissed. It took a lot to make Angel angry, but when something triggered her, it was best to be downwind.

I glanced around, trying to pinpoint anything that stood out in the room. "Listen, we own this house now, and you're not welcome to stick around unless you play nice. *Whoever* you are."

At that point, a sound to the side alerted me and I ducked as the lid from one of the paint cans flew off and sailed across the room like a Frisbee. It passed by me, right where my neck would have been.

"Mother pus bucket!" Whatever freakshow ghost this was, it meant business.

Angel shouted as the paint can suddenly rose in the air and lurched across the room at me, spilling paint everywhere on the floors. I ducked again, and while the can missed me, the paint did not. A wide splash of lilac splattered across me.

"*Fuck you, too.*" I was pissed now. Annoying us in our own home was rude, but we could deal with it. Trying to behead me, then covering me with paint? *Not* so forgivable.

There was a noise on the stairs as Viktor came racing into the room, followed by Herne and Talia. Yutani was hot on their heels.

"What the hell happened?" Herne looked around, staring at the paint can and lid and the paint that was splattered everywhere.

"We seem to have a visitor. Or rather, a temper tantrum–throwing spirit who seems highly incensed that we are in this house." I finished on a shout as I tried to wipe a glob of paint off my face, but all I succeeded in doing was smearing it into my hair and down my chin. "Fuck."

Herne was staring at me, his eyes glittering.

"Don't you laugh," I warned him.

"I'm trying not to." But he wasn't trying very hard.

"Hey, that damned ghost tried to behead me." I told them about being pushed toward the window and the flying lid and can, and that seemed to sober him right up.

"You're right, it's not a laughing matter. Paint is one thing, but when you're being attacked, that's quite another." The smile vanished off his face and he glanced around the room. "We need someone who can deal with ghosts, and we need them pronto."

"What about Kamaria?" Talia asked.

Yutani groaned. "Can't you think of somebody *else*?"

"Not if you want top of the line." She crossed her arms, then turned to Viktor. "Can you grab a roll of paper towels for Ember?"

He raced off, looking relieved to be out of the conversation.

"Who's Kamaria?" Angel asked.

Herne let out a sigh. "Kamaria is a medium. She's really good, but she's arrogant, and she can be annoying as hell. But we've had to call her in a few times to take care of matters for us and she's the best, if you need serious help. All right, give her a call, Talia."

"We were planning on cleansing this place after we painted," I started to say but Talia shook her head as she pulled out her cell phone.

"Nope. You don't want to wait. Not with a hostile spirit situation. For one thing, these events can escalate quickly. For another, do you *really* want to try to paint the house with something waiting to mess up everything you do, if not outright harm you?"

"Good point." I accepted the paper towels from Viktor as he returned. I headed into the master bath to try to clean up. As I ran the water, I stared in the mirror. I was absently thinking that the lilac color actually went well with my black hair, and that it was a good thing we hadn't opened the can of green yet, when the mirror fogged up. My stomach lurched. I didn't have the water running hot enough to steam up the glass.

The fog covered the mirror and I blinked, suddenly finding myself standing in a forest clearing. A circle about ten feet in diameter, the meadow was shrouded by a quickly growing mist.

How did I get here?

But my curiosity vanished, replacing by a growing sense of dread, as I felt something staring at me from the depths of the trees. Whatever it was, it was old and angry, and it was creeping around the perimeter of the clearing.

I looked around, trying to find my way back to the bathroom and the mirror, but all I could see were the trees. The sounds of the forest grew louder as night quickly approached. As stars began to appear overhead, I realized that I wasn't sure what to do.

I approached the edge of the circle, only to see that it actually *was* a circle created out of stones. Outside the stones was a ring of brightly colored fly agaric, and outside of the mushroom ring, another ring of a finely ground powder glittered on the ground. I squinted, for the fading light made it hard to tell what it was.

I leaned across the stones and mushrooms to touch the powder and as I did, it felt like I was sliding my hand into a vat of pea soup. As my fingers touched the fine grains, a shock resonated through my body and I shouted, pulling my hand back. The tips of my fingers were blistered, and I stared at the rising welts, a quick burn rushing through my body.

I let out a growl, startled and in pain.

The next moment, something came rushing through the trees, on a direct line toward me. I looked around, frantic to hide. I didn't know what was coming, but whatever it was, my instincts told me I didn't want to be around to meet it. But there was no cover in the meadow. As I started to step over the circle, a shock reverberated through my body equally as unpleasant as when I had touched the powder and I pulled back.

Whatever was on the way was *big*. So big that the trees were beginning to sway. I rubbed my head as a wave of dizziness washed over me. My face felt flushed and my head hurt. With a moan, I fell to my knees and leaned forward, trying to cushion my head. I couldn't escape. All I could do was huddle on the ground, smelling the pungent soil through the verdant grass.

The creature was nearly on top of me now, the nearest trees were beginning to shake, and I tried to force myself to look but every instinct in me screamed *Don't* and so I closed my eyes tightly, waiting for the end.

The ground rumbled and I drew in a deep breath, the smell of mold and decay filling my nostrils. Everywhere, the scent of death surrounded me, and I whispered a prayer to Morgana.

Lady, if it's my time, please make it quick.

As if in answer, the world around me began to spin as I hunched low, waiting for the end.

Chapter 2

"EMBER!" HERNE CAUGHT me as I fell.

I blinked, crying out as his arms swept around me, keeping me from cracking my head against the bathroom sink. He eased me over so I was sitting on the closed toilet seat and knelt beside me.

"Where—how...what the fucking hell?" I shook my head, trying to clear my thoughts.

"When you didn't come out, I got worried. I called but you didn't answer. So I opened the door and there was a weird mist swirling around you. Are you all right? What happened?" He helped me up, then guided me back to the bedroom where the others were waiting.

"I don't know," I whispered. "I was..." I held out my fingers. They were still blistered, all right, and they had been perfectly fine when I first walked into the bathroom.

"What's this? It looks like a burn. Is the water

heater temperature set too high?"

I frantically scrambled for some clue of what had gone on.

"I don't think so. I'm not sure, now." I eased myself onto the floor. The others surrounded me.

Angel rubbed my shoulder. "Tell us what happened."

I told them about the mirror fogging up and then finding myself in the forest clearing, about the triple-circle that had held me captive. I told them about the powder burns and the creature that had been heading my way.

"I thought I was dead. I have no clue what the thing was, but I knew that it was going to kill me and I didn't want to stick around to see it come through those trees." I felt like a coward saying it, but I had long ago learned that accuracy was more important than pride.

"Have you ever been in that forest before?" Herne asked.

I shrugged. "I have no idea. It looked like most of the forests around here. Old growth trees, tall fir and cedars dripping with moss. Thick undergrowth except for the ring I was in. But *my fingers*. Could I have really burned them on the water in the bathroom and not realized it?" I held them up, examining them. They hurt like a son of a bitch, and there was a rash that spread like a red bloom across them. It didn't look like a hot water burn to me.

Talia examined them, squinting. "I don't think the water was the culprit. Are you allergic to anything? That looks like an allergic rash, and there are a number of plants that can blister. Maybe some stinging nettle in the yard? Or could you be allergic to the paint? Do you think that's a possibility?"

"I don't think so. Not that I know of. If I was, the paint's all over me thanks to that ghost, so I'd be blistering on my face and neck and arms if that was it." I winced. My fingers hurt bone-deep, though the blisters had stopped swelling, at least. "I think they're about as bad as they're going to get." Frustrated, I gathered my knees to my chest, wrapping my arms around them. "Damn it. I never get visions. Not like this. I'd like to know what brought it on."

Angel had been silent. Now, she took one of my hands in hers and opened my curled fingers to stare at the welts. "I don't know about the vision, but I've seen these welts on you once before. Don't you remember?"

I frowned, staring at them. "No, I actually don't."

"We were in the park and a kid racing by on his bike knocked against you. You almost fell and you grabbed the nearest support you could reach, which just happened to be a cast iron bench." She tilted her head. "These look like the blisters you got from that. Even the red rash looks the same."

"I'll be damned. You're right." I stared at my hand. The injuries did look like iron burns.

The Fae couldn't handle iron, at least not in a couple of its forms. When it was blended with other metals, it wasn't so bad. For instance, steel didn't seem to be a problem. But for some reason, our bodies hated cast iron. Iron ore was also bad, and we didn't feel too good when we handled iron pyrite—fool's gold. In fact, if we were body slammed onto an iron bench or table and held down, the burns would kill us before too long. The allergy to iron was in our genetic makeup and we just had to cope with it.

"Iron. That powder that I saw in the triple ring! I'll bet you that was powdered iron!" I lifted my fingers to my nose and took a deep whiff. Sure enough, there was the faintest hint of metal. I sniffed again, thinking maybe I had talked myself into smelling it, but sure enough, the scent was there.

"Iron. Yeah." I frowned. "But that means I actually had to *be* there. I couldn't have been, though, could I have been? There can't be a portal in my bathroom." The thought that my bathroom might have a portal that could transport me to another realm was terrifying. What if I wanted to take a shower and found myself naked, deep in the woods, with a monster chasing me?

Herne headed over to the bathroom. I held my breath, waiting.

"Breathe," Angel said, touching my shoulder.

I slowly exhaled, smiling at her. "Thanks."

A moment later, he reappeared. "There's residue energy in there, that much I can tell you, though I can't find anything to trigger a portal to open. So, what do you want to do? Regardless, we should call Kamaria."

"I'll try her again. I was about to call her when Ember screamed," Talia said. She stepped to the side and pulled out her phone.

I glanced around the room. I had really wanted to get a good start on fixing up the house. Who knew how long it would take to get the medium out here?

"Let's try to get some painting done tonight. But if you have to use the bathroom, maybe use the one next to Angel's room?" I grinned. "Or take a buddy who doesn't mind standing there while you pee."

Viktor laughed. "I'm not sure I consider any of you good-enough friends for that, but what the hell. Let's get this room painted, at least. Did you want the ceiling the same color as the rest of the room?"

I shook my head. "The wall with the window is going to be the forest green. I want the rest of the walls to be lilac, along with the ceiling. The bathroom will be lilac, too. We'll need to get more paint, though, given that damned poltergeist wasted a can of it."

"Okay, tape off the one wall and we'll get started." Viktor motioned to Yutani.

"Dude, my arm's beginning to hurt," Yutani said, bowing out of the process. He had broken his arm when we were on a case up on Whidbey Island, and the cast had just recently been removed. He wasn't back to his full range of motion yet, but he was working on it daily.

Talia rejoined us. "I'll help. Kamaria said she can come over Thursday evening to check out the house. She'll meet us here at seven." She pocketed her phone and helped Viktor finish off the taping, then picked up one of the paint rollers. Herne insisted that Yutani and I take a break while the rest of them made quick work of the first coat of lilac in both the bedroom and bath.

Yutani was rubbing his arm.

"Does it still hurt?"

He shrugged. "Only when I overdo. Doctor wants me to ease back into physical activity."

"Take off your shirt and turn around."

Blinking, he obeyed. I sat on my knees behind him and began gently rubbing his shoulders, using the palms of my hands so I didn't hurt my blistered fingers. I was surprised by how muscled the lanky shifter actually was. I used my elbows to dig into the knots.

"Tell me if I hurt you. I'll try not to dig too deep. But man, you've got knots on top of the knots in your muscles." I could feel the resistance as I kneaded his shoulders. There were pockets of adhesions that felt like they had been there for years. "Dude, you need to start getting regular massages. You're a tangle."

Herne glanced over at us, and I had the distinct impression he wasn't all that thrilled that I was massaging Yutani's shoulders, but I didn't care. Yutani was in pain and I could help. I blew him a kiss and the veiled look vanished as he winked at me.

As they finished the first coat on the walls, I handed Yutani his shirt.

"Thanks, Ember. That felt really good." He gingerly rotated his shoulder, then let out a relieved sigh. "That took care of the spasm that felt like it was waiting to attack."

"As I said, find a good masseuse." I stood up, looking around. The paint definitely changed the way the room felt, even though the accent wall wasn't done yet, and it still needed a second coat. Without further ado, we trooped over to Angel's room. By nine-thirty, both rooms had their first coats of paint.

"Can we treat you guys to a nightcap?" I asked.

Talia shook her head. "Thanks, but I need to go home and feed the mutts." She had two greyhounds, and doted on them. She carried the brushes into the bathroom, Yutani following to help her. Together they washed out the brushes and changed the paint rollers, disposing of the foam coverings. We were set for the next night.

"You guys planning on coming back to help out?" Angel said. "Hint, hint."

Viktor snorted. "Of course. After what happened tonight, we're not going to leave you alone here until Kamaria figures out what's going on. Though I don't know if the ghost and the portal have the same origins."

"They don't." I didn't know how I knew it, but my gut insisted they were separate. "I don't know what that vision was, or how I got burnt with iron, but the ghost and the portal weren't connected. Unless the overflow of ghostly activity boosted the portal's ability to manifest. And that's a distinct possibility."

Angel stared at me. "How do you know any of that?"

"I don't. I'm making a reasonable guess." I grinned at her. "When in doubt, speculate."

She crossed her arms, giving me an indulgent look. "Okay, then. But I do think you're right, at least as far as any connections between the ghost and the portal are concerned. They don't have the same feel, if you know what I mean."

"Why don't we get out of here for now," I said, realizing that I was getting increasingly uncomfortable. "I don't want to be here too late, and I want to see what Kamaria has to say before we spend much more time here." As I said it, I realized that I was now frightened of being in my own house alone. And that couldn't be good.

HERNE RETURNED TO the condo with us. Angel rolled her eyes.

"Guys, can you try to keep it down? You think you're being discreet but I swear, when the two of you go at it, it's like sleeping in a room next to a cat in heat. Or I suppose the better analogy would be a rutting stag. Right?"

I blushed, but Herne just laughed. "We'll try. At least when you're moved into the new house, you'll have more insulation. And you're not quite on top of one another. So to speak."

"So to speak." Angel shook her head. "All right. I'm going to take a shower and then go to bed. Tomorrow's still a workday."

"I thought it was *my* job to say that." But Herne waved at her as she sauntered down the hall to her bedroom. "I think we all need showers," he said, turning back to me.

"Yeah, we do. But we'll have to wait until she's done. The water heater in this condo can only handle so many requests at once. Come on. You want something to eat?"

"You mean after dinner and the snacks we brought, you're still hungry?" But he was teasing. He followed me into the kitchen.

I stuck my tongue out at him. "Yes, so deal with it. The Fae have voracious appetites. I eat like a trucker." I poked around in the fridge, looking to see what we had in the way of leftovers. I didn't cook—that was Angel's department. Oh, I could make sandwiches, scramble eggs, or bake an occasional cake if I had a mix, but I didn't have anywhere near the talent that Angel did. I spied some leftover fettuccini Alfredo and pulled it out.

"Want some?"

He shook his head. "Not really, but I'll take a beer if you have it."

"Dark ale all right?" I didn't drink much and neither did Angel, but since our workmates had been coming over more often, we kept it around because all of them liked it.

"Sounds good." Herne accepted the can and sat on one of the bar stools as I heated up the pasta in the microwave. "So, what do you think the vision was about?"

I glanced at him as I waited impatiently for the bell to chime. Then I laughed. Microwaves had only increased the instant-gratification trigger in people. Human or Fae, it didn't matter. Three minutes seemed a long time to wait for a piping hot meal.

"I don't know, but it scared me. And I don't frighten easily. You know that." I hadn't wanted to broadcast just how worried the incident had made me in front of the others, but now, I let out a long breath and leaned against the counter. "Herne, whatever that force was, it terrified me. I felt like it was aiming directly at me. The thing was big and ominous and I was certain I was going to die."

"You don't think it was Blackthorn, do you?" He opened the microwave and carried my plate over to the table for me, pulling out my chair. Herne was all about the gestures, but it came naturally to him and didn't feel like a show.

I gratefully accepted the seat and stirred my noodles to cover them with the sauce. A forkful of heaven later, I leaned back and closed my eyes.

"Do I think it was Blackthorn?" We both knew the Ante-Fae had taken too great of an interest in me, but this had felt less cunning and more direct.

"No. Blackthorn's clever and smart, but he's like a spider weaving a web. This was brute force, and filled with anger, rather than hunger. Whatever it was, it hated me, and I'm not sure why. Thing is, I didn't get any sense of a *personal* vendetta. Just the will to destroy me. The desire to see me dead. Blackthorn doesn't want me dead, though if he ever got hold of me, that would be preferable to the crap he's capable of." The Ante-Fae had a taste for pain and I didn't want any part of the King of Thorns and his games.

"You're right. Blackthorn doesn't want you dead. Could it have been someone from the Light or

Dark Courts? They don't like you."

I thought about it for a moment. Herne was right about that. Neither the Light nor Dark Fae liked me. I was an abomination in their sight. In fact, my very existence offended both.

MY NAME IS Ember Kearney. My mother was Light Fae, and my father was Dark Fae, and that little fact got them both murdered when I was fifteen. I've hated both my bloodlines ever since because I knew full well that either the Dark or Light, or both, were responsible. The Fae don't like to acknowledge that half-breeds exist, but they take *particular* offense to the rare few who have mixed Dark and Light heritages like me.

Anyway, until a few months ago, I had been a freelance investigator. Then Angel's little brother disappeared and she asked me to find him. That led to a precarious situation that ended up with us both being recruited to work for the Wild Hunt Agency.

Now, here we are, helping to smooth out the wrinkles that the Fae Courts cause with their petty warring. In between, we take on whatever cases Herne decides we can solve. With Cernunnos and Morgana at the helm, we navigate the murky waters underlying the SubCult community, attempting to solve whatever situations are brought to our attention. Some cases are easy, some are dangerous, but one thing we can definitely say: the work is never boring.

I SHOOK MY head as I forked a mouthful of noodles into my mouth. After swallowing, I said, "No, I don't think it's the Fae. At least not this time."

"Maybe something to do with your grandparents wanting to see you?" He paused as I set down my fork, then said, "You're going to have to answer them sooner or later."

"Maybe, but later is better."

I wanted to sidestep the conversation. Herne wanted me to find out what they wanted. I, on the other hand, had no desire to see the people I blamed for my father's and mother's deaths. One way or another, I couldn't help but feel that both their families had been in on the kill.

"I'm not asking you to call them right now, but Ember, they're not going to go away. Your grand-father seems determined to see you." He paused again, but I said nothing. Finally, he shrugged. "Whatever the case, it's your choice. I won't press you any more."

"I'd be grateful if you didn't. If I see them—and that's a big *if*—it has to be on my own time, when I'm ready. I thought about it earlier today. I truly did, but I can't bring myself to call Farthing back. I'm just not ready to hear him out. Whatever he has to say to me." I finished my food and carried my plate back into the kitchen, rinsing it out and putting it in the dishwasher.

Herne joined me, wrapping his arms around my waist. He nuzzled my neck. "I love you, you know."

I leaned back against him, closing my eyes. "I love you too, you big lug."

We stood there, rocking gently back and forth, until Herne took my hand and led me toward the bedroom. I silently followed.

As I started to slide off my clothes, I could hear Angel's door open.

"I'm done with my shower," she called before her door shut.

I motioned for Herne to follow me into the master bath.

I stripped, dropping the rest of my clothes in a pile on the floor, and turned on the water, setting the temperature to a warm rainfall. The evening had taken a turn and the air felt stifling, like we were headed into thunderstorm weather. My hair was plastered to my head from both the remains of the paint and the sweat brought on by the adrenaline rush of the night. I stood back, staring at Herne as he pulled off his muscle shirt to expose his broad, smooth chest. He had chest hair, but it wasn't thick, and his abs gleamed in the soft lighting.

He was built, muscled to perfection, with a few scars that crisscrossed his back and sides. Even gods could get hurt. My stomach tightened as he reached for his belt and I held up my hand, motioning for him to stop. I padded forward, taking hold of the leather strap to slide it out of the belt loops. I dropped it on top of my clothes, then reached down to unbutton his jeans. As I slowly lowered the zipper, I could feel him pressing against the front of the denim, and a moment later, his cock sprang free, rising to attention, firm and hard.

I resisted the urge to touch him, and instead, placed my hands on either side of his jeans, pulling them down to the floor, where he stepped out of them. I was on my knees again, this time facing his groin. I licked my lips as I stared at him. I could barely fit my fingers around his shaft, and now, I closed both hands around him, bringing his cock to meet my lips.

I slowly pressed forward, creating suction, as he placed his hands gently on the back of my head. I tightened my lips to offer just enough resistance so that he had to force his way into my mouth. Inch by inch, I took him in, loosening my throat muscles so that I could fit as much of his meaty cock into my mouth as possible.

Herne let out a groan, swaying against me as I licked his shaft, then slowly began to slide my mouth up and down.

"Don't stop," he whispered, his eyes closed as he dropped his head back.

I sucked harder, licking his length, running my tongue along the ridge of his cock, and he let out a delighted laugh of pure joy as I worked him, securing my lips tightly around the head of his shaft. He tensed, and I paused, waiting.

"Stop! Get up, get in the shower with me, woman." His voice was throaty, and he reached down to take me under the arms and lift me up. He leaned down, pressing his lips to my left breast, sucking and teasing the nipple until it stiffened under the fluttering of his tongue.

I groaned and stepped over the edge of the tub, into the pouring shower. Herne joined me, reaching for the body wash. As I stood under the warm spray, he lathered me up, soaping my body, running the lather over my breasts and down between my legs, where he slipped his fingers into me, thrusting gently as I braced myself against the tiles.

"I don't think I'm dirty there," I managed to say, but he shushed me.

"Oh you are, my beautiful wayward dirty girl." He motioned for me to turn around. As he loomed over me, I slid back, straddling his cock as he penetrated the folds of my sex. He let out a groan, maneuvering his way inside me, firmly holding me by my hips.

I pulled away and knelt on the floor of the tub. He crouched behind me, once again sliding deep into me, thrusting hard as the water poured over us. I arched my back, grinding back against him as he drove forward. He picked up the pace, pumping harder. With one hand, he held my waist and with the other, he reached between my legs, finding my clit to circle the nub. I closed my eyes, the water streaming over my face, as my hunger for him grew. Every time we had sex, the bond seemed to deepen. Every time he was in me, it felt like I couldn't get enough.

"Harder," I moaned as he quickened the pace. He split me open, laid me wide, touched a place inside me that no one else had ever been able to touch. When he was inside me, it felt like Herne *knew me.* He knew me fully, knew every nook and crevice of my body and soul, and found none of it wanting.

He said nothing, just continued to drive himself into my secret recesses until I felt like I was at the edge of the cliff. He gave one final tweak to my clit and I lost my balance, tumbling over the edge, coming so hard I let out a shriek.

Herne growled, and then he, too, came. His orgasm caught me in its wake, rushing over both of us. We were poised, frozen, as the water streamed over us, and for a moment, I thought I could hear the crashing of the tides.

"WE'RE BONDING," HE whispered as we lay together in my bed. My hair was freshly washed and in a ponytail, and we were cuddling atop the sheets. "Can you feel it?"

I nodded. "Yes, I can. It feels like each time we have sex, we not only renew our connection, but strengthen it. Is this normal with you? I never really felt the same way before."

In fact, a couple of my lovers had died—one a victim of my freelance investigations, and the other of a heart attack during the act. A third had been a boyfriend but not my lover and he had been attacked by a goblin when he tried to help me after I told him to stop. Now, Ray Fontaine had turned into a stalker, convinced he was missing out on something by not being with me.

"I don't know whether this is normal. I have to say, most of the women I've been with have been content enough when the relationships ended. I seem to have a way of breaking things off that don't leave them in pain. Most of them. But Ember," he said, shifting so that he was staring into my eyes. "I've been with a lot of women over the years, but none have ever meant as much as you do. With you, it feels right." He stroked my cheek, then kissed my nose.

I wasn't sure what to say. There was still so much that I didn't know about him. Dating a demigod wasn't something that I did everyday.

"Whatever it is, I like it." I paused, then decided to bring up a potential landmine. "Listen, I saw your look when I was rubbing Yutani's shoulders tonight. Don't get jealous on me, Herne. I'm not a woman who juggles men. You should know that by now. But if a friend of mine needs a backrub or a shoulder rub, I'm going to offer them one, regardless of whether they're male or female. Ray Fontaine wants to own me, but what he doesn't understand is that *nobody* owns me. Not him. Not you. Not the Fae Courts. *Nobody.* Now, or ever."

I pushed myself to a sitting position. Herne rested his head on my lap.

"I know. Trust me, I do. But you also have to understand that if I claim you as my woman, I will do everything I can to make certain you're safe. If you ever want to be free, you have only to say so, but until then, in bed—and in my heart—you're mine. And only mine." He traced his fingers down my leg.

I shivered. The gods had their own ways, and I knew that Herne was easygoing, for the most part. But there was a hint of possession in his voice that told me relationships meant serious business to him. He really *wasn't* a love-'em-and-leave-'em sort of god. Or man.

"I'm yours," I whispered. "And you are mine. And for now, wherever it is that we're headed, I'm happy."

THE NEXT MORNING, after feeding Mr. Rumblebutt and spending some time playing with him, Angel and I took her new car in to work, while Herne drove by himself. She had been up in advance, fixing waffles and bacon. Fully fortified, we arrived at the office ready to face the day.

The Wild Hunt Agency was in downtown Seattle, on First Avenue. The city had aged well. It was beautiful, a mix of the old and the new, with wide tree-lined streets and a constant flow of foot traffic in most of the neighborhoods. But beneath the surface, the city had its problems. The population had grown till it spilled over into the suburbs.

The rich—both old money and the nouveau riche—had moved to the suburbs in the north and to the bedroom communities on the Eastside.

The Fremont and Broadway districts, like the downtown area, thrived with lower-income residents, who did their best to keep up the city that they loved.

There was a rhythm to downtown Seattle, a beat that was most apparent during the summer months. The streeps—the street people who hung out on the stoops and in the alleys and homeless shelters—brought their own culture, a continuous rhythm from the constant barrage of music and cars backfiring and the vibrant cacophony of mingled voices that echoed through the streets. From spring until the early autumn days, life poured out from open windows and on the stoops. Come the rainy season and winter, the city was quieter, more muffled.

Right now it pulsed, crackling and ablaze.

We parked in the parking garage down the street. There was never enough street parking so we rented monthly spots for a premium price. Angel and I had rented one between us, and when we both had to drive in, we took turns finding street parking.

As we drove past a group of three young men who were dancing on the corner, a box set out for spare change from passersby, they waved at us. We had seen them every morning the past few weeks, and they were actually quite good, providing a lively show. I suspected they were runaways. I knew they were some form of the SubCult, but I wasn't sure if they were Fae.

Both Angel and I reached into our bags and tossed them a handful of coins as we went by and they waved their thanks.

"Chill day, ladies," one of them said, bowing. "If

you want to see us dance, we be happy to oblige."
He was young, probably eighteen, and I wondered
how many doorways he had slept in during his
young life. He smiled at me, but there was a hunger in his eyes and it wasn't just for food. The boy
he looked beaten down already. I suddenly felt
lucky that Mama J. had taken me in when I was
orphaned. I had missed out on the street-life experience, and I was grateful for it.

"Thanks, brah," Angel said, then she paused,
turning back to them. "How old are you? For real?
And what's your handle?"

"I be Toby." He shrugged uncomfortably. "I'm
sixteen, mebbee. Jozey, here, he's my little bro—
he's fourteen. And Sha-Na, he's almost seventeen."

They were just kids. The three of them suddenly
took on a reality bigger than just being streeps.

"When's the last time you had a really good
meal?" Angel cocked her head, and I could see
Mama J. reflected in her eyes. Angel's mother had
run a soup kitchen once a week out of her diner,
and she had never turned people away who were
hungry. The streeps had known her and guarded
her restaurant from any looters, and they swept
around her like a cloak around a queen.

Toby shuffled a moment, then shrugged. "I
dunno. A week, two. I take care of Jozey and Sha-
Na." He motioned for the two others to stay where
they were and moved closer to us, lowering his
voice. "Sha-Na, he's not quite right. He doesn't
learn very quickly. I watch out for him and for my
brother. Sha-Na's our cousin."

"Where are your parents?" I couldn't help but

ask.

Again, Toby shrugged. "I don't know. My mother comes home once a month or so, if that. I don't remember my dad, and we dunno who Jozey's dad is. Sha-Na's parents kicked him out because they have too many other kids to feed." He paused, then his eyes flickered over me. "You're one of the Fae, right?"

I nodded. "And you and your cousin…"

"We're savines, but Sha-Na, I think he's half-blood."

That answered the question as to their ability to sing and dance. Savines were land-based sirens, but they weren't usually as nasty tempered as their aquatic cousins. They had a natural ability to charm, but tended to be more reclusive.

Herne joined us right then. I pulled him aside and told him about the boys.

"They need help, I think."

"So do a lot of people nowadays, but bring them with us. I'll talk to my mother. If anybody can figure out something to help, they can." He just shook his head and headed for the building.

"Hey guys, we might have some chores you can do to earn some money," I said. "And we have sandwiches—or we can make them. Come on."

The boys brightened up, and like a flock of lost ducklings, followed us into the building.

Chapter 3

THE WILD HUNT was housed in a five-story brick building, across the street from an array of fetish brothels. The brothels didn't start jumping till later in the evening, usually after we had left for the day. We took up the entire fourth floor, while an urgent care clinic was on the first floor, a daycare and preschool was on the second, and the third floor housed a yoga and dance studio. The fifth floor was still empty. The landlord was having a hard time finding anybody to rent it.

We got the boys settled in the break room and Angel was fixing them sandwiches, when Herne's phone rang. As he took the call, I headed to my desk and began to sort through the last of the paperwork that I needed to tie up. From the day we started work until about two weeks ago, Angel and I had been run ragged. The Wild Hunt had been swamped with cases, mostly private.

Although there *had* been a few incidents we had had to quash regarding the Fae. Now, I was on the last-gasp efforts to tie up the loose paperwork still floating around and I hoped things would die down for a week or two.

I had just started to process a few of the remaining forms when Herne popped his head into my office. "Break room. Immediately. Tell Angel to find another place for those kids. We have a code red from Cernunnos."

Fuck. Code red was *bad*. Code red meant emergency.

I dropped the file folder I was holding on my desk. "Where should I tell Angel to put them? They don't have any home, it sounds like. And one of them is special needs."

Herne groaned and waved me off. "I don't have *time* to find shelter for them right now. Tell Angel to rent them a cheap hotel room for a few days and we'll figure it out later. But right now, break room—*stat*." He vanished around the corner and I heard him talking to Viktor.

I left everything in a pile on my desk and grabbed my tablet, a notepad, and a pen, then dashed down the hall to the break room where Angel was talking to Sha-Na.

"Angel, we have an emergency." I motioned for her to join me in the hall.

"What is it?" She glanced back through the door at the boys. "I'm worried. I think Sha-Na has a respiratory infection."

"Herne wants you to clear them out of the break room *now*. He said for you to go ahead and rent them a hotel room, but we've got a code red."

She froze, staring at me. Neither one of us had worked on a code red situation since the first case we had been assigned.

"Uh oh. All right." She looked around. "Will Herne want me at the meeting?"

"I'm pretty sure that will be a big 'yes.'" I paused. "What about the urgent care clinic on the first floor? Send them there and ask the nurses if they can watch after them for us until the meeting is done. Pay for their exams, or something. That should take some time. If Sha-Na is sick, the others might be as well." I was pretty sure Herne wouldn't quibble over the doctor bills and if he did, then I'd pay for them myself.

Angel nodded. "Good thinking. I'll take them down there right now." She headed back into the break room, gathered the boys, quickly whispering to Toby, and then led them out of the room, over to the elevator.

A moment later, Herne exited Yutani and Talia's office, followed by the pair. Viktor trailed behind. I poured myself a cup of coffee and set out another box of doughnuts. The boys had eaten their way through the first one.

As we gathered around the table, Angel came dashing in.

"All set. The boys are getting exams." She paused as Herne gave her a puzzled look.

"Never mind," I said. "We'll tell you later. What's going on?"

Herne cleared his throat, focusing on his tablet again. "I just talked to my father and Morgana. We have a serious problem on our hands."

"What are they doing this time, and which Fae Court?" I knew it was snarky but it was par for the course. Code reds didn't usually happen with private cases.

"That's just it," Herne said, setting his tablet on the table. "This time, it's the Fae who are in some sort of trouble. This morning, Morgana received a plea from both Saílle and Névé. It seems that there are Fae in both courts coming down with a serious disease and it looks like it's spreading. It hits hard and fast, and Morgana's afraid it may turn into a plague."

I winced, my smirk vanishing. While my people were usually a bunch of assholes, even they didn't deserve this. "Why are they calling *us* in? We're not doctors or healers," I said.

Herne leaned forward, clasping his hands on the table. "It's still too early to tell, but the healers in both courts agree that they've never seen anything like this. It started a couple weeks ago, and it seems to be spreading. There have been twenty-five deaths in TirNaNog, and eighteen in Navane. And there are at least a dozen or more sick in each city."

"Forty-three deaths in less than two weeks?" Angel asked, her eyes wide. "Very few diseases ever spread that fast, at least among the human community. What are their symptoms?"

Herne glanced at his notes. "It seems to start with abdominal pain and a rapid heart rate. Within a couple hours of complaining, the victims were beginning to vomit blood, and their throats were blistered. By the time of death, they had blisters breaking out on their hands and faces, bleeding ulcers, and they were going into seizure."

None of us said anything for a moment, then Yutani broke the silence.

"Does this appear to be Fae-specific? Has anybody else been infected?"

"I don't know but I think not." Herne shrugged. "The fact is, the healers didn't realize until a day or so ago that the cases were spreading throughout both Courts. But when they couldn't come up with a solution and people started dying, the medics went to Saílle and Névé, who immediately went to Morgana. That's when they realized it was happening in both Courts."

I felt dutifully chastised. My snark had crept away to hide under the floorboards. I scratched my head. "How long between contact and death?"

"That's still being determined. TirNaNog has the time from first symptoms to death pegged at between four to five days. Navane, three to six days. So I am thinking it looks to be somewhere between three to six days, which gives us a median of a little over four days." Herne leaned back in his chair, staring glumly at the table.

"Why do they think we can help?" Talia asked. "This seems like a medical issue, not one we can do anything about."

"That would make sense except for a couple of things. One, the healers can't find any source of infection. It just seems to have spontaneously erupted. That's not normal. Two, the deaths run across the gamut—elderly, young, thin, fat, patients who were in good health to begin with, to victims who were sick as a dog to start with. The only common denominator is that everybody who got it is Fae. Full-blooded Fae. As to where we come in, Morgana is wondering if there's some concentrated effort to target the Fae communities, since they're the only ones getting sick. So far, no humans, shifters, half-blood Fae, or anybody else seems to be coming down with whatever they're catching. At least, not that they've picked up through the medical grapevine."

"So you think someone *planted* the disease to target the Fae?" It seemed plausible. There were plenty of hate groups and they weren't all made up of stupid *dogwoods*—the dumb good ole boys who clung to the past. But once again, there didn't seem to be much we could do about stopping a plague.

Herne nodded. "Yes, that seems to be the general consensus at this point. Morgana wants us to find out who started it and take care of them. We know it's not from either Court. The Fae may be petty but they're not stupid."

Viktor drummed his fingers on the table. "Where do we even start?"

"Névé and Saílle have agreed to meet with us at ten-thirty this morning. They'll have their healers there to answer questions, so we don't have much time to prepare." Herne paused, glancing at me. "We'll meet with them in an authorized way station. They refuse to come here, and they sure as hell won't visit the other's Court."

When I realized what he was saying, I shook my head. "*No*. I'm not going. For one thing, I'm Fae blood. I can be infected by whatever this is. For another, neither will welcome me in their Court. So you have to let me off the hook."

A pained expression slid across his face. "I'd agree with you, normally."

"But...?" I could hear the word all but falling off his tongue.

"But Morgana and Cernunnos have asked that you attend. Except instead of asking, it was more of an order. Morgana specifically *instructed* me that you are to accompany us." He looked like he'd rather be doing anything else in the world rather than giving me that piece of information.

I groaned, rubbing my forehead. "I suddenly have a horrendous headache."

"That won't get you out of it, I'm afraid. When my mother calls—"

"I know that." I cut him off, irritated. I wasn't pissed at Herne, but at the situation. "All right, I'll go. But don't expect me to be nice."

He let out a sigh. "My mother expects you to behave. Which means you will curtsey to the Fae Queens, and you will be diplomatic and polite. I'm sorry, Ember, but as a member of the Wild Hunt, you represent us."

I stared at him. "You want me to be diplomatic with people who killed my parents?"

"I'm not the one making the rules here." He paused, taking a deep breath before he lowered his voice. "Morgana specifically gave me instructions. If you don't like them, *you* take it up with her. You're *her* acolyte, not mine."

And that was enough to shut me up. I crossed

my arms, feeling churlish and powerless. And yet, he was right. I was pledged to Morgana, just as my mother had been before me, and when the gods ordered you to obey, they expected loyalty. That she was Herne's mother was beside the point. It wasn't his fault. I knew he would spare me this if he could.

He wavered, eyeing me cautiously. "Are we good to continue?"

"Yeah," I muttered. "Go on."

"All right. We'll head over to the Eastside to meet with the Queens—"

"Whoa, hold on. You mean the pair are actually going to be in the same room *together*? Should we take a contingent of armed guards to stave off open warfare?" Yutani asked.

I couldn't help but grin. Yutani caught my gaze, winking at me. Feeling mollified, I uncrossed my arms and straightened up. Like it or not, I needed to act like an adult.

Herne snorted. "You'd think, wouldn't you? They've agreed to act on a temporary truce... treaty...whatever you want to call it. There won't be bloodshed today, at least not at the meeting. If things get too tense, we'll call it off."

Viktor gave him a long look. "If those two get into it, we'll run like hell. Dude, they won't listen to *us*. They can't hurt us, given the covenant, and especially not when they called us in, but they can go at each other for blood."

The thought of the two Fae Queens rolling around in a wrestling ring flashed through my head and I began to laugh. I leaned forward, tears

pouring down my cheeks, but I couldn't stop.
The others stared at me, except for Angel, who
wrapped her arms around my shoulders. When the
laughter finally settled, I hiccupped and tried to
mop my eyes. Talia handed me a box of tissue, and
gratefully, I took it. My eyeliner had taken a beating, even though it was waterproof.

Finally, I let out one last hiccup and looked
around. "I'm sorry. I don't know why that seemed
so funny. I couldn't stop."

"I know why," Angel said. "Tension. You haven't
had to deal with the Fae except when you chose
to. Today, you have to face them and you aren't
ready." She glared at Herne. "How can you force
her to go? She's still suffering from PTSD."

Herne looked distinctly unhappy at being challenged. "I told you it's not my call. You want to
take it up with my mother, be my guest. But I
know better than argue." He shook his head when
she started to scold him again. "Stop. Angel, I appreciate you standing up for Ember, but Morgana
will do as she sees fit. If she thinks Ember needs to
be there, my mother has her reasons. I've learned
to keep my mouth shut. Once either of my parents
gets a bee in their bonnet, you might as well just
knuckle under and accept the inevitable."

I held up my hand for peace. "Angel, thanks, but
don't bother. Herne's right. I am pledged to Morgana and so far she's been easy on me, but I think
that's about to change. I owe her my obedience. I'll
cope with this. Anyway, if I can face the Queens
of Light and Darkness, then maybe I can face my
grandparents and tell them what I think of them."

I didn't want Angel angry at Herne. While I wasn't looking forward to this, I knew full well that he would have kept me out of the meeting if at all possible.

"If we can move on, then? We have to leave in a few minutes." Herne was quickly losing patience. I could hear it in his voice. We didn't argue often, but when we had, the impatient grumpiness had thrust itself forward.

"Please do," I said.

"Where are we meeting them? What way station is willing to host a meeting so fraught with the possibility of imploding?" Talia asked.

"All Waystations are required to host parleys when asked, but I think this will work well. Ginty's, on the Eastside, will be the meeting point. Both Névé and Saílle agreed. That's why we have to leave in a few minutes."

"Ginty's? Oh hell, yes. He can keep them in check if anybody can," Viktor said, laughing.

"Who's Ginty?" I asked. I vaguely knew about Waystations but never had reason to go into one.

"Ginty is a dwarf. As in *Lord of the Rings*, the Norse Eddas type of dwarf. The bar doesn't allow the use of magic inside, so when we go in there, no spells, no tricks. Got it?"

That made me laugh. "You mean to tell me that Névé and Saílle are going to show up at a bar named Ginty's that's run by a dwarf? That boggles the mind." I had never laid eyes on either of the Fae Queens, but the idea seemed preposterous. It was like hearing that the Queen of England was going to pop in at the local neighborhood pub. It just didn't track.

"Ginty is...how can I put this? He's instrumental in the history of the Fae. Though dwarves aren't Fae and they generally don't get along with either the Fae or the Elves, they're definitely one of the more important players in the SubCult realms. You just don't hear about them much because they act behind the scenes. Like the vampires, they have their fingers in a lot of financial pies, though unlike the vamps, they don't look for power through money. They're more about the actual wealth than the power that goes with it. They factor into a lot of the old-money businesses, and are fiscally conservative."

Angel and I looked at each other, blinking. I knew there were dwarves, just like I had known about ogres, but for most of my adult life I had avoided a good share of the SubCult realm except for those who hired me, and most of *them* were shifters. I was beginning to realize just how sheltered I had been, given my circumstances.

"Do we have to dress up?" Angel asked.

Talia laughed. "No, but don't show up with a grubby face, either."

"Angel, you'll stay here to mind the shop." Herne glanced at the clock. "Everybody else, let's go. I suggest we take two cars. Yutani, you and Viktor take your car. Talia and Ember can ride with me."

We scattered then, Angel looking visibly relieved. As I brushed my hair and touched up my makeup, she leaned against my office door.

"Will you be okay? I wish I could be there with you, but I'm kind of glad I'm off the hook."

"I have to be okay, don't I?" I put down my compact. "I wish I didn't have to go, but if Morgana wants me there, I don't have a choice." I stared at the desk for a moment. "I knew someday I had to face this moment. I don't necessarily mean meeting the Queens—not every Fae gets to meet the Courts, but...facing my fears."

"Just take it easy, okay?" She gave me a quick hug. "Don't lose your temper. Don't let them rattle your cage"

I nodded, gathering my purse and tablet. "I'll try, Angel. I'll try."

THE TRIP OVER to the Eastside was a breeze. Traffic was light, given it was nine in the morning and the rush hour was mostly over. Around the greater Seattle area, rush hour extended from about seven to nine in the morning, and from three until six-thirty each afternoon. Other times, traffic was catch-as-catch-can, sometimes bogging down, but mostly, fairly smooth.

We drove across the 520 floating bridge. One of the longest pontoon bridges in the world, it was a testament to the love of convenience, the massive spans arcing over Lake Washington.

"Where is Ginty's?" I asked as we reached the Eastside. "Is it in the UnderLake District?" Angel had lived there until she moved in with me. It was a dark area of town, with a lot of dangerous creatures, and UnderLake Park itself was creepy as

fuck, with a number of unexplained deaths attrib-
uted to whatever forces were lurking within.

"No, it's halfway between TirNaNog and Navane, on the outskirts of Woodinville." Herne kept
his eyes on the road, maneuvering around a stalled
car.

The cities of TirNaNog and Navane had taken
over the area around Woodinville, and the area
there was mostly inhabited by the Fae, just like
the Bothell area had an influx of shifters. No one
was ostracized from moving into those areas just
because they were human or any other race, but
here and there tensions flared that were difficult to
ignore.

The Eastside was a beautiful area. The intense
urban sprawl had given way as the Fae had built
up the natural environment again, blending it
seamlessly with housing and shopping develop-
ments. I had to give props to my people. They
knew how to preserve the environment, making it
possible for people to coexist with nature without
sacrificing their little luxuries.

We wound through the suburbs until we approached the outskirts of Woodinville. I cringed as
we passed A Touch of Honey, Ray's bakery.

"I hope he doesn't see us pass by," I said.

Herne cleared his throat. "*He'd* better hope he
doesn't see us pass by, for his own sake. I'm in no
mood to deal with him, and if he lays one finger on
you, I'll break him in half."

I blinked. Herne had tossed Ray around once
or twice before when he showed up at work and
wouldn't leave me alone, but he hadn't said much

about him otherwise.

"You really would do it, wouldn't you?"

"I would. He's had ample time to wrap his head around the fact that you don't want him around. You've told him to back off, and if he doesn't, *I'll* take action. I won't put up with anyone who thrusts themselves uninvited and unwelcomed into someone else's life."

Herne sounded so grumpy that I wondered if something else had happened to trigger it. Granted, Ray had quickly made himself into one of my least favorite humans, but I just had the feeling something was wrong.

"Are you all right?" I lowered my voice, knowing full well that Talia could still hear us, but it just seemed appropriate.

Herne hesitated, then shook his head. "Don't worry yourself over it. A private issue that I can take care of on my own. It's nothing to fret over, but thank you for asking." He glanced at me, blowing me a kiss. I knew he wasn't telling me the truth, but let it go for now. We all had our secrets that we needed to mull over in private, and he was no exception.

Talia leaned forward. "Not to change the subject, but I haven't been to Ginty's for several years. You think he's still got that gorgeous shifter acting as bouncer?"

Herne laughed. "I have no idea, but don't go wandering off looking for him until the meeting is over. We need to have all ears on board for this. I don't trust either Saílle or Névé to tell us everything we need to know, so listen for nuances, anything that sounds off-kilter or unsaid."

"We should have brought Angel. She'd know if they're lying." I frowned, wishing she could have come with us. She helped me keep myself grounded in a way nobody else did.

"Angel is the receptionist and she needed to stay back at the office. Each of us has our job for a specific reason, and Angel's good at organization and light on self-defense and fighting skills. That's the same reason Talia's a researcher, but Yutani doubles as a field investigator."

Talia sobered, a distant look in her eyes. "Don't be so sure, Herne. I may have lost my powers, but I'm still a formidable foe. However, I prefer to remain on the sidelines. I spent too much time on the hunt, angry." She paused. "I wonder, sometimes, if my powers suddenly returned, would I be the same Talia that I was before I met Lazerous?"

I was watching her in the rearview mirror. The distant look grew cloudier. "Who was Lazerous?" I had never asked Talia about the loss of her powers, though I knew roughly what had happened. We were friends, but not so close yet that I felt comfortable prying into such a personal subject.

Herne shifted, glancing at her in the rearview mirror, but she shrugged.

"I might as well tell you. You'd find out sooner or later. You can tell Angel. I know you two talk about everything, anyway. Lazerous was a liche—one of the undead, but he wasn't a vampire or a ghoul or a zombie."

"Liche are magical, aren't they?" I had never encountered one and never wanted to.

She nodded. "Yes, and Lazerous was a powerful sorcerer. Anyway, Lazerous lived—and died—in Greece over a thousand years ago. I was young, barely moved away from my mother's nest. I lived near what is now Mount Olympus Park. I was out hunting for dinner one night and didn't realize I was near an ancient burial site. It wasn't a church-yard in the traditional manner of thinking, but a creaking hulk of a mausoleum. Anyway, I was chasing a rabbit into the burial grounds, when I saw something move near one of the gravesites." She paused, rubbing her head.

"You don't have to talk about it, if you don't want to."

"Don't sweat it, girl. It's one of those memories that I'll never be able to shed." She let out a long sigh. "I lost track of the rabbit, but my curiosity compelled me to find out what was going on. My mistake. I came face to face with Lazerous as he was exiting from a marble tomb. He was the most hideous thing I had ever seen. He was a walking corpse with fiery eyes. His skin was desiccated, like a mummy without the wrappings. I can still hear the crackle as he moved, like old paper rustling on the wind. I had time to get the hell out of there, but I was young and foolish and full of my own pow-ers. In other words, I was like every other teenager who thinks they're hot shit." She laughed, though it sounded strained.

"I think we've all been there. Some of us more than others," I said.

"In my case, it changed my life forever. I flew down to land in front of him and he turned on me.

I guess he hadn't fed for some time because the next thing I knew, he was draining away my powers. I struggled to get free, and finally managed, but I could barely fly out of range. I landed hard on the ground and broke both wings. I eventually made it home by walking, dragging my wings on the ground. I don't know how long it took me—weeks, I think. My memory from that time isn't clear. It's as though a fog descended as the liche drained me. I don't know how I made it home, to be honest."

"I think we all have that instinctive drive that leads us home when things are bad. There have been one or two times I've driven by the house from my childhood without realizing what I was doing. I suppose I wanted to touch base with the past, to see if maybe it was all my imagination and my parents were still alive and living there, waiting to welcome me in."

Talia nodded. "Yes, *exactly*—the homing instinct. When I finally arrived home, my mother wasn't pleased to see me. Once we leave the nest, we're on our own. But she mended my wings. It took a long time for me to heal. At least a hundred years, they were still so broken and I was so weak. When it became apparent my powers weren't going to return, my mother kicked me out. Weakness isn't considered a virtue with my people, and neither is deformity. I spent a long time hiding in the forests. I tried to hunt, with some success, but I couldn't fly except for brief distances, and my screech had vanished along with my song. I could still sing, but I couldn't mesmerize or harm others."

"A harpy without her song is handicapped in more ways than one," Herne said softly.

"True, very true," Talia said, shifting to lean back in her seat.

"As a race, we don't get along together, and I was attacked by others of my kind when they realized I was vulnerable. So I learned to hide, and I taught myself how to fight with a sword and use a bow and arrow. There were times I thought that I'd go crazy, but I grew reclusive, and kept myself hidden. Eventually, time passed and the world began to change."

"How did you meet Herne?" I asked.

She laughed. "That's another story. I couldn't keep still, because there was too much chance of being caught. So I traveled, mostly at night, through the mountains and back roads. I left Greece and eventually I found myself up along the coast near the Strait of Dover. It occurred to me that maybe I'd have better luck across the water, so I stowed away on a ship. From there, I lost myself in the forests until one day, I happened to be chasing a doe when a massive silver stag raced through the area and intercepted me."

Herne's lips tilted at the corner, a gentle smile spreading across his face. "I'm grateful that I was out there that day. Otherwise, we might have never met."

"What did you do?" I asked.

"I stopped her from hurting the doe. The deer was pregnant, and well...baby deer grow up to make more deer. But as angry as Talia was, she didn't try to hurt me."

"I knew you were a god. I could tell," Talia said. "And when you offered to take me home for a good meal, my instinct prompted me to accept, although I had barely talked to anybody in months." She leaned forward to pat him on the shoulder. "He took me to his father's palace and that one night changed my life. I met Morgana, who took pity on me and offered me a new chance. My wings and talons scared people away. She couldn't restore my powers, but she could change my form with a permanent glamour."

It occurred to me how chance meetings altered our lives so often. If I hadn't been searching for Angel's brother, I might not have met Herne. Except Cernunnos had hinted that it was my destiny to join the Wild Hunt. Maybe Talia had been fated to meet Herne as well.

"What made you choose the form you did?"

"I thought about it a lot. If I chose to look forever young and beautiful, I'd constantly be fending off unwanted advances. I wanted respect. I wanted to blend in without being too homely or too pretty. I decided that an older woman, attractive but not too much so, still active and strong...that felt right. It would give me a lot of freedom in many ways." Talia shrugged. "Herne offered me a job with him, and I accepted. Morgana gave me freedom from both my broken wings and my natural shape. I had been given a second chance. A do-over, you might say."

"And you've been with the Wild Hunt since then?"

She nodded. "Yes. I've been through four human husbands, and five stepchildren. Countless dogs and cats, and once, when we were still in the UK, a horse. I doubt that I'll ever marry again, though I date. But I'm content in my own company and I love my pets, and I'm good at my job. So here I am."

I was about to comment when Herne pulled into a parking lot. I realized that Talia's story had carried us through the drive to Ginty's.

The bar was homey-looking, like a place that you'd go back to for not only drink and food, but for friendship. It was a standalone building, at the end of Way Station Lane, off of Paradise Lake Road near Bear Creek.

Ginty's had a rustic exterior, rough stained lumber with bronze trim, and it was a single story high. The parking lot was large enough to hold at least forty cars, and I wondered just how many people could fit into the bar. As we exited the car, the warm breeze filled my lungs with the scent of wildflowers from a meadow to the left of the bar. The steady drone of bees echoed even from where we stood, and it felt as though everything else—all the city sounds—had been muffled.

Herne looked at us, then back at the bar. "Well, are you ready to go meet the Queens of Light and Dark?"

I simply nodded, even though that was the last thing I wanted to do.

Chapter 4

YUTANI AND VIKTOR had pulled in right behind us. They joined us as we crossed the nearly empty lot to the front doors. The double doors were wood, with bronze handles—no wrought iron, no silver, which made them friendly to shifters, Fae, and vampires alike.

"Peace bind your weapons before we go in," Herne said.

I snapped the sheath closed on my dagger. Peace binding wouldn't stop us from drawing our weapons, but it would be obvious if we tried, giving the other party time to act.

As we opened the door, a very large man gave us the once-over. "You are now entering Ginty's, a Waystation bar and grill. One show of magic or weapon will get you booted and banned. Do you agree to abide by the Rules of Parley, by blood and bone?"

"We do, by blood and bone." Herne said, giving the hulking bouncer a solemn nod. "By blood and bone" was an oath essentially putting your own blood on the line, should you break your word. At risk? Forfeiting anything from a hefty fine to indentured servitude, depending on who was running the parley.

As we moved past him, toward the bar, I looked around.

The inside of the bar was as homey as the outside. The bar itself was polished mahogany with brass fittings and a granite inlay. The surface gleamed, polished to a high sheen. Booths skirted the edges of the bar, and a number of tables filled the center of the room.

A large rack of antlers hung over the center of the bar, and there were paintings of Mount Rainier and the other Cascade volcanoes scattered around the room. The walls had a log-cabin feel, though they were less rustic than most log cabins, and the lighting was bright enough so that all the wood didn't feel claustrophobic. A large picture window stretched across two-thirds of the front wall of the bar, and to the right and left, windows lined the upper third of the walls. A stairway behind the bar led up to a second floor.

I paused, frowning. "I didn't see a second story to the bar outside."

"That's because there isn't one. Not in this dimension. That staircase leads to private chambers that are under the sanctuary rule. Nobody is allowed back of the bar except those who come to parley, those claiming sanctuary, and Ginty and the wait staff. And even then, everybody who works here undergoes a number of background checks and security training." Yutani glanced around. "Not a very big crowd today."

"It's barely ten-fifteen," Herne said.

"What are the hours here? I thought most bars didn't open until noon or later." I glanced around, looking for anybody who might look like a Fae Queen, but mostly, I saw a few scattered shifters at one table eating pancakes, and a lone Fae woman at another, who was absorbed in a book.

"There's always somebody waiting to open the doors if a person arrives seeking sanctuary. But I think the regular hours are from nine A.M. until midnight. No booze served until noon." Herne motioned for us to follow him to the bar, where we situated ourselves on the stools.

"What's the difference between a Waystation and a sanctuary house?" I hadn't even been aware of the existence of either thing before six months back. I had kept my head in the ground far too long. Even though I wasn't interested in my people, I should have taken time to get more involved in the SubCult community.

Herne leaned across the bar to ring the bell that hung from the transom. Made from stained glass formed into the shapes of leaves and flowers, the transom was illuminated from behind. I wondered how many hours it had taken to create.

"You know how sanctuary houses are run by the United Coalition?"

I nodded. "Right, and all four groups that make up the coalition agree to the rules."

The government—the United Coalition, or UC—was composed of the Human League, the Fae Courts, the Vampire Nation, and the Shifter Alliance.

"Well, a Waystation is pretty much limited to the SubCult population, aimed toward those belonging to one of the SubCult—or Crypto—races, whereas a Sanctuary House is open to those of human blood as well. And usually, those seeking sanctuary at a Waystation are fleeing from some inter-Crypto skirmish."

"So, similar but with a slightly different focus. What does the UC think about the Waystations?" It occurred to me that they had to have some policy about them.

"They work with them, actually," Herne said, ringing the bell again. "Often, those brought into the Sanctuary Houses first seek shelter at a Waystation."

At that moment, a door at the back of the bar opened and a dwarf appeared. He was about four foot five, and burly as all get out. He had a blond braid that hung down to his mid-back, and a glint in his eye that sparkled like gems. He was a ruggedly handsome man, well-proportioned, and my first thought was that I wouldn't want to meet him during an altercation. He was wearing a pair of jeans and a polo shirt, and a pair of motorcycle boots. He grabbed hold of the bar, and the next moment, he was staring us straight in the eye. There had to be a running board back there.

"Herne, you old dog. Good to see you, my man." Ginty clasped Herne's hand and they gave each other a bro-shake, along with a grunt.

"I wish we were here for fun, rather than on business," Herne said.

"Yeah, I know. They're waiting upstairs in the meeting room. I don't envy you, lad. Not in the least." Ginty's voice was gruff, but a sympathetic look crossed his face. He glanced down the bar at the rest of us. "Viktor, Yutani, merry meet. Talia, how are you, sweet cheeks?"

Talia snorted. "Good as ever, Ginty. And it's good to see you, too." She winked at him. "Any time you decide to fly solo, just let me know." But she laughed as she said it.

"You know it, girl. But Ireland would have me by the balls if I thought of it."

Herne grinned as he introduced the rest of us. "Ginty, this is Ember Kearney."

"Before you ask," I said, "yes, I'm a tralaeth." Everybody blinked, but I mustered up my courage. "I've decided to just reclaim the fucking word and make it my own."

Tralaeth meant someone of half–Dark Fae, half–Light Fae parentage and was used as a slur, an insult that meant tainted blood. But I had decided that I wasn't going to accept it in that manner any more. I was who I was, and the purists of the Fae community could kiss my ass.

"Well then," Ginty said, a smile slowly crossing his face. "That makes matters easier. But be aware, Ember Kearney, I do not allow racial epitaphs to slung around the bar, so if someone uses that word against you in a way not to your liking, tell me."

I held his gaze for a moment, and in the depths

of his eyes, I saw time unfolding. Ginty was old, as old as the mountains that were his home. I had no idea where he had originally come from, but in those summer-blue eyes of his, compassion and understanding mingled with a glint of gold. He felt as solid as the mountains, and as sturdy as the tall timber of the forests. He searched my eyes and what he found, I could not know, but he seemed satisfied as he turned away to greet the others.

Herne reached out and stroked my hand.

"So, they are waiting for you. Shall we go up? I will join you, given I can best defuse any hostilities not permitted beneath this roof." He turned around to the door out of which he had come and called, "Wendy?"

A hulk of a woman immediately popped out. She was at least six-two, and her hair was bound back in a similar braid. She was golden brown, and wore leather pants and a tank top that fit her form so well I could see the six-pack beneath it. Her biceps put mine to shame, and she strode out to Ginty's call.

"Watch the bar. I'll be up in the meeting room with our guests." Ginty handed her the bar rag and Wendy said nothing, just nodded.

Herne motioned for us to follow Ginty as we headed toward the stairs. The steps were roped off, but Ginty waved his hand over the rope and whispered something. The rope opened on its own, then closed again behind us. I glanced at it as we passed by. It looked almost like a snake or some eel-like creature. I had the feeling it sensed my scrutiny, and I thought about touching it, but my hand wouldn't move and I realized that my self-preservation instinct was warning me to keep my fingers to myself.

There were four steps to a landing before the stairs turned to the left. Fog rolled through the passage as we ascended the staircase, and after a moment, it occurred to me that we should be at roof level by then, yet the steps kept going. I wondered what happened if somebody couldn't climb the stairs, but decided that they must have figured out some fix for that.

The walls of the stairwell were difficult to see, though the railing was easy to find. The fog rolled around us, a swirling vapor that tangled around our ankles and clouded our sight. I reached out, trying to touch the moisture in it, but it quickly became apparent that this fog was magical. It wasn't made of water vapor at all.

Another moment and Ginty vanished through an opening at the top of the passage, and then Herne, and then we were all through, standing in a long hallway. The hallway stretched three doors down on either side, to a door at the end that seemed to be glowing from behind the solid wood. Ginty led us to the first door on the left. There was a bronze glyph hanging off the doorknob, and he touched his hand to it. There was a click as the door swung ajar. The dwarf turned to us, gave us a nod, and pushed open the door.

THE FIRST THING I saw when we entered the room was a U-shaped table. On the left side, center, sat a woman who had to be Névé. She was dressed in pale green, a gossamer gown that swathed her in layers of translucent veils, embroidered with metallic gold flowers, and pops of red. Her hair was spun platinum, caught up in a tall chignon, held in place with a glittering emerald and diamond tiara. Emerald earrings hung from her ears, and a matching necklace. A solitary emerald the size of a silver dollar on a chain encircled her neck. Her eyes were dark, as brown as rich dirt, with flecks of gold, and her lips formed a brilliant red bow. She crackled with the smells of fire and summer heat and lightning.

To the right, opposite of Névé, sat Saílle. Where Névé was summer and heat, Névé was winter and ice. Saílle wore a silk gown, cinched at her waist with a low sweetheart neck that emphasized her bust. The silk shimmered with crystal beads that mimicked stars across an indigo expanse of sky. With every movement, the beads scintillated, scattering rainbow prisms. Saílle's hair hung loose and curling, a halo that surrounded her like a cloak. Black as my own, black as a raven, it cascaded down her back. She, too, wore a tiara, composed of brilliant sapphires mingled with diamonds, and around her throat was a choker—five strands of amethyst beads, and amethyst chandelier earrings hung from her ears. Saílle's eyes were the color of blue ice flecked with hoar frost, and the steady sound of the wind howling on autumn nights echoed from her aura.

I stared at them, unable to look away. I had never imagined what kind of power the queens of my bloodlines must have. I had imagined them merely as petty dictators, squabbling women in a perpetual catfight. I had never envisioned the amount of power that flowed through this room. The walls reverberated with their magic.

Herne was standing beside me, and even he seemed affected. He caught his breath as he gazed at the two Fae Queens, then bowed deeply, nudging me. I did my best to follow suit, all my anger fading as it was replaced by a healthy fear of what they could do to me. Viktor and Yutani also bowed, and Talia lowered herself into a curtsey.

Ginty, however, seemed less affected. He strode to the front, where he nodded, then took his place at the center. Herne followed him, along with the rest of us, and we took our places on either side of the dwarf. I sat beside Herne, while Talia, Yutani, and Viktor sat on the other side.

I couldn't bring myself to look at Névé or Saílle. Their power crept through the room like a thief, sneaking into every nook and crevice, surrounding every chair and filling every corner. It vibrated and sang, a resonant melody from Névé and a deep bass harmony from Saílle. Their powers clashed and collided, and yet they made up a single song that made me want to cry. My reaction both frightened me and humbled me. It frightened me because neither one of them thought I should exist. And it humbled me because they could snuff me out like a candle flame.

Ginty stood. He cleared his throat and held up

what looked like a golden wand with a dark crystal on the end of it. "I hereby declare the Lughnasadh Parley of the Courts of Light and Darkness, in the year 10,258 CFE, open. Under this mantle, all members are bound to forswear bearing arms against any other member of this parley until the meeting is officially closed and all members are safely home. I also remind the Courts of Light and Darkness that they are forsworn by the Covenant of the Wild Hunt from inflicting injury on any and all members of the Wild Hunt team, under the sigil of Cernunnos, Lord of the Forest, and Morgana, Goddess of the Sea and the Fae. Let no one break honor, let discussions progress civilly, and remember that I—Ginty McClintlock, of the McClintlock Clan of the Cascade Dwarves—am your moderator and mediator, and my rule as such supersedes all other authority while we are in this Waystation."

He paused, then held up what looked like an extremely long scroll, covered in fine print and appearing to be very old. "If you stay, you agree to the rules. If you disagree, leave now, or be bound to the parley. I have spoken, and so it is done."

I blinked. Essentially, Ginty had just given us the terms of service contract. By staying in our seats, we were clicking "I Agree."

Another heartbeat, and no one moved.

"Then, I open the parley to Herne, son of Cernunnos." Ginty put the wand back on the table and sat down again.

Herne cleared his throat and leaned forward in his seat. "The Wild Hunt is here at the bequest of Névé and Saílle. We know the barebones of your issue, but please give us an in-depth description of what has happened. I trust you have brought your healers with you so they might give us the facts as they know them?"

Névé and Saílle had been staring straight at us the entire time. Now, Névé reluctantly glanced at Saílle. The look on her face was unreadable but somehow, I didn't think she was thrilled to be here. She inclined her head at the Dark Queen.

Saílle returned the look and, again, the slow nod. She turned to Herne.

"My healers came to me a week ago when they first began noticing the problem. A strange illness had hit our populace, and lives were beginning to fall. At first, we thought it merely a few isolated cases. But then, people began to take ill at a faster rate, and each time, the end result was death. We've had twenty-five deaths so far, and we have at least another dozen ill with the same disease."

Névé waited a beat, and when it was apparent that Saílle had stopped talking, she said, "Ours is a similar story, only we've had eighteen deaths and we have twenty in the wards right now. Nothing our healers have been able to do has helped. It's obvious that something serious is wrong, and that our city is under siege. We had thought, initially, that it was an attack from TirNaNog, but they are suffering the same fate and we no longer believe that."

Saílle looked at her and, for the first time since we had arrived, spoke to her directly. "You thought we were attacking you, and we thought you were attacking us. Perhaps someone looking to set us on each other? It's obvious to me that both of our great cities are in danger from an outside source."

Herne held up his hand, then stopped, picked up the golden wand, and held it up. "What makes you think this is an attack rather than a natural outbreak sweeping through the Fae community?"

Neither Fae Queen seemed to agree.

Névé shook her head. "I would be more inclined to agree *if* my healers could identify the disease. But this contagion, whatever it is, eludes the scope of my medical community. M'Sáille, what of your opinion?"

Sáille shrugged. "The same. My healers have no clue what's going on or why the people are dying. The symptoms are violent and painful, and so those things alone bind me over to thinking that someone has planted it in the midst of our community."

"What are the symptoms?" Herne asked, motioning for me to take notes.

Sáille gestured to the man sitting next to her. "Val, if you would?"

The man stood. He looked around my age but I had the feeling he was far older. Once the Fae reached thirty to thirty-five, the aging process slowed. I would look like I did now for centuries to come, unless I allowed myself to get out of shape. But time's stamp would slow to a crawl, barely ticking along with the passing years.

Val bowed to Névé's side of the room, then to us.

"I am the lead healer for the Court of Darkness. To answer your questions, the symptoms of my patients have been a high fever, vomiting, and nausea. This leads into vomiting blood, abdominal pain, ulcerations in the back of the throat. Within a few days this turns into bleeding ulcers in the stomach, then seizures begin to break out. Blisters and boils erupt on the skin, and finally, coma and death."

"How quickly do the symptoms progress?" Viktor asked.

Val glanced at him. "The symptoms progress quickly, so quickly that we are powerless in the face of them. We've tried every remedy we can think of, but nothing has done any good. The disease is contagious, though we haven't yet pinpointed how it's spread. It doesn't seem to affect every person who comes into contact with those who are ill, and we haven't been able to pinpoint what factors make some more susceptible than others."

I thought over what he said.

Névé's healer—at least I assumed that's who she was—stood on the other side of the room.

"My name is Jena, and I'm the primary medic for the Court of Light. I concur with my colleague. That's precisely how the symptoms have been progressing among our people. We, too, have tried everything we can think of to stop or slow the progression, but to no avail. We have cordoned off the ill in hopes that we can prevent the disease's spread, but until we know how it's passed from patient to patient, I'm afraid nothing will do any good."

I cleared my throat, nervous about speaking. Névé and Saílle and their healers wouldn't take kindly to me, I already knew that. But I had thought of what seemed like an important question.

"Excuse me, but it occurs to me that the patients who initially contracted the disease had to have something in common. Do you have any clue of what they might have all done or ate, or anyplace they might have gone together. It might enable us to figure out where ground zero for the disease was."

Saílle stared at me long and hard. She looked offended, and I had the feeling she was going to ignore my question, but Val spoke up.

"After three patients came in with the same complaints, we started asking them where they had been. I first thought they might have some form of food poisoning and wanted to make certain that we put a stop to it. What I found out is that four of the initial patients attended Fae Day. That was the one common denominator."

"Fae Day. Of course," Talia said.

Fae Day was a local festival celebrated at the Farmers Market, located dead center between the TirNaNog and Navane. The Fae from both courts came together to eat and drink and play games and whatever else might be on the agenda. Although Fae Day was a truce festival when both Light and Dark agreed to lay down their battles during the day, I never attended. The generosity of spirit didn't extend to my kind. It was always celebrated two weeks before the festival of Lughnasadh as a pre-harvest festival.

I glanced at my calendar.

Today was actually Lughnasadh, so Fae Day had

to have been a couple weeks before.

A Celtic festival of sacrifice, Lughnasadh was considered the first harvest—the harvest of grains, and was a reminder that the grain god died at this time of year to sacrifice his body so that people might live through the long winters. It was celebrated by the Fae and humans alike, although most humans had long forgotten what it was. Time had a way of twisting festivals and so did conquering nations. I usually didn't go out of my way to mark it in any major fashion, but I always remembered what the day stood for.

"Who ran Fae Day this year?" Herne asked. "I keep meaning to attend one of these years, but it always seems to slip my calendar and Morgana, my mother, forgets to remind me." The way he casually dropped his mother's name was a power play. Even I could see that and I wasn't all that astute with politics.

Ginty frowned, glancing at a folder of notes in front of him. "Fae Day is funded by both Courts, but it's run by a neutral third party—a small organization handpicked by your mother. They're called the CMO—the Courts Management Organization. I'm not sure who's in charge at this point, but Morgana handpicks every person on there and they're all deemed acceptable to both Courts."

Névé let out a snort. "The CMO pokes its nose in where it's not wanted, but we aren't given a choice. It's part of the *grand* covenant."

"That *grand* covenant allows you to remain here and not be deported across the Great Sea," Herne said, a warning in his voice. His eyes flashed as he stood, staring at the Queen of Light. "Do not abjure that which my mother sees as necessary or you may find yourself on a boat sailing for home."

"Your mother. Yes, your mother would do *just* that. But, Lord of the Hunt, the Light Fae agreed to the covenant centuries ago, and we hold by it, even though we may not like it. The world was a simpler place when humans were fewer, and we were allowed to exercise our full powers." Névé turned to Saílle, smiling coolly. "What say you, Darkest Star?"

Saílle returned the smile, fox to the fox. "I say that we miss our old ways, but in this world, sadly, we must abide by agreements. However, one good turn deserves another. Let Morgana and Cernunnos have their day in the sun. The night still belongs to all creatures lurking in the shadows. And we never know what the future holds."

The tensions in the room bristled as a silent conversation seemed to unfold. I couldn't hear the words, but I could sense the implications and cautiously watched the three-way standoff between Herne and the two Fae Queens.

Ginty stood, holding up the scepter again. "*House rules*. Remember, all of you."

"Politics will never be far behind when it comes to the Fae, Ginty. Accept it and move on. But I suggest we continue on with the parley." Herne kept eye contact with the Fae Queens even as he answered the dwarf.

"Where were we, then?" Névé broke the impasse.

"Val was stating that the one thing the first few

patients had in common was they all attended Fae Day," Ginty answered.

"Oh, yes," the Queen of Light said. "Jena?"

Her healer nodded. "That was our experience as well. Our first four patients had spent the day at the festival. I asked them what they ate, in case it was food poisoning, and the only dish they had in common was the ginger chicken." She motioned to Val. "Did you, perchance, ask the same of your patients?"

Val blanched. "I did, and the answer is the same as yours. We had five initial patients, and they all ate the ginger chicken. That was the one thing we could find in common that they had consumed. Of course, it could be contact with someone there that set it off, but it seemed a place to begin. I assumed, for a few days, that it was simply food poisoning, but then the cases began to multiply and the latter patients hadn't eaten the food, and several of them hadn't even attended the festival."

I was furiously scribbling notes. We had a total of forty-three patients dead, another thirty-two sick, and nine of those had attended the Fae Day festival and eaten the ginger chicken.

"Who was the catering company, if anybody knows?" I looked up from my notes.

Val answered. "I asked. Apparently the Constantine Catering Express took care of the banquet. I don't have any information on them. After I realized not all the patients had eaten the chicken, I moved on to the assumption that the disease had to be caused by something else. Don't you think?" He looked puzzled. "I mean, if they didn't all eat the chicken, then it couldn't have been that."

Talia tapped the table with her pen. "I don't know. Something feels very odd about this. Whatever the case, do you think it's still spreading?"

"Yes," Jena said. "We took in another two patients this morning, so it's definitely contagious, whatever is causing it. And it's fatal. Which means if we don't find an answer, then both Navane and TirNaNog are in trouble."

Herne was sitting quietly, rubbing the scruff of his beard. He looked troubled, and a chill ran down my spine as it hit me just how deadly this disease was. I might not like my people, but this could put a serious dent in the populace of the Fae nation. Granted, most of the Fae didn't live in the two cities, but a great many did, along with the ruling courts. An infectious illness sweeping through the inhabitants could effectively put a dent in the entire Fae race.

"I think we'd better move quickly," Herne said. "We have to find out what this disease is, and then we have to find out how to stop it. My father's best healer will set to work on the problem, if he hasn't already. I assume you gave my mother your notes?"

Both healers nodded.

"Good. So we're a leg up there. What have you been doing to quarantine those who are infected? And their families. We have to curb this now."

"We've taken that precaution," Val said. "Trouble is, there are so many people the victims have come into contact with. And we suspect that the disease is contagious during the incubation period, which presents a whole new problem. In fact, given how few of our healing staff have come down with it, I'm beginning to think that the highest chance of contacting the disease is during the incubation period."

"That would make it even more lethal," Yutani said. "If you don't know you're sick, then why bother avoiding others?"

Jena nodded. "Right. We've been seeing that pattern, too. But this would mean putting both cities on quarantine, because we don't know who has come in contact with the victims. By the time they show up at our doors, they're already incoherent from the fever."

"Are any other races affected by this?" Talia asked.

Jena and Val both shook their heads.

Herne replied, "I don't think so. Mother said it seemed to be strictly confined to the Fae community. So we're facing a disease targeting the Fae, it's lethal, and it spreads quickly."

"In other words, a plague," Ginty said. "Or it might as well be that."

THE MEETING WOUND down from there, and we prepared to leave.

Névé had led her contingent out already, with the promise that they would keep in touch if anything new was discovered, and they agreed to keep us updated on the number of the sick. I leaned against the table, waiting for Herne, who was talking to Ginty. Talia, Viktor, and Yutani were gathering up their notebooks.

As I stood there, I realized that Saílle was heading directly for me. I straightened, reaching behind me to tug on Herne's arm. Strictly speaking, we were still under the rules of the parley, but who knew what the Queen of the Dark would think to do?

"Ember Kearney, I wonder if you would meet with us in another parley before you leave?" Saílle asked, looking vaguely irritated. Whether it was because of having to meet with Névé, or actually talk to me, I didn't know.

I frowned. "What about? What do you want?"

Herne turned around, his gaze fastened on the Dark Queen's face. "What do you want with Ember, Saílle?"

She ignored him, her focus glued to me. "I brought someone with me who wishes to meet you. He's attempted to get in touch with you for some time now, but you haven't answered him." Pausing, her lips curled into a feral smile. "I brought your grandfather with me, Ember. It's time you met your family."

Chapter 5

"SAY WHAT?" I stared at the brilliant queen. Her frost-chilled eyes frightened me, but even the power that emanated from her couldn't scare off the anger that I felt. "You brought *him* here? No. I refuse. I don't want to see him."

"Think carefully before you decide," Saílle said. Her words were precise, and I had the distinct impression there was a threat hidden somewhere. The Fae Queen was tall than I was, but as I stared at her, I realized we had similar features.

"Why should I see him? Your people—my *family*, on both sides, deny my existence. I'm a tra-laeth. My parents died for their love. They were murdered because they dared to say 'fuck you' to the thrones and to the hatred and the incessant warring." I was just getting warmed up. It felt like I had been waiting all my life for this moment. I wanted to rub her nose in my life, in the fact that

I was one of the things she hated most and—*too bad*—I was still here, I was still alive.

Saílle turned to Herne, who was watching the interplay cautiously.

"Talk some sense into her, son of Morgana. You may be her lover and she may be protected under the covenant, but I think it wisest if she at least hears her grandfather out."

Herne wrapped his arm around my waist. "Ember can make up her own mind. But I guarantee you, if she does meet Farthing, at the first sign that he's harassing her or threatening her, I *will* take action. And so will my mother."

The Fae Queen gave him a long, sultry look. For a moment, I thought she might be flirting with him, but then she let out a barely audible huff and turned back to me.

"Will you *please* meet your grandfather and hear him out? He has much he wants to tell you, and I promised him I would try to get you to listen. If only for your own sake."

It was then that I realized that no matter how hard I tried, I'd never be able to shake him. Not until I actually sat down and heard what he wanted to say. I had been running from him since he first contacted me, not wanting to hear anything that might stave off my anger. Not wanting to let the bitterness in my heart go. But if he had convinced Saílle to bring him with her to a parley, then there must be something important he wanted to tell me.

"Fine. I'll talk to him. But he gets *ten* minutes to make his case. After that, if I decide to walk away, then he never tries to contact me again. Promise me this, Saílle? And we meet here. He can say what he has to say in front of everyone. I won't be alone with him."

As I laid my conditions on the table, the Queen laughed, her voice rich and throaty. It wasn't a comfortable laugh. It put me in mind of hidden secrets and dark rooms and the laugh of somebody who had already won the war.

"Very well. I give you my word. Ten minutes. If you chuck him out after that, I will bind him to stay away from you." She swept back toward the chair she had been sitting in. "This should be rich. And before you ask, I have no idea what he wants. I didn't bother asking." She said the latter as though she were tossing away an old tissue.

"Are you sure?" Herne asked me, as Ginty went to fetch Farthing. "You don't *have* to do this."

I stared at the table. "I'm not sure about anything right now. But if nothing else, this will get him off my back. I don't want to talk to him, but if ten minutes can buy me a lifetime of peace..." I trailed off.

Herne tugged on his collar, then kissed me on the forehead. "I'm here for you. And remember: You are under the Wild Hunt's protection. If he tries to hurt you, I'll break him in two."

"That's what you threatened to do with Ray. Is that your standard fallback maneuver?" I laughed, grateful for the break in tension, as brief as it was.

The next moment, the dwarf reappeared, and behind him was a man who looked scarcely older than me, although there were centuries of experience in his eyes. He *felt* old, rather than looked it, and old in that ancient way, not as in "old and feeble." He was wearing a long black tunic over a pair of black trousers, belted by a silver sash. It was a simple outfit, but it looked expensive, and I had the feeling my grandfather was a man of means.

He strode up to stand in front of me and I saw that his rich brown hair was sprinkled with silver. Not enough to notice right off the bat, but it belied his age. His eyes were emerald green, the same as my own, but his smile was pinched, and I thought he looked like a cruel man.

"Ember, how are you?" He didn't touch me, didn't offer a hug or even a handshake.

"You have ten minutes. What do you want?"

I wasn't about to stand on ceremony. This wasn't some long-desired family reunion. He was an enemy, as far as I was concerned, although I recognized that I nursed an uncomfortable hope that perhaps something would shift, that he would offer me proof that he hadn't been part of my parents' deaths, that he had been locked in a tall tower, unable to contact me until now. The fairy tale of Rapunzel was alive and living in my heart.

He glanced around. "I see we have an audience."

"It's either this, or no meeting," Saílle spoke up from her chair. "And I admit to a certain amount of curiosity as to what you are up to, Farthing." The way she said his name was far too familiar for my tastes.

"As you will, Your Majesty." He shrugged and turned back to me. "I've come to offer you an olive branch, from your grandmother and me. Your grandmother is ill."

"Does she have the…" I started to say "plague" but stopped, not sure of how much he knew about what was going on.

"She has a bone disease that is destroying her mobility. She isn't on her deathbed, but there's no returning to health from this condition." He paused, and I detected only a flicker of movement to indicate that this upset him at all.

I thought over my response. I probably should say I was sorry, but that wasn't really true. The truth was, I felt numb as he spoke, and I knew I had gone into self-protection mode.

"What do you want? Do you want me to see her? Does she even *want* to see me?"

Only then did he shift, just enough to tell me that he was more nervous than he let on. "When she dies, I will be the only one left in our family, other than you. We have amassed a fortune. I have been doing a great amount of research and I have discovered a possibility that would benefit us all." There was the faintest hint of hesitation in his voice.

He started to reach out and I quickly took a step back. I needed space, I needed to be out of his grasp. I felt like I was a nice plump fly being courted by a mealy-mouthed spider. His energy wasn't evil per se—not in the way I had come to think of as evil, but it was grasping and greedy, and self-centered.

I glanced at the clock. "You have seven minutes left."

"Well, then, I'd better get on with it." He backed

away to one of the chairs and sat down, motioning to the one opposite him. "Please, sit."

Reluctantly, I joined him.

"I've been doing research and have come across an arcane ritual. It requires a powerful sorcerer, but we shouldn't have too much difficulty finding one."

"What kind of ritual?" I asked, still not trusting him.

"When properly performed, the ritual can strip away parts of your heritage. We can eliminate the Light Fae side and cleanse you, leaving you solely with the blood of your Dark Fae ancestors. *My* family's blood. Then, Ember, you can enter the Court. And you would become my sole heir, after your grandmother."

EVERY LIFE HAD its defining moments...marriage proposals, weddings, deaths, and funerals. Even great success or failure, every major event changes us. But when my grandfather told me he wanted to reach inside of me and rip out my mother's blood, it left me reeling.

I stumbled out of my chair, almost falling over it in my haste to back away from him. The echo of his words ricocheted through me.

"You might as well offer to tear off my skin, to put me in a different body. You want to make me into someone I'm not." I stared at him, loathing the sight of him.

"You're not just offering to transform my blood, but to change the core of what makes me, *me*. Regardless of the difficulties, regardless of the way I've been treated, I have *never* in my life wished I wasn't tralaeth. I have never been ashamed to be who I am, except when I see people like *you* claiming a connection to me." I stared at Farthing, unable to mask my disgust. "I can't believe you'd ask me to forsake my mother, to purge my blood of her history?"

He blustered, his eyes narrowing as he jumped up.

"Well, I'm not about to ask you to purge your father's blood, am I? Face facts. Wouldn't life be easier if you were to cross over to one side? *Of course* your grandmother and I want you to follow your father's footsteps. You could be the daughter we never had. Our son fell so far, like a star crashing to earth, when he lost his head over that tramp." His eyes glittered as he took a step toward me.

"How *dare* you speak of my mother that way?" I shoved a chair between us. "How dare you call her that? Don't you taint her memory with your slurs! The only thing you know is that she was your enemy because she was Light Fae. You not only persecuted her, but you turned your back on your son. On *me*. Did you also play a part in their murders?"

The anger of all the past years came sweeping back and I threw the chair to the side, feeling a wave of power rise up. I wasn't sure where it came from, but it buoyed me. I could hear the crashing of ocean waves.

"*Tell me,*" I said, lowering my voice to a growl. "Tell me, how did you manage it? Did you work alone, or in concert with the Light Fae? Who made the decision on how they were to die? Was it you? Did you give the orders?"

Farthing paused, an uncertain look in his eye. He cocked his head, cautiously eyeing the distance between us. "What does it matter? It's been fifteen years."

"It matters. Trust me, *it matters*. You stand there, talking about your son without a tear in your eye. Why this interest now? Why not when I was young? Why not when my parents died? Where were you then? Why so eager for me to join you *now*?" I wanted to slap him, but I kept my hands to myself. We were still under parley rules.

He flared. "Confound it, girl, just do as we ask. Cease with the infernal questioning. You don't need to know. You just need to obey."

I forcibly restrained myself, gripping the back of a nearby chair to keep my hands occupied. "Answer me!" I held his gaze, forcing myself to stand steady.

Farthing raised the ante. He slowly approached, raising his hand. I wanted to squirm away, but held firm. I refused to flinch. I refused to let him best me.

He slowly stroked my face, his fingers cool against my cheek. As he gazed down into my eyes, the challenge grew. We were in a battle of wits. A battle of courage. But I had one thing my grandfather didn't have. He might have experience, but I had very little to lose. I had already lost so much.

I reached up and grabbed his hand, holding it tightly, squeezing hard. He was strong, but I was stronger. His eyes narrowed as I tightened my grip.

"So, are you going to tell me what part you played in their deaths, and why you're coming to me now? If you don't, you might as well turn and walk out the door." I could feel Herne's eyes on me, but he didn't interfere. A sideways glance told me Saílle was watching, an avid look on her face. She was enjoying this.

"Are you so certain you want to know?" he asked, his voice unwavering even though I was seconds away from breaking his hand.

"I want to know the truth." I gripped his hand even harder and felt a faint snap as a small bone gave way.

Farthing didn't blink, didn't wince or budge. "Very well, but remember, *you asked.*"

I let go of his hand and stepped back.

"Your other grandparents worked in tandem with us. For once, the Light and the Dark worked together, and we agreed that our children had disgraced not only both families, but both Courts. Your maternal grandmother and I hired the sub-Fae to rid our families of both stains. Only *you* weren't there. Oh, we would have killed you too, if you had been. And that would have been an end to it. But you lived, and now you are here, and I offer you redemption."

And there it was, out in the open. Everything I had always suspected, laid on the table for everyone to see. My grandparents had worked together to kill my mother and father, and they would have killed me, too, had I been home.

I circled Farthing, a seething knot of emotions. Everything in the room felt distant except for the man who stood in front of me. It was as though we were the only two in the room, and everyone else fell away. I came to stop in front of him again.

After a moment, I finally found my tongue. "If we were not in parley, in a Waystation, I would kill you. The next time I see you, once parley is over, you're fair game. *That* is my answer to you."

He blinked, a look of surprise cracking the self-assurance. "Think carefully, Ember. Your grand-mother and I are worth a fortune. You would have a noble seat in the Dark Court." He glanced over at Saílle. "Your Majesty?"

Saílle didn't bother standing, but from her seat, she gave an impassive nod. "You would. If you undergo what he's suggesting, you will be accepted into the Dark Fae Court as his heir, and that in-cludes his seat in the nobility."

I couldn't tell what she was thinking about all of this. She had been watching closely, but her expression wasn't exactly that of a cheerleader. It was more like she was...*weighing* the proceedings, searching them for something.

"What do you think of this, Your Majesty?" I addressed her directly, not certain of the deco-rum involved but deciding that it didn't matter. I was already damned in the eyes of both Light and Dark, so my actions wouldn't make a whit of dif-ference.

Saílle blinked, looking surprised. She straightened, glancing over at Herne, whose focus was fixed on Farthing and me. Then she cleared her throat.

"I think this is a matter *you* must decide. No one can make your decision for you. I cannot imagine not agreeing to such a generous offer, but then again, I am biased." She was choosing her words carefully, that much I could tell.

I frowned, surprised that she hadn't instructed me to take the offer and run.

I glanced at the clock. Two minutes and my ultimatum would time out. There was no question, of course. I couldn't believe that Farthing had even bothered. That he could think I'd even be interested was beyond me, but narcissistic people never could look beyond themselves. In fact, most narcissists believed the entire world revolved around them.

"Here's my official, final, answer, Farthing. You can take your offer and shove it up your ass. I hope you and my other grandparents—on both sides—have painful, excruciating deaths. I wish for you an end as bloody as the judgment to which you sentenced my parents. If we weren't in parley, I would do the job myself, with no regrets. So take your ritual and your money and title and fuck off back to TirNaNog. Know forever in your heart that your granddaughter takes pride in being a tralaeth, and that I will count the days until your death."

I wanted my blade, I wanted to make him bleed. I wanted him to experience the same hurt and the terror that I had come home that day to find.

Herne must have seen the bloodlust in my eyes, because he slipped over to my side and wrapped his arm around my shoulders, moving me back a few steps. He then turned to Farthing.

"You have your answer. Leave now."

Farthing looked stunned and I realized that he had somehow expected me to jump on the idea. Did he truly think I was so miserable that I would leap at the first chance to be accepted by the Court? Or that I was so money-hungry that a title and a fortune would win me over?

"I ask you one last time. Will you come with us? Will you become one of us?" He ignored Herne, focusing his question to me.

"But Farthing, I already *am* one of you. Like it or not, I am full-blooded Fae. Light or Dark, it makes no difference to me, because I really don't see a lot of difference between the two Courts. The distinction is arbitrary. Fae against Fae, what does it all do?" I turned to Saílle. "What good does it do? The Dark and the Light have been fighting since the beginning of time, and why? What distinction can you make between the two?"

Saílle stood, rising up to her full height. She no longer looked fascinated, but a terrible expression crossed her face and I realized I had gone too far.

"I will not listen to a tralaeth disparage tradition. We were born at odds, and we die at odds. Our existences bring balance. We cannot help our natures. My people live in the shadows, we take our cues from the dark hues of the palette, from the clouds and the mist, the stars and the night and the frozen wastes. There will never be *one* Fae race. There can *never* be a blending that breeds true."

She motioned to my grandfather. "You have received your answer. Come. No more of this nonsense. Her taint can never be cleansed."

As Farthing left the room, Saílle paused, then turned back to me. "Even if you had accepted his offer, you'd never truly be one of us."

"I didn't ask to be. Just leave me alone, and others like me. Leave us to form our own community. You don't have to like us, you don't have to accept us, but stop hunting us down." I wasn't about to back down now. Herne and Ginty would protect me, at least here.

She gave me a considered look, then nodded. "I will admit one thing, Ember Kearney. You stick to your position. I had expected you to cave. You didn't. That alone shows courage of heart. Even though such courage breeds foolish decisions." As she swept toward the door, she called over her shoulder. "Contact us when you have any further information on the plague."

"We will," Herne said, frowning.

When Ginty was the only other one remaining in the room with us, Talia let out a long breath and dropped into a chair.

"I thought we were about to see bloodshed," she said. "You kept your temper better than I could have."

I stared at the door, trying to process everything that had happened. I wasn't sure how I felt, but it sure wasn't pleasant.

"Ember, are you okay?" Herne tilted my chin up.

I stared into his eyes, not certain how to answer. On one hand, the final crack in my heart had broken when Farthing had confirmed my suspicions about my parents' deaths. On the other, the entire incident had only increased my dislike of my own people. And yet a third factor crept in: the fear I had felt when Farthing had told me about the ritual. That part had actually bothered me most—that they had discovered a way to strip away a part of what made up the very bloodline, the very nature of a person.

"Did you know about the existence of the ritual he spoke of?" I asked Herne.

He shook his head. "I've never heard of it until now. I'm suspicious, though, as to whether it's actually possible."

"I hope not," Ginty said. "If it can be done, then anybody could use it as a weapon."

"My thoughts exactly," Herne said. "I'm going to have a talk with my mother about it. Perhaps she can forbid the use of it among the Fae. We need to find out if this is a new form of magic, who created it, and exactly how it's being used. I think we'll have to bring the United Coalition in on it."

I returned to the table. "I'm sorry I spouted off like that. I know we're supposed to be diplomatic, but Farthing pushed me to the edge. And over." I paused, then asked, "You guys think I made the right decision, don't you?"

"Don't doubt yourself," Yutani said. "What he asked of you went beyond the pale. And how he could expect you to just fall in line after what he told you about your parents speaks volumes about his character."

I nodded, slowly. "I have the nasty feeling this isn't the end, regardless of what Saílle told Farthing. I feel targeted now." And truth was, I did feel like I had a big red bull's-eye on my back.

"We'll watch out for you," Herne whispered, brushing my hair back away from my face. "As to your decision, I would have been highly disappointed if you had made any other."

"So what now? Where do we go from here?" I tried to shake off the past twenty minutes, to focus on what we had learned about the disease sweeping through the Fae Courts, but it was difficult. My grandfather's words kept running through my mind, coloring all of my thoughts.

"Back to the office," Herne said. "By the time we get there, maybe we'll be over the shock of what just happened." He turned to Ginty. "Thank you for holding the parley. I'll contact you when we get back to the agency so you know we've arrived safely and you can note the end of the meeting."

"My pleasure, Lord Herne, although I can't say I expected quite so volatile an event." Ginty showed us back through the hall, down the stairs, and to the front door.

As we headed out of the bar, Herne glanced at me. "Parley doesn't officially end until both parties are back at home. We always go directly to our home base after such a session. When every party has checked in with Ginty, the parley is officially ended. That way if someone is waiting to ambush the other party, it counts as breaking parley."

I slid into Herne's car and fastened my seat belt.

Talia patted my shoulder before she got into the back seat, following suit. All the way back to the agency, we said nothing, both of them allowing me to process my feelings in silence. But it would be a long time before I was able to process the fact that my grandfather had been willing to sacrifice my mother's blood in me, in order to make me acceptable in his eyes.

ANGEL WAS WAITING as we entered the lobby. Viktor or Yutani must have called her because she immediately jumped up when she saw me, the look on her face telling me she knew all about what had happened.

"Meeting in fifteen minutes after we all get situated. Grab whatever snacks you can to hold you through till we're done." Herne headed into his office, after a quick glance at Angel and me.

Angel steered me into my office, handing me an iced mocha. "Four shots," she said. "I thought you might need it." She paused, then dove right in. "Yutani called to tell me what happened. I don't even know where to start."

"Don't even try. If you think it's hard to know what to say, how do you think I feel? My grandfather offered to strip me of my mother's blood so I could be acceptable as his heiress. There's nowhere to go with that. And in the same breath, he admitted to hiring the thugs who killed my parents, to conspiring with my mother's parents on *her* death, and to planning to kill me—only I was late from school that day. I don't know how to process all of this. I really don't."

"Yutani said you threatened to kill your grandfather?" She sat down beside me.

I pulled a big sip of the mocha. "Not exactly. I told him that if we hadn't been in parley I would gut him like a fish, though, so I guess that's tantamount to the same thing. And if we hadn't been under Ginty's watchful eye and still under the terms of the parley, I would have done just that." I shivered, thinking how easily he had tripped my temper. I didn't like thinking of myself as a time bomb, but it was true.

"Is there any way you can turn this into a positive?" Angel had been studying the law of attraction for a while, and while it worked, there were times when even the biggest stretch couldn't bridge the gap between *totally fucked up* and *make lemonade out of lemons.*

"Um, no. If he ever comes to our door, I'll throw him headfirst into the basement. Or let Herne break him in half."

I closed my eyes, the adrenaline suddenly washing out of my body as I thought about what had transpired. I began to shiver, then a knot formed in my throat and I burst into tears.

"Angel, Farthing killed my father. *His own son.* Sure, he hired someone to do it, but he killed my father and he got away with it. There's nothing I can do." I leaned forward, resting my head on my desk, all the fear and horror of finding my parents dead on the floor flooding back.

Angel put her hand on my shoulder, murmuring to me. "Cry, Ember. Let it out. You know now. At least you know."

I heard Herne's voice from the door behind me, then Angel saying, "She'll be okay. Give us a few minutes?" Then she was back, her arms loosely draped around my shoulders as I shivered, feeling absolutely gutted.

"I wanted to kill him, Angel. I wanted to wipe that sneer off his face. I wanted to trample him, to scream, *How the fuck do you think I'm going to accept your offer now that I know what you're like?* But I didn't. I couldn't. And still, he was so sure. So *arrogantly positively certain* that the lure of money would win out. How could he think I'd ever consider such a proposal?"

She waited for a moment, then said, "Sit up. Drink your mocha."

Sniffling, I obeyed. "I feel devastated."

"You confirmed what you already knew, but the shock of knowing for sure can do you in." She paused, then said, "But tell me the truth. Did you really expect anything different?"

I thought about her question as I accepted the tissue she held out. Blowing my nose, I realized that there had been a part of me that had nurtured hope. The teenaged girl who had come home to discover her parents dead on the floor had wanted more.

"Logically, no, but there was a part of me that... hoped to find a grandfather who would miraculously open his arms and welcome me in. Who would say, 'Come home, a dragon kept us apart but we've slain him and you're free to come back home, into our hearts.' "

Angel tilted her head, smiling. "You wanted your family. But love, they *aren't* your family. Blood means nothing if hatred is involved. *I'm* your family, though, and DJ. And we love you. And at the end of the day, I'm here beside you, and Herne, and Yutani and Viktor and Talia, and we are your family."

I bit my lip, nodding. "I know," I said after a moment. "I just... Cinderella dreams. Fairy tales and fairy godmothers and the prince rescuing the princess. Sometimes, all those lies people tell their children still infect my thoughts."

"They're not all lies," Angel said, handing me a candy bar. "After all, you've found a prince, and I'm your stepsister, of a sorts, and we have a new home to call our own."

As I cleared my throat and bit into the chocolate, welcoming the rush of sugar and fat, I realized she was right. I had found my fairy tale, even if it was a slightly lopsided one. And the villains of the world, well, it didn't matter whether they were of my blood or not. In the end, they really didn't matter at all.

"Come on, let's head to the break room," I said, licking my fingers. "And Angel? Thanks. Thanks for always having my back."

"We have to stick together," she said. "It's a cold, brutal world out there."

Nodding, I followed her out of my office, toward the break room.

Chapter 6

HERNE HAD CALLED the meeting to order by the time I splashed cold water on my eyes and joined the others. Angel was talking as I entered the room.

"I found Toby and his brother and cousin a hotel room after they left urgent care. I have to say that Toby is a good egg. He's tried so hard to take care of the others. I'm worried about them, though. They're all malnourished, and his cousin is sick with a serious respiratory infection. It only affects savines, and it can be deadly. The doctors said he needs to be in bed for at least three weeks, but none of them will agree to go to a hospital because of the costs."

Herne frowned. "Unfortunately, in this economic climate, most hospitals probably wouldn't admit him without some way to cover the bill. You said you found them a hotel room?"

She nodded. "Yes."

"Tell them to eat what they want and not worry about the cost or how long they'll be staying. Meanwhile, I'll put in a few calls and attempt to find them a host family who will look after them." He scribbled a note on a pad of paper. "I think we have some Water Fae around that might take care of them. If worse comes to worst, maybe we can get the Foam Born Encampment to take them on. They're hippocampi, but they're Water Fae and they might be willing to look after the boys for a while."

"Will do." Angel paused, then added, "Thanks, Herne."

He flashed her a smile and it hit me that Herne spent a lot of his time looking out for the under-dogs of society, so much that he should probably add "social worker" to his resume. He truly cared, which was more than most people did.

"All right, Angel, I assume you've been filled in on matters?"

She shrugged. "I heard about Ember's grandfa-ther."

Herne arched his eyebrows. "Yes, well, for now, let's focus on the disease that's sweeping through the Courts. I want to organize our notes. Talia, can you start researching the catering company? An-gel, if you would, please collate all our field notes and start a file. This isn't exactly a typical case, but we'll just have to approach it like any other. We have forty-three dead bodies, almost three dozen more sick, and the possibility that somebody intro-duced this illness as a weapon. I suppose we just go from there."

After that, we began compiling our notes, and spent the rest of the afternoon tying up loose ends on some of our other cases.

I WAS IN the forest, trying to figure out how I got there. All around me tall timber rose into the heavens, dark sentinels against the night sky. Overhead, I could see the glittering stars of Caer Arianrhod, and I kept wondering if I was in Cernunnos's forest, in Annwn. I pushed through the undergrowth, trying to keep the waist-high ferns from slapping me with their fronds. Everywhere I looked, more shrubs and bushes sprang up, and I would think I managed to make it through one clearing when another patch of vegetation appeared to block my path.

I heard a rustle in the bushes behind me. As I turned, I saw a white fox dart past, then vanish into the foliage. Overhead, a flurry of crows winged past in the dark, as though they had been startled awake and scared out of their nesting trees.

My heart was racing as I tried to figure out why I was here. I couldn't remember what I had been doing, and I kept looking this way and that, trying to find Angel or Herne, or anybody familiar. But I was alone. I pushed through yet another thicket of bushes and suddenly found myself on a mountaintop, staring over a sweeping valley below. The night gave way without warning, and the sun rose into the sky, brilliant and blood red as though behind a thick layer of smog. It rose fast—so fast that I sank to my knees, dizzy.

As it approached its zenith, I realized I was staring straight at it and wondered that I hadn't gone blind. But there was something mesmerizing about the blazing globe that lit the sky ablaze. It arced over the sky, from east to west, as the valley below spread out in a panorama of bluish ice, glacial sheets that spread across the horizon. The mountain was steep, but there were more mountains in the distance, and they, too, were covered with glaciers, the ancient ice holding sway against the warming planet. They were silent, rising like monoliths, keeping guard over the world around me.

I managed to stumble to my feet, and was about to head down into the valley when the sun reached the west.

I can't have been sitting here all day. It's only been...

But it hit me that I had no clue how much time had passed. I might have been sitting there on my knees for an hour, or a month.

Once again, the night began to approach, the sunset blushing against the snowbound mountains. But this time, I was exposed, out of the forest, and my heart began to race. There was nowhere to hide. In fact, I couldn't find the forest. I was standing atop the mountain, and all around me, the ice sheets were melting, their waters racing in a mad dash to expose a quarry—a wide swath of rocks and stones sweeping through the valley.

A deep-seated fear began to take hold, and I looked for any place to hide. There was a large boulder to my left, and I crouched behind it, holding my breath as the sound of thunder echoed in the distance. Something was coming, out of the valley, and its footsteps shook the mountainside. I wanted to run, but there was no place to go.

I began to hear screams all around me, as ghostly figures rose up.

The Unseen.

Between worlds, they were, between life and death, caught forever in a loop from which they couldn't escape. I recognized them as *my* people— both Light and Dark Fae—and they were running, trying to escape whatever force was approaching. But as I watched, they fell, one after another. In droves they died, screaming and as they hit the ground, they vanished into mist, going down in ghostly flames. The smell of burning skin surrounded me and everywhere I turned, it clogged my lungs as the screams grew louder.

"Where the hell am I?"

I crept from behind the boulder I was hiding behind to another, bigger one, but a thumping of drums echoed from the other side of the mountaintop, growing louder. Something was coming. Something huge and dark and terrifying.

I had a feeling of déjà vu. *I have been here before. I've run from this before.*

I scrambled to remember, but my memories were foggy, and all I knew was that I had woken up to find myself in the forest. I knew my name was Ember Kearney. I knew that I was a tralaeth. I knew that I worked...*who did I work for?* I couldn't recall, it was on the tip of my tongue, but not quite willing to come forth.

Another rush of ghostly figures came racing by me, fleeing whatever it was that lurked in the darkness. I stared into the sky, awaiting the monster who was poised to come striding over the hill, traversing the hilltops, leaping from mountain to mountain with his great threshing rod, rooting out the Unseen who were dying around me, their misty forms vanishing as I watched.

There was a moment when I could feel him rising up. He was coming now, and he sensed that I was there, and that I was still alive, unlike the spirits who milled around me.

I stood. It was no use hiding, no use secreting myself behind a rock. The storm was gathering, and there was no shelter.

"EMBER, EMBER! WAKE up!"

Angel's voice echoed through the mist. I struggled to follow it, to follow her lead out of the ghostly fog that wrapped around me like a burial shroud.

"Ember!" This time her voice slid through the edges of the Phantom Kingdom and pulled me out, like a quivering baby from its mother's womb.

I shot up in my bed, screaming. "Don't let him get me! Don't let him catch me!"

"Ember, you're okay. You're here, in your bed.

Come back to me, love. Come back." Angel held my
shoulders, shaking me lightly until I opened my
eyes.

I was in my bed, covered in sweat, and she was
holding me then as I burst into tears and rested my
head on her shoulder.

"There, there. You're safe. There's nobody here,
nobody's after you."

I choked on the phlegm in my throat, coughing. She leaned over to my nightstand for a box
of tissues, handing me one, then she grabbed the
water bottle I kept by the bed in case I was thirsty
at night. I swallowed a mouthful of the cool liquid,
dabbing my eyes. Coughing again, I blew my nose
and pulled my legs up to my chest, wrapping my
arms around them and resting my chin on top of
my knees.

"Fucking hell, that was terrifying." I nervously
glanced around the room, but in the gentle light
of the bedside lamp, there was nothing out of the
ordinary. The shadows made me nervous, though.
"Can you turn on the overhead light?"

She obliged, flipping the switch to flood the
room with light. "Better?"

I nodded, blowing my nose again. "Yeah, better.
Was I screaming?"

"Yeah, pretty much. I had gotten up to take a
piss and I heard you screaming on my way back to
my bedroom. What the hell happened? Nightmare,
I assume?" Angel sat on my bed, folding her legs
into the lotus position. She leaned back, resting her hands on the mattress behind her. In her
pajama shorts and long sleep tunic, without her

makeup, she looked more cute than gorgeous. She didn't look thirty, that was for sure.

"No, I don't think so. Not exactly." I paused, shaking my head. "I think I was in the Phantom Kingdom."

Angel paled. "Phantom Kingdom? I've never heard that term before and somehow, I have a feeling that before you're done explaining it, I'm going to wish I never had."

I groaned and leaned back against the headboard. "I don't know much about it, but it's like the Dream-Time. It exists outside of time and space. There, all worlds can intersect—this world, the dream world, the spirit world. It's not limbo, but it's definitely a place where spirits wander who haven't gone to their rest. I'm really not clear on it, so that's about all I can tell you."

"What happened?" She settled in as I told her about the dream. "So, you didn't really know who you were. I mean, you knew your name but..."

"I knew my name and that I was Fae, but not much else. I couldn't seem to remember anything about my life."

"I hate to state the obvious, but do you think that the 'he' you were terrified of seeing represents your grandfather? Could this dream be triggered by what happened at Ginty's today?" Angel gave me an apologetic smile.

"I know it sounds all Psych 101, but that was a major shock to your system. Couldn't it just be a nightmare brought on by a combination of all the crap that went on? After all, the Fae were dying around you, and that's happening in TirNaNog and

Navane right now. And some ominous male figure that seemed huge was coming closer. Your grandfather would be an authority figure in terms of the way we usually think of grandparents, so he would be 'bigger' than life, perhaps?"

I thought about what she said. It made sense, but it didn't click the way things do when they finally fall into place. After a few minutes, I shrugged.

"I don't know, I really don't. But I'm sleeping the rest of the night with the light on. And a bag of chips in hand." I opened my nightstand and pulled out the half-finished bag of potato chips that I had stashed there. I offered Angel one but she shook her head.

"Thanks, but I'm good. If you need me, I'm just in the next room." She headed toward the door. "Do you want me to leave the overhead light on?"

"No," I said after a minute. "Just leave the small lamp on. It will be enough."

But as she shut my door behind her, I began to panic again. I slipped out of bed and slapped the light switch, once again flooding the room with light. I pulled out my tablet and began flipping through old shows on Vex—a streaming video service. After finishing off the bag of chips, I was calm enough to lie back down, but it was at least another hour before I was able to drop off to sleep again.

WE DRAGGED OURSELVES into work, me with a quint-shot latte in hand. Both Angel and I were tired, me from my nightmare and lack of sleep, Angel because she had apparently stayed awake for a while to make sure I didn't call out again.

Herne was waiting impatiently, a worried look on his face.

"Everybody into the break room. I have news."

As we entered the room, Ferosyn was sitting at the table, looking distinctly out of place. The Elfin healer was Cernunnos's eldest medic, though he barely looked old enough to shave. I glanced at Herne. He planted a quick, worried kiss on my lips.

"I'm sorry I didn't have time to drop by or call this morning." Sometimes Herne showed up to drive into work with us, or he would drop by for breakfast if he hadn't stayed the night with me. The house he rented was luxurious and spacious, but somehow we ended up at my condo more often than not. But even when he was busy, he usually called me in the morning.

"No problem. It was a rough night but I'll tell you more about that later." I nodded at Ferosyn. "I take it we have news?"

"Yeah, and it's not good. I have no idea what the hell to think, but maybe we can brainstorm ideas. Long story short, what he's found makes it clear this is an attack on the Fae." He had pulled his hair back into a long braid that hung down his back, and he was wearing a green muscle shirt that showed off his biceps and tight black jeans that hugged his ass.

"I wish we had time to cuddle," I whispered. "And I'm not talking just sex. You smell so safe to me." And he did. Herne smelled like sun-ripened cornfields, and wildflowers in the meadow, and the scent of cinnamon and spice on a cool autumn evening. All things wild and free and wonderful, and yet everything that spelled hearth and home, wrapped up tight together in a very handsome package.

He gave me a curious look. "You're really shaken. What happened?"

"As I said, I'll tell you later."

"Not Ray—" The threat was implicit in his words.

"No, it wasn't him this time. Something else. But I want to hear what Ferosyn has to say first." I slid into a chair, and Angel sat down beside me.

Herne introduced Ferosyn to Angel and then took his place at the head of the table. "All right, the floor is yours."

Ferosyn let out a slow breath. "I've made some discoveries about this virus. I examined blood drawn from all the victims—they kept samples from the deceased, luckily. The virus was mutated—a poison was introduced into it, and that poison now transfers with the virus as it's passed from Fae to Fae."

"A *poison*? So it *is* an attack, then?" Viktor asked.

The healer nodded. "Yes, it's an attack. But there's more. The nature of the poison makes this particularly deadly. The base was created from meteoric iron." He let that information soak in.

I tried to make sense of it. "*Iron*? No wonder there were blisters and burns on their throats and bodies. How does the virus pass?"

"I'm assuming the virus was intentionally used to contaminate something consumed by the target-zero patients, and then passed as contagion. I don't believe that it's airborne. If it was, both TirNaNog and Navane would already be laid to waste. I think it has to be from some form of contact. I've notified the emissaries from both Courts to start question-ing people. It might be kissing, it might be sexual, it might be bodily fluids. We just don't know. The fact that it was an engineered virus means that it was deliberately constructed for one purpose: to wipe out the Fae race. Since it's magical as well, we have to watch for more than the typical variants."

"Can you cure it?" I asked.

"Cure it?" He rubbed his forehead. "I've barely discovered the cause, let alone the cure. That will be my next task. I'll get on it the moment I return to Lord Cernunnos's palace. I understand that all the first victims ate ginger chicken at Fae Day. You might find out who was manning the station, and go from there. If we can find out who did this, we might have a better chance on knowing how to stop it."

"We're on it." Herne stood and Ferosyn rose, bowing low. "I'll have Viktor run you back to the portal. We'll talk to you as soon as we've discov-ered anything."

"M'lord..." Ferosyn paused for a moment. "An-other thing. Meteoric iron is a rare commodity. There isn't much of it in the world, and the Fae are far more susceptible to it than any other form of iron. Not only this, but this particular iron comes from an ataxite meteor, so whoever's behind this wasn't looking to just mess with the Fae. I'm deadly serious when I tell you that whoever it is, is out to destroy the Courts. Someone with that much hate in his heart has got to be dangerous."

Meteoric iron was found in a scattered few meteorites, and ataxite meteors—which had a higher nickel content—were rarer still. It would take some serious searching, perhaps for years, to find a meteorite of that class.

"Understood," Herne said. He motioned to Viktor. "Can you run Ferosyn back to the portal? You know where it is."

"Yep. Your back yard."

"That's right." Herne waved as Ferosyn followed Viktor out of the room.

"Well, that answers one question," I said, slowly pulling the box of doughnuts to me. "It's deliberate, and it had to be planned out in detail. Whoever instigated it had to find a source of meteoric iron, and ataxite on top of it." The very words shook me up.

"What do we do now?" Talia asked, quickly typing notes onto her laptop.

"Start searching for any sources of ataxite meteorites that cropped up recently, or were sold recently. There are markets out there devoted to collectors who look for meteoric iron." Herne rubbed his chin, thinking. "Perhaps whoever's behind this bought a piece. We can't overlook the possibility. Yutani—how much have we found out about the catering company?"

"Very little so far. If the source of the poison was the ginger chicken, that gives me more to go on. I'll do what I can to find out who was manning that station. I should have something in an hour or so." He pulled his laptop closer, burying his nose in the screen.

"I don't know if it has anything to do with what's going on, or perhaps it was just brought on by working the case, but my dream last night feels related."

I told them about the dream, slipping into a mild panic as I laid out the events that had occurred. "I was hiding from whatever it was. All around me, Fae were dying. Light and Dark, it made no difference. But they were ghosts, they weren't actual people. I think they were dressed differently than most of the Fae dress today, so maybe I was seeing into a different time period. I couldn't escape. Whatever it was, it was so huge and powerful."

"Just like the other night. When you went into trance in your bathroom and you were in a circle and something was coming for you," Talia said, glancing up from her keyboard.

"Yes, and if you remember, I burned my fingers. I still have the welts." I held up my fingers. They were on the mend, but the raised bumps were still there.

"If you *are* dreaming about what's happening, then we should dissect everything you can remember. I wouldn't want to ignore anything that might help us. Angel, why don't you record everything Ember can remember about both incidents? See if there's anything you can dredge up that you left out." Herne headed for his office. "I'm going to contact a few friends I have, see if there have been any stirrings against the Fae from any of the major hate-groups lately."

With that heavy thought hanging over our heads, we moved into the rest of the day.

BY THAT EVENING we had accumulated a lot of information, but none of it was usable yet. We had to leave on time in order to meet Kamaria at our new house to deal with the ghosts. Yutani and Viktor decided to work on rebuilding the broken fence posts in our side yard until she arrived. They headed outside as Angel and I cautiously entered my bedroom.

"Holy crap." I stared at the walls. In what looked like blood streaming down the freshly painted walls were the words "Get Out Now." On one hand, the sight freaked me out. On the other, it pissed me off.

"Is that blood?" Angel asked.

I walked over to the walls. It was dried, whatever it was. I leaned in and sniffed it. There was the faint scent of ozone crackling in the air.

"I don't think it's blood, but I have no clue what it is." I stared at the letters, wondering if I should touch them. I reached up, then paused. But I had learned the hard way about touching things when I wasn't sure what they were.

"Let me," Angel said. Before I could stop her, she rubbed one finger down the "O" in "out" and then pulled her hand away, staring at the congealed glop that rested on her skin. "I have no clue. It feels nasty, like slime."

"Ectoplasm," Herne said from behind us. "Leave it alone so that Kamaria can get an accurate reading on it."

"Ghost-poop?" Angel asked, laughing.

I cracked up then, grateful for the chance to laugh. "Oh man, we have a rude ghost on our hands."

Herne grinned, shaking his head. "Well, that's one way to put it."

He paused as the doorbell rang. Talia was downstairs, waiting for Kamaria, and a moment later we heard footsteps coming up. Talia came first, followed by a tall, lithe woman with flaming red hair, with Yutani and Viktor behind her.

"May I present Madame Kamaria?" Talia said, inclining her head toward the woman.

The medium was probably in her mid-forties. She had a dancer's build and wore an off-the-shoulder top—a brilliant crimson—and a long flowing black skirt. A delicate silver and black shawl was draped around her shoulders, caught by a silver clasp in the center. Her hair was long, almost the color of her top, and flowed over her shoulders. She wore ballet flats, and she was carrying an old-fashioned carpetbag.

Kamaria looked at me, then held out her hand. "Ember Kearney?"

I nodded. "Yeah, that's me."

She held my hand for a moment, gazing into my eyes.

"You are at a crossroads, my dear, and very shortly will have many decisions to make. Be prepared to choose, or the choices will be made for you. But the spirits show me no more than that." She glanced around the room. "Your house is riddled with spirits and ghosts and past memories. Luckily, most will be easy to deal with. But there is one creature who is problematic. If you'll give me a few moments."

She didn't wait for further introductions, merely shooed us out of the room.

"Should she be in there alone?" I asked, worried. The poltergeist had nearly taken my head off with a paint can lid and then tagged my walls with graffiti. I wouldn't put much beyond it.

"She can more than take care of herself," Herne said. "Kamaria is scary wicked when she wants to be. Her parents were Russian, and she grew up steeped in the tales of her homeland. She was born a medium. Her mother was told that her daughter would grow up under the shadow of ghosts, and so she accepted Kamaria's fate and fed her mythology and legend for breakfast, lunch, and dinner, so the girl would have a grounding to help her cope with her gifts."

"Is she a witch?" Angel asked.

"Not exactly. I wouldn't know quite how to describe her. Kamaria is...Kamaria."

There was a shout from my room, and a loud crash. I rushed to the door and opened it. Kamaria was standing there, arms overhead, and I could see a spirit bearing down on her that reminded me of an octopus with a human face. The tentacles were tendrils of mist, and the face was enraged.

"I will contain you," Kamaria shouted at the spirit. Then, without even glancing my way, she added, "Get out and shut the door. I'm busy."

I quickly retreated. "Cripes, she's fending off something that looks like it's out of a monster movie. I don't know who I'm more worried for—her or the ghost."

"I'd put my money on Kamaria," Herne said. He glanced at me as I stared at the door, forcing myself to keep from running in. "I can see you want to help her. Why don't you go outside and check on what Yutani and Viktor did? If you interrupt Kamaria, things could go very wrong."

Reluctantly, I turned toward the staircase, but the next moment, my bedroom door slammed open so hard the door splintered and put a hole in the wall behind it. Inside, Kamaria was in midair, arms and legs stretched out as the ghostly creature held her, misty coils wrapped around her neck, ankles, and wrists. She was trying to scream, but the tendril around her neck was squeezing her throat.

I charged in, with Herne on my heels. The others were right behind us.

As I crossed the threshold, my head began to swim and I found myself beginning to float up toward the ceiling. I tried to recover my balance, but with my feet in the air, there was no way to steady myself. It was as though a giant cloud had formed beneath me and was buoying me up toward the ceiling.

I barely realized that I was heading toward the ceiling when I slammed into it. The cushion of air that had buoyed me up vanished and I plummeted to the floor, landing flat on my back. The thud shook the room.

"Fucking hell."

I blinked twice, trying to shake out of the haze of pain that ran through my body. My next thought was to assess whether I was hurt. I shifted carefully, but nothing felt broken, just jarred. I started to sit up, wondering why nobody had run over to help me, but then I understood why. Yutani was trying to fend off a ghostly tendril intent on wrapping around his waist. Herne was trying to yank Kamaria out of the clutches of the spirit. Talia was trying to protect Angel, who was holding out her hands to ward off the creature. And Viktor was thrashing his dagger toward the mist and vapor.

I had a sudden idea. I didn't know if it would work but right now, anything was worth a try. I rolled over and pushed myself to my feet, wincing as my back creaked. Sprinting for the bathroom, I slammed the door behind me and turned on the water full force in the tub, plugging the drain. As the tub began to fill, I sent out a call for any water elementals who might be riding the waves through the city water pipes. And sure enough, I felt the questioning touch of one as the tub filled. I dropped to my knees, plunging my hands into the icy water, and pushed all of my fear and need into an image of the creature that was in my bedroom.

We need to disrupt it. Can you help me?

The water elemental hesitated, then came the hesitant sensation that *yes*, it would help. But I got the clear impression it would need form to do anything. With a sinking heart, I realized what it was asking. It needed my body.

I had never been possessed—giving permission or not. I had never lowered my guard enough to allow anything to take over. The thought terrified me, and yet...the elemental could help if I conquered my fear. Fear warred with need. But a scream from the other room shook me out of my frozen state and I broke down, lowering the wall. I shut off the water and let out a long sigh.

Very well. You may use my body. Just please, help us.

A cool feeling began to trickle through me, as though someone had injected me with a steady flow of rain, filtering through my veins drop by drop. Like liquid silver it flowed, a wave of energy that spread through my body. Round and round it began to spin, creating whirlpools and eddies throughout my spirit. The elemental crashed against the sides of my veins, then oozed slowly into the capillaries. After a moment, a steady wash began to surge through my veins, saturating my muscles and joints. I began to retreat, stepping to the side as the elemental took the helm. I could still see through my eyes, but it was as though I were watching a film, observing from a distance.

I stood and raised one hand, looking at it with wonder. My skin sparkled with a blue luminescence. My form felt malleable, shifting and reforming with every step as I reached out and unlocked the door.

The elemental sharing my body was curious and yet concerned. It felt my concern and worry and reflected them till they echoed around me, amplifying my emotions. If it could amplify my worry, I wondered, could it amplify my power?

My focus began to narrow into action. I had to destroy the spirit. I zoomed in on the thought: *Drive the spirit out. Disrupt it.*

The elemental responded.

As I reentered my bedroom, Yutani managed to free himself. He halted, staring at me, wide-eyed, then slowly began to back away. Talia stiffened as I approached the center of the room, and then she pushed Angel out the door.

The spirit's attention was on Kamaria. It wanted to hurt her, and I could feel the waves of her fear and pain. I nurtured my rage. This spirit didn't belong here. It was out of sync. Around it, a nimbus writhed, jammed with the forms of sub-demons, of psychic leeches, and all things that fed off of the living.

The elemental let out a growl, and the growl echoed from my throat. I raised my hands and channeled the raw power of Mother Ocean, the raging force that drove her gales and hurricanes across the surface of the world. The elemental brought the power of the storm raging in and the blast tore into the spirit.

Kamaria began to fall, but Herne caught her. He was staring at me—at us, for the elemental and I were one—and yet he didn't move. Warily, he handed the unconscious medium to Viktor, who carried her out of the room to safety.

"Get out," I said to Herne. "Now."

He retreated with the others.

When they were out of range, I let go of that last little barrier inside, and the elemental took over completely. As the full power of the Ocean Mother began to boil and twist, the spirit let out a long howl. The vortex I—or rather, the elemental—was creating tore its vapors to shreds. With a shriek, a waterspout caught up the spirit, and I found myself staring directly into its face. It reached out, trying to mark me, but then another wave crashed over it, and it split asunder, its cords to the house severed. The water washed it away on the current of sparkling magic. I watched it go, impassive, and then the elemental began to retreat.

The next moment, the world went black, as I tumbled into the void that it left as it withdrew from my body.

Chapter 7

THE CEILING HAD a scorched look to it when I opened
my eyes. I blinked, my entire body feeling like a live wire.

What happened? Why was I flat on my back, staring at an octopus-shaped soot mark?

I sucked in a deep breath and found out that breathing hurt—though not in the break-your-ribs kind of hurt. I winced, carefully prodding my stomach and chest, trying to ascertain what kind of damage I had taken.

It was then that I realized I was soaking wet, as though I had jumped into a swimming pool. The floor beneath me was wet. Frowning, I brought my fingers up to my nose and took a shaky breath, inhaling. It was fresh water, that much I could tell. I didn't smell like brine.

I moaned and the next second, Herne was kneeling over me.

"Ember, are you all right?"

I struggled to sit up. "Yeah, I think so." My memory was still fuzzy but as I spotted Kamaria, lying prone on the hall floor outside the bedroom, it all came back in one giant info dump. I thought I could hear sirens, but I wasn't sure.

The elemental. The spirit. Being a walking representation of the Ocean Mother.

"I don't feel so hot," I said, rubbing my head. As Angel smoothed Kamaria's hair off her face, I realized that the medium was seriously injured. "What's the damage? How is she?"

"Whatever that creature was, it hurt her bad. She has at least two dislocated joints, if not broken bones. And it siphoned energy off of her. Her breathing is shallow and her pulse is way too rapid," Angel said, staring down at the woman. "If you hadn't stopped that thing, she'd be dead by now." She glanced up at me, her eyes somber. "That was no ordinary ghost."

"No, it wasn't. I'm not certain what it was, but it wasn't the spirit of any human, I think. Whatever it was, it was old and hungry." I held my hand out and Herne pulled me to my feet.

"Are you sure you're all right?" He stroked my face.

"Yeah, I think so. How's everybody else?" I glanced around.

Talia was nowhere in sight, and Viktor appeared in the doorway, carrying a clean painter's cloth. He handed it to Angel and she gently tucked it in around Kamaria.

"Okay, we'll be fine." Herne paused as the sound of sirens grew louder.

"The sirens—an ambulance?"

Herne nodded. "Talia's waiting downstairs for them." As he finished speaking, voices echoed on the stairway and Talia appeared, leading two paramedics who were carrying a stretcher between them. I recognized them as shifters right away. She pointed to Kamaria.

"There she is." Talia stepped aside.

Angel backed away as they approached.

"She's human?" one of the paramedics asked.

Angel nodded. "Yes. Some sort of spirit creature attacked her."

It was then I realized why Talia had called a Sub-Cult emergency team. Even though they knew all about us, as well as ghosts and other beings, most human hospitals weren't set up to treat injuries on the psychic front.

As they set to checking her blood pressure and heart, I turned to Herne.

"Whatever it is, it's gone now."

"I think it was attracted to the pain and violence left behind by the murders," he said, lowering his voice. "I wish we would have recognized what it was earlier—I've encountered creatures like that on occasion. They're a form of astral demon that feeds on life force, pain, and anger. It must have set up home here and has been feeding on the residual energy left behind by the killer and his victims."

"Or maybe it even attracted him here. I thought it was his spirit, to be honest." I glanced over at the paramedics. "We should pay her medical bills. I will, if the agency can't. I hope to hell she'll be all right. I feel responsible for dragging her into this situation."

"Don't. She's dealt with worse. But yes, the Wild Hunt will pay for her expenses and for any time she loses due to recuperation." He paused, then tapped me on the arm and motioned for me to follow him out into the hall, away from the paramedics working on Kamaria. Once we were there, he took hold of my shoulders, staring down at me. "What did you do in there? What happened? You weren't *you*."

I caught my breath. I had been waiting for the question. "I've never done this before. I didn't even know I could, but I guess my work with Morgana has been preparing me for it."

"My mother has a way of working subtly behind the scenes, and then boom...big changes. But what happened?"

"I summoned a water elemental, called it by filling the tub with water. I asked if it could help and it said yes, but only by taking possession of my body. So I allowed it to take me over."

He froze, his eyes searching my own. "Your magic is evolving. I think you need to visit my mother to talk to her. I'm certain she didn't mean for this to happen without her being involved. Are you feeling all right? Did it leave you, or is there a chance it's left a cord in you, to plug back in when you might not have your boundaries up?"

I shrugged. "I don't know, but I don't sense it anywhere. It left an aftereffect, though. I feel as though I can sense more. The moisture in the air, the water in my own body...I'm more aware of it all. I don't know how to explain it, but as the power of the Ocean Mother moved through me, she left behind a part of herself." I stopped, struggling to find the right words. There was no way to fully explain the sensation that I was feeling. Finally, I shook my head. "Leave it for now. Let's go check on Kamaria."

"All right, but when we get her settled and taken care of, I'm calling my mother." He followed me back to where the paramedics were lifting Kamaria onto the stretcher. Her arm was no longer splayed out at a wrong angle, but her left leg was in a splint, as was her right wrist.

"How is she?" Herne asked.

"She's stable, but she's sustained multiple injuries. She has a shattered kneecap, her tendons and ligaments in her leg are bruised, if not torn, and her wrist seems to be fractured. She's still unconscious, so we need to find a shaman who can enter her mind to see if there's been any damage to her life force." The paramedics adjusted the stretcher, raising it up to carry it down the stairs. "Do you know her family? They should be contacted."

Herne glanced over at Talia. "Do we have a contact for her?"

Talia shook her head. "No, but I can try to find one. I'll go with her to the hospital."

"Good," Herne said. "Meanwhile, we'll take care of matters here."

Talia vanished with the medics.

I was still feeling rough, completely raw and

shell-shocked. The room looked like a war zone. All the new paint had been splattered with residue soot—at least it looked like soot—and right now the only thing I wanted to do was to get out of the house. I need to eat, and I needed to sleep away the massive hangover left in the wake of the elemental.

"I'm beginning to question the wisdom of buying this house," I said, rubbing my forehead.

"Don't," Yutani said. "Wait till morning. We'll come back and see how the dust has settled. Chances are, the spirits will have cleared out, after what just happened."

I smiled him a faint thank-you, and we filed downstairs. Once there, Angel asked Herne to come back to the condo with us. He offered to drive me there, if she drove my car.

"I don't think you should get behind a wheel right now." He steered me out of the house as Angel locked up behind us.

Viktor and Yutani waved good night and headed off.

Angel seconded that. "I agree. And yes, I can drive her car back to the condo. I'll see you there." She headed toward my car. Angel and I had exchanged car keys when we moved in, so we had access to both our cars.

I let Herne bundle me into his car, still feeling rattled. As we pulled away from the house, I leaned my head back against the seat. I was feeling fragile.

"What are you thinking about?" Herne turned the ignition and pulled onto the street.

"Opening up. I've never let anything crawl inside

me like that before. Hell, I have a hard-enough time letting people inside my *life*, let alone opening my psyche to a creature in order to let it control my body. But Kamaria needed help, and she needed it fast. I didn't have a choice."

"There's always a choice. You had the choice to do nothing, but you decided to act instead. You stepped over the boundary of fear and into the unknown to help someone. That's the definition of courage, in my book." Herne flipped the turn signal, then changed lanes so we could make a turn.

I realized he was complimenting me, but right now I didn't need a thank-you for what I had done. I wanted to *understand* it, to know how I had been able to create a path for the water elemental to enter my body. I wanted to be able to control it, so I could both do it again, if need be, and prevent it from happening if somebody else tried to force it.

"You said you'll call Morgana for me? It's so much easier than for me to try to reach her through a ritual." Having a boyfriend who had a direct cell phone link to the gods was one perk I hadn't counted on when Herne and I had gotten together.

"I'll do that as soon as we reach your condo." He paused, then added, "Do you think that whatever is chasing you in your dreams might be trying to possess you?"

I shook my head. "No, whatever that creature is, it's out for blood. It wants the Fae dead. Which is why I believe that my visions—dreams—whatever they are, have to do with the plague that's sweeping through TirNaNog and Navane."

I thought for a moment, not wanting to say what I was about to, but it needed to be said. "Listen, if by any chance I catch the iron plague—"

"You won't," Herne said, cutting me off.

"I hope not, but Herne, I *am* Fae. Full blooded, even if my bloodlines are mixed. If I *do* catch it and it turns out there's no antidote, then I want you to help me. I don't want to go out in pain. Do you understand?" I snuck a glance at him. I realized what I was asking, but he was the Lord of the Hunt, and his nature was both brilliant and dark. The Hunt was a force of death, as well as a force of nature.

"You're asking a lot," he said.

"I know. But...I *am* asking." I held his gaze and he finally nodded.

"I'll do what's necessary. But you're not going to catch it."

WHEN WE REACHED the Miriam G Building, which housed my condo, Herne guided me to the elevator. Angel had already arrived home and by the time we reached the front door, she had opened up a can of soup and had cheese sandwiches grilling. Angel nurtured through food, and no matter what she cooked—whether from scratch or out of a can—it was prepared with love.

I eased myself into a chair. Not only had I been body slammed by the astral demon, but the elemental's energy had left me aching and weary.

The adrenaline rush had worn off and now I just wanted a warm bubble bath and a soft bed.

"I'm just grateful we figured out what was there before we actually moved in," Angel said, setting our plates in front of us. She looked almost as tired as I felt.

"Yeah, me too. I wonder if there's anything left behind. Speaking of which, Talia hasn't called with any news on Kamaria." Regardless of what Herne said, I felt terribly guilty for exposing the medium to the creature.

"I'll give her a call, then I'll contact Morgana for you." Herne somberly walked away from the table and pulled out his phone.

I took a bite of the sandwich. The molten goodness oozed in my mouth and I let out a satisfied sigh. Not only had Angel used sharp cheddar, but a creamy provolone as well. The bread was sourdough, and altogether, the sandwich was simple and yet, perfection. The soup was a rich tomato with just a bite of spice behind it.

Angel and I locked gazes.

"Do you think that thing was there when he murdered the girl and her grandmother?"

I thought about her question. "I think it could have spurred on the murders. Or maybe it just grew out of them. Astral demons don't usually just show up out of the blue. There's almost always some factor that opens the gate for them."

"How do we keep it from coming back?"

I dipped my sandwich in the soup. "I don't know, but we can ask Herne to find us someone to help."

Herne returned to the table at that point. He didn't look happy.

"How's Kamaria?"

"Physically beat-up but stable. But she's still unresponsive. I gave them the name of a shaman to call in. One of the best. He can retrieve her soul. She's disconnected from her body and unless we return her to her body, she'll sink into a permanent coma."

He must have noticed my expression because he reached out to place a hand over my wrist. "I told you, it's not your fault, Ember. She took the risk. She's taken a lot of risks over the years on the spiritual realm. Kamaria has always felt it's her mission to help people. This could have happened in numerous other cases. She just managed to beat the odds...until now."

I stirred my soup with my spoon. "I know, but I still feel responsible."

"Don't go down that route. Hell, if you want to play the blame game, Talia and I were the ones to suggest her." He paused, then shrugged. "There's nothing we can achieve by regrets. I put in a call to my mother. She should get back to us soon."

We ate in a silence punctuated only by the clink of our spoons on the china. When we were done, I crossed to the sofa where Mr. Rumblebutt was waiting, purring up a storm. He began to knead my chest, licking my face, and I gathered him into my arms, kissing his head.

"It's been a rough day, Mr. R.," I whispered.

In return, he rubbed my chin with the top of his head and leaned against me, making biscuits on my chest. In another moment, he had dozed off in my arms. I gently kissed his nose and then deposited him on the sofa beside me.

Angel sat cross-legged on the wide ottoman, and Herne stretched out on the floor, on his back. He crossed his arms over his face and we sat in the comfortable silence, each wrapped up within our own thoughts. Ten minutes later, his phone rang and we all jumped. Mr. Rumblebutt was so startled that he dashed off the sofa, shaking his head and glaring at Herne as though he held him personally accountable for the disruption.

"Hello? Yes, she's here with me." He held out the phone to me. "Morgana."

I took it, still wondering over the fact that the gods had taken to cell phones and technology. The next thing you knew, they'd be setting up websites. In fact, they probably had.

"Hi, this is Ember," I said as I took the phone and held it to my ear.

"We need to talk. *In person*." Morgana wasn't much for chitchat, apparently. "I want to see you tomorrow morning. Around ten-thirty."

"All right." I hesitated, not wanting to sound stupid. "Um, how do I get to you?"

When she had claimed me, *she* had come to *me*, at the Wild Hunt Agency. But I didn't expect her to show up at the office every time.

"Herne knows the way. Tell him to drop you at the portal on my dock. He'll know what I'm talking about." And with that, she hung up.

I handed his phone back to him, relaying her message. "Do all of the gods have portals around here that most of us never notice?"

"Yeah, I'd say that's pretty much the way of things. Tomorrow we'll head out there from the office. It's not far." Herne glanced at the clock. "It's late. You and Angel need to sleep."

I walked over to him, leaning against his chest as he wrapped an arm around my shoulders.

"Will you stay?" I asked softly.

He kissed my forehead. "I'd love to, but I need to get home. I have some work I have to attend to for my father."

I reached up, placed my lips against his and lingered in a long, leisurely kiss. As he wrapped his arms around me, gently massaging the small of my waist, I rested my head on his shoulder and we stood for a moment, in silence. Then, with another kiss, he pulled away and tilted my chin up. His gaze locked onto me, burning a hole through my heart.

"I love you, Ember," he said, placing two fingers over my lips when I began to answer. "Shush, love. You're tired. Rest."

And then, he headed for the door, bidding good night to Angel.

MORNING ARRIVED AND with it, I felt much better. A hot bath and a cup of chamomile tea the night before had left me tired enough to fall into a—thankfully—dreamless sleep. I woke stiff, but a long shower seemed to put me to rights, and I lingered over my wardrobe, trying to decide what would be dressy enough to meet Morgana, yet active enough for work. I finally decided on a pair of black jeans that had enough stretch in them that I could run easily, along with a bustier that zipped up the front. It had a built-in bra that was stiff enough to hold up the girls, and while it had leather strips on the sides, it breathed for summer.

The sun was glinting through the bedroom window. The weather forecast called for a hot day in the mid-eighties, so I chose a pair of sneakers over ankle boots, and brushed my hair back into a high ponytail. After putting on my makeup—I did more than my usual slap-and-dash—I joined Angel in the kitchen. She had whipped up a pan of blueberry muffins, and sliced some gouda and cheddar.

"I hope you don't mind a quick breakfast, but I had to drag myself out of bed." She yawned, sipping her tea. "Last night really took it out of me."

"I think last night made all of us her bitch. Muffins and cheese are fine—in fact, better than fine. The muffins smell heavenly, and you know my love affair with cheese." I bit into one of the muffins and the taste explosion filled my mouth. "Bag some up for snacks?" I asked, speaking around the crumbs.

"Already ahead of you." She pointed to a box, where I saw that she had packed a dozen for the office. "You look dressed up today."

"Remember? I get to talk to Morgana today. This will be the first time I've seen her face-to-face since the day she claimed me. No way am I going to show up looking piecemeal." I stuffed my phones—both work and personal—and tablet into my bag. "I had no clue I could channel water elementals. I wonder what else I can do. My magic is growing, Angel. And I admit, I'm a little bit afraid." I glanced at Mr. Rumblebutt's dish. "Thanks for feeding him."

"He was stomping on my feet while I was baking, trying to convince me that we've been starving him. So I decided to bribe him to keep his fur out of the batter." She paused, then asked, "How far do you think you'll go with the magic? How much is she going to expect from you?"

"I don't know," I answered. "I suppose I'm hoping to find that out today. While I've adjusted to working with the Wild Hunt, you have to admit that both our lives have changed drastically since Beltane. Since we met Herne. I feel like we hopped on a merry-go-round and it turned into some wild Tilt-a-Whirl ride."

"What do you want to happen? Or do you even know?" She picked up the box with the muffins as I slung my purse over my shoulder and opened the door for her.

As I closed the door, I thought over her question. What *did* I want? Where did I expect to go on a magical level? But the answers eluded me as we headed toward the car.

BY THE TIME we arrived at work, Herne was in the break room, and we went directly there instead of stopping at our respective desks.

Talia was first to report in. "Kamaria's stable as far as her physical condition goes, but she's sinking deeper into a coma."

"I've called in a shaman who specializes in soul retrieval and he'll arrive today. He's coming here first, so we can give him the rundown on what we were fighting. He should be here within the hour." Herne tugged on his collar, looking uncomfortable.

"What's his name?" I asked.

"Kuippana. He's Finnish by blood."

"He's coming all the way from Finland?" That seemed like a long way to travel for one patient.

"No," Herne said. "He's coming from Camano Island, where he runs a woodland retreat. He moved over here from Finland a long time ago." He fell silent, and I recognized the signs that he didn't want to talk about it anymore.

I blinked, trying once more. "That's all?"

Herne ignored my question. "When he gets here, Ember, I want you to fill him in on what went down last night. You'll have to be brief since you have an appointment with my mother at ten-thirty. Viktor will drive you down to the pier." He consulted his notes. "Yutani, you're next. Bring us up to speed on what you've found."

"This morning I came in early and put in a few hours. I've managed to identify the waiter who was manning the ginger chicken station on Fae Day. His name is Nigel Henderson. The catering company said that he was a late fill-in for one of their regulars who was in a freak accident. Nigel was recommended by some day-labor company, supposedly, but I can't find any record of them in the books. FMR Labor, but they don't show up anywhere. The owner of the catering company—Marie Shill—was pushed to the wall with everything going on and apparently didn't check the referral. She assumed he was vetted."

"Do we have an address for Nigel?" Angel asked.

"Yes, we do. I phoned but there was no answer. I left a message asking him to return the call. Meanwhile, I've started looking into him, but he's been very good at hiding his tracks. I did, however, discover that he rooms with a vampire named Charlie Darren."

"A vamp? Is Nigel also a vampire?" Viktor asked, but then answered himself. "No, he couldn't be if he was out in broad daylight. Right?"

"Right. The event was outside. No, as far as I can tell, Nigel is a run of the mill human. I tried searching on FMR Labor, but I've come up with squat. Nothing—not even a whisper." He shook his head. "In this day and age, a company that doesn't have a website is a company geared to fail, not to mention, setting off red flags. I'll check with licensing and see if they have a business license."

"They don't even have a website? That's odd. And you say the catering company never used them before?" Herne asked.

"Nope. As I said, she was pushed to the wall and when her regular called in sick, she apparently hired the first person who showed up. I have the caterer's number and address, in case you want to talk to her later on."

"All right," Herne said, scribbling down notes.

"We might just do that. Also, check on the regular waiter—what kind of freak accident? It seems a little too coincidental to me. The waiter who was supposed to man the station was injured right before the event? I wonder if he had some help."

"That's a good point," I said. "Anybody know how they're doing out at TirNaNog and Navane?" Thinking about the meeting with the Fae Queens made my stomach tense, bringing up visions of my grandfather again. I was still pissed.

"Yeah," Herne said, a gloomy look washing over his face. "Three more deaths in Navane this morning, four more ill. TirNaNog has two more deaths and five more ill. So it *is* spreading somehow. There have been absolutely no reports of anybody with blood other than Fae coming down with the disease."

"What about those who aren't full blood? I know that neither side wants to admit their existence, but there are half-Fae around." Talia tapped away on the keyboard.

Herne's phone beeped and he glanced at it. "Kuippana just texted me. He's on his way up. Angel, can you unlock the elevator?"

She nodded. "Should I just open up shop now, or do you still need me here?"

"Go ahead. We're almost done." As she headed out of the room, Herne continued. "In terms of half-Fae, we don't know. None of them live in TirNaNog and Navane, and neither side will claim them so we have no clue if anybody attended Fae Day who was half-Fae. Yutani, why don't you alert the hospitals to let us know if there's anybody coming in with symptoms that match the disease? Don't even specify race—while this appears to be limited to the Fae, we have no clue of how this illness could progress."

As we began to clear up our notes, Angel returned, a tall man following her. With skin that was finely tanned to a light golden brown, and eyes so dark that I found myself falling into them at a single glance, he was striking. His hair brushed his shoulders and he had a full beard and mustache, all a rich brunette. His lips were full, and he wore a V-neck sweater in forest green, and a pair of camo pants. Both his ears were banded with earrings—at least four on each side, and the center of his lower lip was adorned with two silver rings, side by side, looped around his lip and through—a dolphin bite piercing. Herne was a beautiful specimen of masculinity, but he had his match in this man.

"Kuippana," Angel said, her eyes lingering on him as she spoke.

Herne held out his hand. "Kuippana, thank you for coming," he said quietly.

Kuippana inclined his head. "I answer when needed." He paused, then added, "Do you mind me working the case?"

Herne shook his head. "I wouldn't have contacted you if I did. Bygones and water under the bridge. As long as you remember this is *my* team."

"I'll be on my best," Kuippana said.

I detected a slight smirk behind the words. I was beginning to get the feeling that the pair had some baggage behind them.

"Allow me to introduce my team, then. Talia, our

resident researcher. Ember, one of my investigators." Herne paused, then added, "She's also my
girlfriend. Understand?"

Kuippana's eyes twinkled. "I believe I do."

"Our receptionist, Angel, who brought you in."
He pointed to Yutani, "Yutani, our IT specialist and an investigator. And then there's Viktor,
another investigator." Herne's gaze never left
Kuippana's face.

"Pleased to meet all of you. Please, call me
Kipa, it's my nickname, and easier to pronounce."
Kuippana motioned to the table. "May I sit down?"

"Please do. Would you like some coffee?" Angel
hovered by his side.

I glanced at her. She looked smitten. I could see
it in her face. I glanced back at Kipa. He was absolutely gorgeous, but like Herne, there was a darker
edge behind the smile, and I wondered just how
much we could trust him.

As Angel poured him some coffee and pushed
the box of muffins over to him, Herne cleared his
throat, glancing at me for a moment.

"Ember will brief you on what we were fighting
last night, then Talia will take you to the hospital."
He paused, looking uncertain. "Ember, can I speak
to you in my office for a moment?"

"Of course. Angel, keep Kipa company, would
you?"

I wasn't sure whether it was a good idea to
encourage her or not, but then again, nothing
could happen with Viktor and the others there. As
I followed Herne into his office and shut the door
behind us, he turned to me, a serious look on his

face.

"I want you to be cautious around Kipa. Seriously."

"What's wrong? Is he dangerous?"

Herne blinked. "We're *all* dangerous, love. Regardless of our nature. But I want you to be cautious of him because, in the scheme of things—you might consider him my distant cousin. Except he's got light fingers. Not only did he steal my girlfriend, but he was thrown out of Mielikki's Arrow. He crossed paths with Tapio when he tried to seduce Mielikki. Kipa is the Lord of the Wolves, and to say he's a wolf himself would be an understatement."

Chapter 8

I STARED AT Herne, not quite registering what he was saying. Then it hit me.

"Kipa is a *god*? Like you?"

He shook his head. "Not quite. He lives outside of time. He's one of the elemental forest spirits. He is Lord of the Wolves, the Packmaster. He's a trickster, much like Coyote, except sometimes he spins out his games for fun, rather than for a lesson."

I stared at the door, thinking of how much havoc someone like that could cause. "Should we trust him?"

"You can always trust him, to be exactly who he is." Herne paused, twisting his lips. After a moment he said, "Ember, one thing to accept about the gods—you can never fully trust any of us, not if you're looking for safety. We move outside of the range of safety and security. We don't operate like people do, or even the Fae. But most of us do our best to keep to our words. Kipa...he has good intentions, until something distracts him and he forgets. As I said, he's a distant cousin, in the sense that we are joined by the forests, but would I trust him around you? Absolutely not. He'll try to seduce you—wait and see. And when he does, I'll beat the crap out of him."

I laughed at that. "You'll have to go through me first. But don't worry about me. I'm not interested in him, even though he's a very pretty man."

Herne frowned, but said nothing.

"Can we trust him with Kamaria? Will he help her?"

The frown slipped away and Herne nodded. "Of that, I am absolutely certain. Kipa is the best at what he does, and he will do what he can to save her, having given his promise."

As we turned toward the door, I asked one more question. "Did Talia suggest bringing him here, or did you?"

Herne ducked his head. "I did. We need the best, and he's the best there is."

KIPA AND I were sitting alone in the break room. Herne had strategically left the door open, and I could see that Viktor was talking to Yutani, but was standing where he could keep watch on me. It seemed ridiculous. There wasn't anything Kipa could do to me without them hearing, but I let them play protector.

He leaned forward, a cunning smile on his lips. "So, you are Herne's new woman. And you are... Fae...Elven?"

I blinked. I wasn't used to being called somebody's "woman."

"I'm Herne's girlfriend, yes. I'm Fae—mixed blood. Both Light and Dark."

His eyes narrowed briefly. "I see. That's an unusual blend. You wear it well." His voice was smooth, and it slid over me like slow honey.

I shivered, realizing just how much effect he could have. "Let's talk about the astral demon."

"As you wish. As you will." He leaned forward across the table.

I pulled back, straightening in my chair. "I thought it was just a poltergeist at first." I went on to describe what had happened, and how I had invoked the water elemental to fight it.

Kipa's eyes lit up, flaring. "So, a water witch?"

"Yes, more or less. Speaking of which, I have an appointment, so I'll leave you to the others." As I stood, I bumped against the table and blushed, feeling clumsy.

Kipa let out a low growl, then laughed as I jumped.

"You could be a lot of fun," he said with a lazy smile. "I see why Herne put his claim on you."

Tired of being talked about like somebody's toy, I rested my hands on my hips.

"Listen, dude, Herne didn't raise his leg and pee on me. I *choose* to be with him. In fact, I choose who I want to be with. Period." I headed toward the door.

He threw back his head, laughing as he slapped his thigh. "Oh, you are a lovely wench. Go on, then, to keep your appointment. I shall not make you tarry. But *Ember Kearney*, I hope to see you again."

I paused, turning back to him. "Oh, we probably will. But mind your manners, do you hear me? If you don't, I'll make you wish to hell you didn't have a dick. Got it?"

He reined in his laughter, though I still detected a smirk. "I will be the epitome of a gentleman, I promise. Unless you want something else."

Infuriated and yet slightly breathless, I hurried out of the room. Yutani gave me a long look and I shook my head. "Watch him," I mouthed, as I stopped in my office to drop off everything before I headed out to see Morgana.

VIKTOR DROVE ME down to the docks. The water in the sound was choppy as the wind drove the waves to ripple along the docks. While the sun was streaming down through ribbons of filmy clouds, the breeze had picked up, causing the temperature to drop. The disconnect between the bright morning and the cool air was disconcerting.

"So, which dock is Morgana's?" I was nervous, and talking helped me avoid thinking about what was to come.

Viktor flashed me a sideways glance. "Calm down. You haven't done anything wrong."

"True, but I'm not certain what she's going to say about what happened with the water elemental. I'll be honest with you, Viktor. That scared the hell out of me. I've never had that happen before. I've never been possessed by *anything*. It was creepy as hell to have somebody in my head, looking through my eyes while I stood to the side, only able to observe."

Viktor paused for a moment, then asked, "What did it feel like?"

I stared out the window, letting my mind drift back. "In a way, it was beautiful, almost as though the water elemental and I were one. But I was terrified. The elemental could have done anything, and I wouldn't have been able to stop it. It could have killed any one of you, and all I would have been able to do was watch." I licked my lips. "You know, I don't understand how mediums like Kamaria can allow spirits to talk through them."

"That, I agree with. Having someone pry around in your brain isn't my idea of a good time."

Viktor fell silent as we drove along First Avenue, swinging a right onto University Street. We were headed for the I-5 freeway. As we sped up onto the interstate, I was grateful to see that traffic was moving at a good pace. We had managed to miss the morning rush, and we weren't into the noon crunch yet. It didn't take us long before we came to the 168A exit. From there, we headed to Portage Bay, which housed a number of private docks.

"So Morgana isn't downtown on the waterfront?"

Viktor shook his head. "No. Too much traffic

there. But Portage Bay is an extensive boat marina, and there's a boat that has a portal in it that leads to her realm."

It made sense, when I thought about it. Madonna was a goddess of the sea as well as a goddess of Faerie, so a portal in a boat was logical.

"Do you know how I'm supposed to cross through?"

"No, but the gatekeeper will. Herne assured me there will be someone there to meet you."

"Good." I paused before asking the next question. "What do you think of Kipa?"

Viktor cleared his throat. When he spoke, he sounded wary, as though he wasn't sure how much to say. "Kipa has his uses."

I waited, but he said nothing more. After a moment, I asked, "That's it?"

"What do you want me to say?" the half-ogre said. "Herne is my friend. Kipa's a distant relative of his, and we need his help. But Ember, be cautious. There are dynamics playing out in that familial relationship that you couldn't pay me to get involved in."

"Have you ever met Kipa before?"

Viktor nodded. "Once, indirectly. I happened to be in the area when Herne was talking to a wolf, and then I saw the wolf turn into Kipa and dart through the woods. This was about fifty years ago. When I asked him about it, all Herne would tell me was that he had been talking to his cousin, and to leave it at that. He didn't seem happy, so I didn't press it."

After another pause, Viktor added, "Ember,

please don't get too involved. Kipa isn't malevolent, not in the way you or I would think of it. But he can do a lot of damage. He's screwed Herne over more than once, and I'd hate to see it happen again. Why he's even allowed in the office of the Wild Hunt, I'm not sure. He was soundly thrashed and kicked out of Mielikki's Arrow. But I suppose Herne feels the benefits outweigh the liabilities."

I realized what Viktor was worried about.

"Dude, I'm not asking because I find Kipa attractive, although I have to admit, he's gorgeous. However, I'm not interested in complicating my life. I love Herne. I just want to get a feel for who we're dealing with, and while Herne told me a little, I have a feeling there's a whole lot of history between the two that I could stumble over."

"That's putting it mildly. And Ember, even if you aren't attracted to him, watch yourself. Kipa has a way of getting under your skin. He's charming and a lot of fun. But when the chips are down, he usually takes off, not willing to help pick up the pieces of what he's destroyed."

We were headed north on Boyer Street when Viktor swung a left onto Fuhrman. Shortly after that, we turned right onto a side street—Misty Lane—and parked in a small lot. There was room for six cars, and two slips were marked "Reserved." Viktor parked in one of them, next to a pale silver sedan.

"See the blue houseboat at the end of the dock?" He pointed to the dock to our right. There, three houseboats lined the pier. The one at the end was painted a cobalt blue. Single story, it looked about the side of a large bus. The deck was lined with planters of herbs.

"That's the boat?" I slipped on a pair of sun-glasses, staring at the boat as it rocked gently on the waves.

"Yes. I'll let you go alone. I'll be waiting here when you return."

"What are you going to do while I'm in there?" I hated to think of him sitting out in the car, getting bored.

"Probably head to a coffee shop. You want me to bring you back something?"

I shook my head. "I'll get a latte on the way back to the office. All right, here goes nothing."

Summoning my courage, I opened the door. As I shouldered my purse, a surge of adrenaline racing through me. I steeled myself and headed for the pier.

The water to either side was a dark green-gray and the wind was whipping it into frothy waves that splashed over the pier. I passed the first two houseboats, glancing at them, wondering about the people who lived on the water's edge. That life appealed to me, in many ways, but I needed more space in which to stretch out.

As I came to the third boat, I glanced at the name painted on the hull—*Fantastica*. Think-ing that seemed the perfect name for a houseboat leading into the world of Fae, I swallowed my fear and knocked on the door.

The gatekeeper was a slight woman, looking to be Fae, and yet I had the feeling she wasn't full blooded. She blinked, her wide eyes a glittering green. They matched my own, but her hair was the color of gold, hanging to her waist, and she was thin and petite. She welcomed me in.

"You are Ember?" she asked, and her voice chimed on the wind, almost as though she were singing.

"Yes." I reached for my purse. "Do you need some identification?"

She laughed. "No, you wear Morgana's mark in your aura. I can read the signature."

That was news to me, but handy to know. "And you are..."

"Aoife." She pronounced it *ee-fa*. "I'm a priestess of Morgana."

A sofa stretched along the right wall. The room was long and narrow, and a set of bunk beds rested against the end of it. A door, half-open, stood to the right and behind it I caught a glimpse of a toilet and shower. There was a second door next to it that was closed.

A kitchenette covered half the wall to my left, and the rest of the length was taken up by floor-to-ceiling windows. A square table sat in front of the windows with two chairs. A ladder next to the door to the bathroom was flush against the wall, leading up to an exit to the roof.

The walls were painted a silvery-gray, and strategic uses of white mimicked the look of waves racing across the walls.

"Do you live here?" I asked, looking around. It was artful, and lovely, but minimalistic.

Aoife shook her head. "Only every other week. Another priestess and I share the duties of watching over the portal. If you'll put your purse on the table, I'll keep it safe until you return." She pointed toward the table. There was a vase with a single white rosebud in it sitting on the walnut surface.

I sat my purse down next to the flower, and took a deep sniff of the petals that had just begun to unfold. The scent pierced my senses, reminding of jasmine or lotus instead of a rose.

"So, how does this work? What do I do?"

"First, you should change. It won't do to have you appear before her dressed like that, not when you're in her court." She crossed to the second door and opened it, bringing out a flowing gown on a hanger. "You can wear this."

I reached for the dress. It flowed to the floor, layers of material draping like petals on a flower. I wasn't sure what material it was, but it felt like silk, light and wispy. The color was that of the twilight sky. All over the gown, hand-sewn beads sparkled, scintillating under the sunlight that flowed in through the windows, causing the gown to flash with rainbow fire.

"This is too beautiful. I can't wear this—"

"You can and you will," Aoife said. "And you will go barefoot. Now take the dress into the bathroom and change. If you need help, just ask."

Properly chastised, I carried the dress into the bathroom and shut the door. The bathroom was almost as large as the rest of the boat, with a Jacuzzi, a walk-in marble shower, and two vanities, each with its own sink. The toilet seat looked marble as well. Morgana liked her priestesses to live in luxury.

As I stripped out of my clothes and folded them neatly on the counter, I caught sight of myself in the mirror. There was something different about me—I hadn't seen it this morning when I put on my makeup. But this mirror, large and frosted around the edges, seemed to reflect not only my image, but the energy flowing around me. I stared at the swirling mist that surrounded my body—blue and purple flames floated off my skin, sparkling with a wash of glitter. They swirled and coiled as I watched, reaching out behind me almost like gossamer wings. I was caught by my reflection, mesmerized by the energy that drifted around me.

A moment later, a knock brought me back.

"I'll be out in a minute," I called, hastily taking the dress off the hanger.

It was long, with spaghetti straps to hold up the deep V-bodice. The skirt swirled out, layer upon layer of silken material. I realized the waist was elastic, making it easier to get into, and so I pulled it over my head, sliding it carefully down over my boobs. It really wasn't made for a large-busted woman, but the strips of material that formed the bodice were enough to cover most of my boobs, and I had to hope that I wouldn't pop out if I turned the wrong way.

The material brushed against my nipples, and I caught my breath, glancing back in the mirror. The flames surrounding me flared with a deep magenta, and I slowly ran my hands over my breasts, my nipples stiffening under my caress. Shaken, and yet terribly aroused, I forced myself to open the door.

Aoife was waiting for me, a knowing smile on her lips. "The dress looks perfect on you."

"I think it might need a little more up top to cover my...assets." I stumbled over the words, feeling awkward. But she merely shook her head, placing a light hand on my arm. My skin jumped as she touched me, and I did my best to remain collected.

"Come. I'll take you to Morgana now." She led me over to the ladder.

"You want me to climb that ladder in *this* dress?"

"You'll manage," she said.

As she began to climb, I followed her, rung by rung. She opened the large skylight, but the sun vanished as she did so. I blinked, but said nothing as she climbed through, then turned to lend me a hand. As she drew me out atop the boat, I realized that we weren't in the bay any longer. We were standing on a strip of sand next to a dark, moody ocean. The waves were crashing against the rocks on either side, thundering so that they were all I could hear.

To the left, a short distance up the sand, stood a castle that was built out into the sea. The walls were glossy black, like obsidian, and around the base they were embossed with silver images. I squinted, trying to make out the pictures, and blinked as I saw they were depictions of sirens standing on the rocks, beckoning to boats that rode the waves. Still others were etchings of people I didn't recognize, but all of them were regal, cloaked in mystery.

From the windows, invisible against the jet walls, lights flickered forth, creating the illusion that the castle was on fire. Atop the castle, battlements stretched the length of the walls, their merlons stark against the sky. I thought I could see figures watching though the crenelles, and I wondered if they were fitted with bows and arrows. And *that* thought made me wonder whom Morgana might be braced against. For some reason, I hadn't expected Morgana to live in such a solemn-looking castle.

"That's…" I sought for a word other than *intimidating*. "Impressive."

Aoife seemed to understand my hesitation. "Morgana is of the Fae. She has seen her share of battles. Even the gods of the realm have their conflicts."

I hadn't thought about that. But if the gods of Faerie battled each other, then I wondered why Morgana was pledged to help Cernunnos stop the petty bickering among the Fae who followed her.

"Where do we go?" I finally asked.

"Follow me." She guided me to the path that led to the great castle doors. I was surprised there weren't any guards standing in front of them, but decided to hold my tongue.

The stark cliffs to our left led up to what looked like a forest. What kind of creatures roamed Morgana's woodland? And who lived within her woodlands?

The top of the castle had a footbridge leading to the top of the cliff. The base of the castle was built on the sand, jutting out into the water.

The footpath was formed of cobblestones, but they shimmered like mother-of-pearl, and only underscored that we were fully within another realm. A gust of wind whipped by, catching the layers of my dress and sending them fluttering. I shivered beneath the filmy material.

As we approached the castle, gargoyles appeared, looming out from the castle walls, the same jet color but brushed with a silvery film. It had been hard to see them from a distance. They watched over the walkway, their eyes swirling with a miasma of color.

"Are they alive?" I asked.

Aoife nodded. "They are, but frozen in time until they sense danger. I would not be an enemy and approach these gates. Morgana is a deadly goddess, and wields the power of the Ocean Mother."

We approached the end of the walkway where two massive gates covered the entrance to the castle. They looked to be silver although I knew they had to be stronger than that. They weren't iron, that much I could tell, but exactly what metal they were made of, I had no clue. Near the top of the gates, a large sapphire nearly the size of my head glimmered, the gates meeting on either side of it.

We paused and Aoife held up her hands. Twin beams of light emanated from her palms, burning white, and they hit center on the gem. There was a creaking, and the gates swung open.

Aoife led me inside. The hall was stark, the walls bare except for a continuation of the murals that had glimmered along the outside. We were in a long hall, with doors to either side, and the walls were illuminated by torches that burned with a blue fire from which came no heat. It hurt my eyes to look at it, so I kept my gaze steady, straight in front of me.

Still we had seen no one, but I could feel the presence of beings around me. The Unseen, I thought. They had to be the Unseen. But I didn't have time to ask, because Aoife led me to the end of the walkway, to a pair of ornate double doors. She stepped to the side, placing her hand on a panel next to the door.

As it swung open, I straightened my shoulders. I had expected a large throne room, but instead, we were staring at a long narrow path that led out over the water, barely skimming the surface, to a boulder the size of a house.

"Go now. She's waiting. I'll stay here to guide you back when you are done." Aoife motioned to the path. "Just follow the path and you'll be safe. Do not step into the water, though, no matter how much you may want to."

I gave her a hesitant look. "Are you sure?"

"Yes, Morgana waits for you on her throne. Go now."

I was totally out of my element and I knew it. But I stepped through the doors, onto the path, and the building fell away behind me, like a snake shedding its skin.

I followed the path, which was barely a foot wide, cautious not to stumble. It led through the water, which was just inches below the trail. The path was formed of compacted sand, with bits of shells scattered along the way. Here and there, a patch of sea grass wavered in the breeze, and the sky overhead was seething with clouds that boiled past, heavy with rain. The air was saturated with moisture and it felt almost like I was breathing underwater. I blinked as the scent of brine enveloped me, thick with seaweed and decay.

Halfway there, I began to hear a voice on the wind. It was a woman, her singing so faint at first I could barely make it out. But as I continued along the path, her song became louder, and it sang to me of the open sea, of treasures fair and adventures waiting to sweep me away. I felt a stirring in my heart, a desire to step out onto the water. My feet promised me they could hold me up, that I could race across the surface like running on glass.

Come join us, Ember. You can be one of us. Part of the sea, part of the Ocean Mother. You can live with us forever under the rain-shadowed days. And during the night, we watch as the vast panorama of stars unfolds and they dance with the water, reflecting in its surface. Join us and become one with the entire world, bound together by the rivers and streams and lakes. For we are the chosen ones, we are the singers of songs, we are the weavers of dreams. Come, sister, and we will brush your hair and drape you in pearls and coral.

A crow flew by, startling me with its caw, and I blinked, realizing that I was about to step into the water. I clasped the raven-shaped necklace around my neck, holding tight. Morgana had given it to me as a symbol that I belonged to her.

Focus, I whispered to myself. *Focus.*

I kept my eyes straight before me, avoiding looking over the depths of the water, and sped up. Before long, I had come to the end of the path. The boulder was huge, shrouded on all sides by trees that grew up out of the briny sea. They towered overhead, tall fir and cedar. A massive willow rose behind the rock. In front, steps, formed from mother-of-pearl, led up to a throne. Formed of seashells, the throne was draped in pearls and seaweed. Stretched along the back of the throne perched a murder of crows, all watching me as I approached.

And on the throne was Morgana.

Pale as alabaster, she waited, her skin luminous against the darkened sky. Her hair cloaked her in a raven shroud, and her dress shimmered, the color that iridescent sheen between twilight and dusk. Every time she moved, a thousand beads shimmered, and the sweetheart neckline was cut low against her breasts. A tiara adorned her hair, aquamarine interspersed with amethyst and pearls.

Morgana raised one hand in greeting, and the sleeve of her gown draped down like a gossamer wing. "Well met, Ember Kearney. Welcome to my realm."

I stared into her eyes. They mirrored the ancient moon, and I felt dwarfed as I knelt in front of her. "Lady Morgana, I am here at your summons."

I stood as she motioned me to rise, and waited, my hands clasped in front of me. I was still afraid, but the fear was giving way to a sensation I wasn't used to—pride. It hit me that I was proud to be here. Proud to be one of her chosen. A smile crept across my face.

"You begin to appreciate your place in my world." She held my gaze, and it felt as though she was dipping into my thoughts, reading my heart.

I wasn't sure what to say, so I kept silent.

"Cat got your tongue? Tell me, Ember, what you are thinking. Tell me, what do you want?"

Tripped up by the question, I found myself blurting out the first thing that came to mind. "I want to know what *you* want of me. What you expect of me. You drew me into your service, but I'm not sure what to do. I don't know how to serve you."

"Would you serve me, then? As a full and dedicated priestess?"

I paused. "I don't know what that entails. My life…" I realized I had no clue of how to answer her. I had never thought much about what I wanted out of my life, other than to make my own way and stay under the radar of the Fae Courts.

"Your life does not have to change in a drastic manner. I've been waiting to see how far your powers would awaken. The other night, your potential awoke. It's time you learn who you are." She stood, slowly descending the steps of the throne. She seemed overwhelming in her power, and yet when she stood beside me, she was barely taller than I was, but the energy crackled around her, like lightning over the ocean.

Her words made me uneasy. I knew who I was, or thought I did.

"What do you mean?" I gazed into her eyes, mesmerized by the brilliant tides that flashed through them. It was as though I was standing by the ocean incarnate, and her swirling eddies of energy buoyed me up. I wondered, if I were to reach out and touch her, would my hand pass through her like it would the water?

"You knew how to summon the elemental because you carry your mother's blood within you. No one's ever told you what kind of Water Fae your mother was, nor what type of Fae your father was. But now, you must set out to explore both of your bloodlines. For they are working together to form a new blend—a deadly mix."

I stared at her. "And what do you mean, my bloodlines are forming a new blend?"

Morgana reached out to stroke my face. "Ember, your mother came from the line of the Leannan Sidhe, and your father from a line originally known as Autumn's Bane, a band of Faerie warriors who were descended from the Holly King himself. They are waking up, and you must be prepared."

Chapter 9

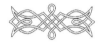

THE *LEANNAN SIDHE? Autumn's Bane?*

I felt weak-kneed and dizzy. I looked around for a place to sit. There was a pile of shells next to the throne. "May I sit here?"

"You may. I realize this is a great deal of information to process. If your parents would have lived, no doubt they would have told you by now. At least, I hope they would have. But do you see why you must know *what* you are, before your powers fully come to fruition?"

I slowly nodded. It was as if I lived in a snow globe and somebody had just picked it up and given it a good shake.

"How...but my mother was *Light* Fae." I frowned, trying to puzzle out the onslaught of feelings that were washing over me.

"One thing you must understand: *Light is not the same as good.* You know very well that the

Light and the Dark are merely two sides of the same coin, and good and evil reside within both bloodlines. The Light Fae love the summer months and the waxing half of the year, while the Dark prefer the shadows of autumn and the cold fingers of winter." Morgana paused, giving me time to take in what she was saying.

"The Leannan Sidhe—are they truly..." My voice dropped away. I wasn't sure how to ask what I needed to know. Hell, I wasn't even sure *what* I needed to know. I had spent my life away from both Courts, and right now, my lack of knowledge felt terrifying.

"The Leannan Sidhe are bloodthirsty. They delight in luring mortal men to their deaths. They're also incredibly inspiring and not easily forgotten."

"Ray." I let out a long breath. "He can't forget me. And two of my boyfriends died thanks to me, even though I had no intention of harming them."

"*Once you have met me, you'll never forget me,*" Morgana said. "The watchwords of the Leannan Sidhe. You will have to be cautious. If you develop your mother's powers, you may be able to drain the life force from someone with your kiss."

"Like a succubus?" I jerked my head up, now terribly afraid.

"In a sense, but the Leannan Sidhe don't *need* to feed on others to survive. They simply enjoy it."

"Trophy hunters, then." I set my lips, thinking that it would be better if I needed to feed on energy—at least I'd have an excuse. "Will the hunger overpower me, if I do develop my mother's powers?"

"It doesn't have to," Morgana said. "I can train you to control it, for the most part."

"That's good to know." I looked up at her. She was standing next to me, staring out into the water behind us. "What about my father? What are the Autumn's Bane?"

Morgana raised her hand to the sky and a bubble formed on it, glistening like a crystal ball. She played with it a moment before suddenly wrapping her hand around it so that it popped.

"The Autumn's Bane are also known as the Autumn Stalkers, because they send out parties during the autumn to hunt down victims. They're pillagers. Across the Great Sea, they continue to raid other Faerie bands. They used to raid mortal villages, as well. They took slaves—women and children mostly—and killed the warriors of the tribes they overcame. They have an inborn knack for hunting and tracking. During the winter, they feast and hang out with the wolves, and during the spring and summer, they sleep, regaining their strength for autumn. There are few of the original bands left, mostly across the Great Sea, but their descendants tend to be ruthless, and possess the drive to hunt."

"Autumn Stalkers." I tested the words on my tongue, trying to examine how they felt. After a moment, I shivered as a cloud seemed to settle around my shoulders. "And I'm a mix."

"And your blood mix is a rare type. I doubt if there have been more than a handful quite like you. The Leannan Sidhe are not easily captured, and the Autumn Stalkers are seldom ensnared by any such as the Leannan Sidhe. Since you are only now reaching the beginnings of the Cruharach, your full abilities haven't come through. We can only surmise what those will be."

The Cruharach.

"Right." I didn't even want to think about that, but it sounded like I was going to have to. For one thing, since I didn't belong to either Court, there was no one to walk me through it, so I had decided to do the next best thing: just ignore it.

The Cruharach was the point that came in every Fae's life where they stopped aging. It was like a second puberty. I hadn't been sure what to expect, so I wasn't even sure if I had gone through it, but apparently, I hadn't. I had been hoping that it would just pass by unnoticed.

At around thirty, the aging process for the Fae slowed drastically. I knew there were rituals that most Fae went through, but given my status as an outcast, I had no clue what to do.

"Tell me about the Cruharach. What should I watch for?" I was suddenly feeling desperate, afraid that I wouldn't know what to keep an eye out for.

Morgana knelt beside me, her gown spreading around me like a sea foam. "You are near the metamorphosis, that much I can tell you."

She paused for a moment, then continued. "When your mother underwent initiation in my service, she was very young. Before she died, during a ritual she and your father asked if Cernunnos and I would watch after you. Your mother foresaw their deaths and wanted to make certain you would be looked after. Cernunnos and I promised we would take you under our guidance."

I bit my lip. "My parents knew they were going to die?"

She nodded. "Your mother had a vision of the Bean Sidhe in her dreams. And the Bean Sidhe only appear to a very few who do not seek them out."

"How did my parents meet?" They had never told me their story.

"We must save that story for another day, but it was fated that Eolin and Breck meet. There are always reasons for why things happen, Ember, even if it seems a remote coincidence, or at odds with all we hold true. Not even the gods can see all of the intersections on the web, but they are there." She held out her hand. "Stand. You aren't one to cower."

I took her hand and stood. "My ability to channel the water elemental, was that part of my emerging powers because of my bloodline?"

Morgana inclined her head. "Yes. That would be the Leannan Sidhe side emerging. Your prowess with weapons, your strength and ability to track things, comes from your father. But the Autumn Stalkers have more powers than those—darker powers, rooted deep within the forest. Cernunnos will be able to help you more than I. Together we will guide you to balance the emerging combination of abilities. And there are some that may not hold, because you are a mix of two such distinct races."

A thought occurred to me. "Are the Dark and

Light Courts aligned with the elements?"

Again, a nod. "To a degree, though there will always be some overlap. Nothing except primal energy confines itself to only one element or season. The Light Fae tend to be connected more with fire and water, and the Dark, with earth and air."

"What should I do? How do I take control of this?"

Morgana handed me a piece of paper. "I've written down the name of a teacher—she's one of my priestesses. She will guide you. I want you to meet with her weekly. She'll also watch for signs that the Cruharach is approaching, though I believe you've already entered into it. We'll devise a ritual to lead you through the gate when it arrives. Ember, this is not simply a phase. It's a gateway through which all Fae must pass."

"What will happen if I don't undergo the ritual?"

"You could die. Or go mad. Or the emerging powers could tear you apart. Half-Fae don't undergo the same transformation, since theirs is gentler on their systems. But you are full-blooded. I imagine that's why your grandfather contacted you. He knew you were approaching the Cruharach and wanted to get to you first."

"He wanted me to give up my mother's side." I told her what he had said.

Morgana stiffened. "He asked you to do that?"

"Yes." By the look on her face, she was taking the request worse than I had.

"I'll have to have a talk with your grandfather. And trust me, he *will* listen to me."

Her eyes had grown dark as night and they

sparkled and whirled. I cringed, afraid I might be in the path of the rising storm. Out on the water, the waves began to crash over the edge of the boulder and lightning split open the sky.

"What will you do to him?" I whispered, trying to keep my balance as the eddies swirled on the water, creating whirlpools.

"Teach him not to be so arrogant. It's none of your concern. Not now." She sighed, then seemed to rein in her power. "Enough. I will save my indignation and apply it where it's deserved. You may go now. Contact your teacher as soon as you can, because I want you to start in on your lessons next week. I'll contact her, as well."

I felt myself calming down. "What happens if I find myself trying to channel another water elemental in the meantime?"

"Resist it. While a number of elementals are benign, there are some who are malevolent. If you contact one of the latter, or if an elemental happens to be controlled by a creature such as a siren or a kelpie, you run the risk of letting their master take you over."

That was a splash of cold water. "You mean that a siren could effectively take possession of my body if I let one of her controlled elementals...*in*, for lack of a better word?"

"Yes, and there lies the most danger." She paused. "Ember, I know you're frightened, but I'll walk you through the Cruharach, and together with Cernunnos, we will guide you in harnessing both sides of your nature. It is a deadly mix, but one that you can keep in control."

I let out a long sigh. "I trust you. I really have no choice, except to trust you."

"Good. Now you may return to your day, and do not forget to contact Marilee. She'll be waiting for your call." And with that, she reached out and touched the raven necklace that hung around my neck.

As her fingers touched the pendant, everything began to waver. I blinked twice, dizzy, and then when I opened my eyes the second time, I was standing on the strip of shoreline and Aoife was there, waiting for me. She reached down and opened a trap door beneath a thin layer of sand and motioned for me to swing down on the ladder. As I began my descent, cautiously making sure my feet were firmly on the rungs and that my dress didn't get caught up on anything, another wave of dizziness hit me and I suddenly found myself climbing back into the boat. Aoife followed me down through the skylight and fastened it firmly.

"Are you all right?" she asked. "Sometimes people get a little dizzy coming and going between dimensions."

I actually did feel a bit weak in the knees, and said so. She poured me a glass of apple cider and told me to sit down for a moment. As I sipped the cinnamon spiked nectar, the dizziness began to pass and my head cleared.

"Well. I didn't expect any of that." Morgana had revealed so much that my head was spinning. I looked up at Aoife, who was standing beside me with a worried look on her face. "Thank you for waiting for me."

"It's my job," she said with a touch of pride. "Morgana depends on me to do as she asks without screwing up."

I nodded, thinking that Aoife seemed content with her life. "How long have you been one of her priestesses?"

Aoife knotted her brow, squinting as she counted under her breath. After a moment, she said, "It's been around six hundred years, give or take a few. I was assigned to this post around thirty years ago. Before this, I guarded a portal in New York City, in a skyscraper. I was getting tired of the unending city, so Morgana transferred me here."

Feeling revived and ready to head out, I thanked her again and she escorted me to the door of the boat after I changed back into my own clothes. During the time I had been aboard, the tide had receded, so I climbed up a ladder next to the dock and, with a final wave, headed back to the parking lot to where Viktor and the car were waiting.

BY THE TIME we got back to the office, it was twelve-thirty. I had spent about an hour of time, at least on our side of the portal, in Morgana's company and another hour to get there and back. I leaned across the counter, staring at Angel who was eating a peanut butter and jam sandwich.

"So, I found out a lot of serious stuff about my background." I glanced around. "Where's Herne?"

"He and Kipa are in his office, talking." She

blushed.

I knew what that meant. "You think he's pretty," I teased.

She waved me off. "Right. Like I'm going to take a chance getting involved with someone like that. I can smell trouble coming a mile away around him."

"Um hmm. You say that now but wait till he invites you to go out somewhere. Just you see."

She stared at me like I was a wayward child. "Will you *stop*? He'll hear you."

"You can tell me you're not interested now, but we'll see." I relented, though. "Seriously, I found out what kind of Fae I am and it scares the hell out of me. I need to talk to Herne. I'll tell you tonight, when we can discuss it in depth."

"Are we going back to the house tonight to work?" She didn't sound too enthusiastic.

"I think Herne has something work-related planned for this evening, doesn't he?"

"What are you talking about?" Herne asked as he abruptly opened the door and strode out of his office. He sounded a little harried. Kipa leisurely strolled out behind him.

"I wondered...weren't we going to do something tonight on the case? I'm all topsy-turvy after my meeting with Morgana, and I need to talk to you about it. It's important." I gave him a long look, hoping he'd hear the underlying message. I did *not* want to talk about this in front of Kipa. I still didn't know him well enough to trust that what I said would be safe.

Herne paused in mid-step as he stared at me.

I wasn't sure if it was the look on my face, or the tone of my voice, but he abruptly handed Angel a file and motioned for me to head into his office.

"I'll be back as soon as I give Angel the rundown on what she needs to enter into the system." He glanced at Kipa, who was leaning against the wall, arms folded across his chest, with an amused smile on his face. "You can wait in the break room. Angel, ask Viktor to take Kipa to the hospital to have a look at Kamaria, would you?"

As he flipped open the file folder and began to point out what Angel needed to log into the files, I headed into his office and shut the door behind me.

HERNE LISTENED SILENTLY while I told him everything Morgana had said. When I finished, he remained silent.

"You're so quiet that I'm starting to get nervous." I had been pacing while telling him the story. Now, I pulled one of the leather chairs over to his side and sat in it, cross-legged.

He licked his lips. "I'm processing all of this and trying to figure out how best to help matters." Again, he paused, then he reached out and took my hands, sitting there, facing me. "The Leannan Sidhe truly *are* deadly. So are the Autumn Stalkers. You know that I never sugar-coat anything, love. You were born with a recipe for death and destruction in your blood."

Somehow, coming from Herne, the announcement seemed more ominous.

"What do you think I should do?" I asked.

"What my mother tells you. Call the teacher today. The Cruharach is a turbulent time in every Fae's life. For some reason, I thought you had been through it already." He gently squeezed my hands. "We'll get you through this."

"I'm afraid," I said, not wanting to admit it. "I don't know what to expect. It's like being told you have some condition that's going to manifest as you go along, but you're not sure what to expect or how it will change your life. Is it wrong that I'm hoping whatever I inherited from my parents is limited? I don't want to feel the urge to become a psychic vampire or a bloodthirsty hunter."

"I understand. And that aversion to those aspects of your parentage is what will help keep you from acting them out." He brought my hands up to his lips and kissed my knuckles. "Ember, we'll all help you. The others will have to know about this. We can help keep watch so that if the Cruharach starts without you realizing it, we'll catch it early."

"You make it sound like I'm going to go crazy," I said, half-joking. The truth was, I was worried about that myself.

"Aren't we all a little crazy?" Herne said, a smile spreading across his face.

I slowly nodded. "Yeah, I guess we are. I'll go call Marilee now."

"Good idea. But first, give me a kiss." He stood, pulling me up. As he wrapped me in his arms, I realized that I was breathing easier. And at that moment, it dawned on me that I had been terrified that Herne would find my bloodlines distasteful, that he'd think I was too high maintenance and break up with me.

I froze. While we had exchanged "I love yous," the full impact of how much he meant to me hadn't hit home yet, until now. Until when I thought maybe he would turn and walk away. Our chemistry had hit hard and quick, with no signs of slowing down, but sometimes it took me longer to process emotions.

"Is something wrong?" Herne stroked my cheek, pushing my hair out of my eyes.

I wasn't sure whether to tell him what I was thinking.

"I see the indecision in your eyes," he said, whispering. "Tell me. You can tell me anything."

"It's just that..." I paused, trying to put into words what I was feeling. "Mortals—whether human or Fae or shifter—our lives are messy and unpredictable. I suppose I've been secretly fearing that one day you'll wake up and say, 'I've had enough.' That you'll get tired of all the issues that surround me. Today, when Morgana told me about my mother and father, it terrified me in so many ways. I find out I'm a ticking bomb—two monstrous bloodlines wrapped into one. I'm near a transformation point and nobody knows just what I'll become. That scares the hell out of me. And then, I thought, *what about Herne*? Will he want to cope with this? Will he have the patience to stay with me as I go through this process?"

Herne placed his hands on my shoulders and

rested his forehead against mine. I fell into his gaze, deep and hard, my heart racing. I was sure he could hear it, thudding in my chest like a runaway locomotive.

"Ember, you know I love you. What you may not know is that I don't say those words lightly. I would never say them to someone who I was just dallying with, and I never have."

I gave him a long look. "You are telling me that in all the time you've lived, you've never used those words to bed a woman?"

He flushed, then gave me a sheepish look. "All right, maybe I have. But it was long ago, when I was young and tearing it up in Annwn. If I were just in this for a fling, I would have told you. But from the beginning you fascinated me. I'm here for you now, and I'll be here for you during the Cruharach. I don't know where we're headed, but I want to find out."

I placed my hand on his chest, feeling the beating of his own heart. It was calm and rhythmic, and I closed my eyes, breathing slowly as I marched my breath with his. As my pulse began to slow, a calm descended over the room.

"I believe you. And it's not easy for me to believe and trust in others. Angel is the only one who has never done me wrong."

"I hope to earn your trust enough so that you can say the same about me."

"Before we move on, I have to ask you something. Why *me*? Why did you choose me?"

He gave me another little shrug, and this time his smile widened. "Why *me*? Why anybody? I don't know if any oracle in the world can analyze what draws two people together. I suppose you could call it fate, or destiny. Or maybe our bio-rhythms match or it's written in the stars. Possibly, we just fell hard for each other. Does it really matter?"

I shook my head. "No, I suppose it doesn't. I suppose that all that matters is we know what we have. Thank you for being here. For being you."

He kissed me then, long and deep, wrapping me in his arms. I felt safe in a way that made me dizzy. I wondered if Herne felt the same, but decided not to ask.

After a moment, he broke away. "I'd love to continue this, but it will have to be later. We're going to pay a visit tonight to Nigel's roommate, since Nigel isn't answering the phone."

"Nigel? Oh, the waiter—that's right. His room-mate is a vampire, isn't he?"

"Yes, so we need to be polite, and we need to be professional."

I hadn't had a lot of dealings with vampires. Our last big case had brought them up close and per-sonal for a brief time, but otherwise, I steered clear of them.

"What's his name again? The roommate? And why would a vampire room with a human?"

"Charlie Darren. Yutani was curious about that, too, so he looked him up. Charlie was recently turned. He hasn't had time to establish himself in the vampire community yet. Apparently, just *being* a vamp isn't enough to secure yourself a good foot-ing. Charlie worked as a baker in a doughnut shop before he ended up as a blood bag, so he didn't have a lot of money. He probably let Nigel move in to make ends meet while he figured out his next steps. At least, that's what we surmise."

Herne glanced at the clock. It was almost one-thirty. "Why don't you spend the afternoon sorting out paperwork. Then we'll grab a bite to eat before heading over to their apartment. If we're lucky, Nigel will be there."

Once I was back in my office, I put in a call to Marilee. She set up a meeting with me for Sunday evening. After that, I got back to work, trying not to think about what I had learned from Morgana. There wasn't anything I could do about it at this point, and if I worried about it, it would only drive me batty.

"OH YEAH, THIS is the way I like to spend my Friday nights," Viktor said, rolling his eyes. He was in the back seat, with Herne driving and I was riding shotgun again. Yutani had begged off, and we decided that the three of us showing up on a vampire's doorstep was enough.

"Does Charlie even know we're coming?"

Herne nodded. "Yeah, I talked to him earlier and set a time. He sounded odd when I asked him about Nigel, almost guarded. Something's not meshing, and I'd like to know what."

"You're probably going to get your wish," I muttered.

Nigel Henderson and Charlie Darren lived in the Beacon Hill district, a tired part of the city where houses often came equipped with bars on the windows and doors. A lot of the streeps tended to congregate there, in flophouses run by slumlords who had found a way to fill a need at the expense of those they exploited. There were some flops that housed twenty to thirty people a night, stretched out on sleeping bags on the floor, for a few bucks each. Showers were extra, as was coffee in the morning and a few prepackaged convenience foods. But when the rainy season hit, a number of the streeps took refuge there, citing that it was safer than some of the shelters run by the city.

"People think this area's dangerous," I said, "but people here look out for one another. I wonder if those kids—Toby, Jozey, and Sha-Na—ever stayed here."

"That reminds me. I need to talk to Angel. I called Rhiannon up at the Foam Born Encampment. She said they have someone who could take the boys in, as long as they adhere to the rules. They'll see that they get the care and schooling they need, and will try to hook them up with savines who will help them integrate into their culture."

"Good. At least we can give them a chance." I thought about the street kids. If not for Mama J. and Angel, I might have been one of them.

"So Darren knows we're coming?" Viktor didn't sound all that pleased.

"Yes, he's waiting for us." Herne paused, then added, "I know you both have it in you to remain composed but remember, Charlie's a young vampire. He might not be all that savvy with how he acts."

"Young as in vampire, yes, but how old was he when he was turned? I don't cut a lot of slack for grownups either, you know." Viktor cleared his throat. "Never mind, I'll be on my best behavior. I always am. Or try to be, at least."

"Actually, young as in when he died, too. Yutani said Charlie Darren checked out when he was barely nineteen. So he wasn't very experienced when his sire got to him. He didn't want to be a vampire, as far as we can tell. Didn't belong to any fangbanger societies, wasn't a groupie of any of the local legends. In fact, he was a math student who was looking to put himself through college. He had the grades for a partial scholarship but was working to fund the rest of his ride when a rogue vamp got to him. The vamp's name was Shelby Jones. Apparently, Jones was taken down by the Vampire Nation, so Charlie's sire is dead. Jones had such violent tendencies that he was a liability for the entire community."

I stared out the window at the houses passing by. "You know, the way the vamps police their own community puts the Fae Courts to shame. Hell, my people need an outside force to keep us in check, while the Vampire Nation takes care of its own."

From the back seat, Viktor let out a snort. "Your people need a makeover, all right. At least as far as attitude goes. When Saílle and Névé were taking potshots at each other the other day, I was certain we were going to end up pulling them apart."

"Hey, don't blame me. Neither one of them like me, and I don't like them."

But that brought me back to thinking about the meeting and my grandfather. Then it hit me—the *Autumn Stalkers*. My grandfather carried them in his blood, and probably my grandmother as well. Which made his nature more understandable. And of course they wouldn't like that the Leannan Sidhe side from my mother might manifest. While it didn't make me dislike him any less, I began to see the pattern of behavior. The fact that he and my maternal grandmother had worked together to kill my parents only highlighted just how violent and angry both sides of my heritage were.

"Enough about that for now," Herne said. "Ember's got enough on her mind without being reminded of what went on after the meeting. But look—ahead. There's the apartment complex."

As he pulled into visitor parking, I glanced over at the building. It was tall, at least fourteen stories high, and a grim gray brick. Perhaps long ago it had been red, but now it looked like a gloomy dedication to the soot and smog that had filtered through the city over the years. The bricks were weathered and chipped, and the windows that dotted the sides of the walls were barred on the outside. I wondered how the residents coped with the feeling of being trapped inside their apartments. A steep set of stairs led to the main front door, which was metal. An inset intercom hid behind bars, allowing visitors to punch the buttons but not reach the panel as a whole. I wondered how many times it had taken for some idiot to destroy it before they got the idea to provide some security. A glance up at the top of the stoop showed a security camera, also behind bars. The apartment owners weren't giving vandals much of an option.

Herne scanned the intercom panel for a moment, then pressed a button. A moment later, the buzzer sounded and the door clicked. I pushed it open and we headed inside, on our way to ask Nigel Henderson why he had served tainted food to the Fae.

Chapter 10

CHARLIE DARREN WAS nothing like I had expected him to be. First, when he opened the door, he was wearing a polo shirt and a pair of jeans. His hair was longish, just down to the top of his shoulders, and he wore a pair of glasses, which seemed odd. Upon being turned, any old injuries were healed, including eyesight. Although if someone was turned who had an amputation, they wouldn't grow back the body part that had been excised. He was carrying a bottle of blood with a straw in it, and in the background, I could hear the sound of a TV.

"Come in, please." He smiled, his fangs descending. As if suddenly aware they were showing, he shut his mouth quickly, pressing his lips together. "Sorry, I didn't mean..." He rubbed his head, his skin the pale alabaster that always marked a vampire who had been Caucasian during their lifetime.

"Don't worry yourself over it. I'm Herne, head of the Wild Hunt. Allow me to introduce Ember Kearney and Viktor Krason, two of my investigators."

I blinked. I had never heard Viktor's last name before and, indeed, hadn't thought he had one. Following Herne's lead, I held out my hand.

"How do you do?"

Viktor followed suit, and Charlie shook our hands, his fingers cold against our own.

He led us into the apartment. It was small, with gray walls and a smoky-colored sofa against the wall of the narrow living room. The other side was given over to two desks. One was neat and tidy, and the other was a shambles. The kitchen, which we could see through the doorway, was tidy as well, though it was so small it was only big enough for one person to stand in at a time. Three other doors led to what I guessed were bedrooms and a bath.

Charlie motioned us to the sofa. "Please, sit down. I'm afraid we don't have room for a table, but will the sofa do?" He seemed to be good-enough natured and eager to please.

"Thank you. Is Nigel home, by any chance?" Herne asked.

Charlie shook his head. "No, and I wanted to talk to you about that. When you said on the phone that you're an investigator, I thought you might be able to help."

"What's the problem?" I asked.

"It's about Nigel, actually. He went missing about two weeks ago, and I haven't heard from him. I reported it to the police, and all they would say was that he's an adult and will probably show up at some point. But I know something's wrong. He never does this. He's practically a recluse, except for work and when he goes to meetings twice a month." Charlie sounded worried.

Herne frowned. "We couldn't find out much on him. You say he vanished two weeks ago?"

Nodding, Charlie jumped up. "Hold on, let me get a picture of him. It's a printout of his profile picture on Home-Time, that new social media site." He crossed to his desk—the clean one—and sorted through a stack of papers, pulling one out to hand to us.

Nigel was human, all right, average height and altogether too slender. He looked slight, even, with blond hair and a thin scruff of beard. He wasn't a handsome man, but rather plain—someone you'd see at the bus stop and your gaze would skip over as you perused the crowd. There was a look in his eyes, though, that made my hackles rise. Something about him set my teeth on edge.

"Where do you think he went?" Viktor asked.

Herne glanced at the photo, and he gave me a look that told me he saw what I did.

"I don't know, frankly. He belongs to a couple groups, but I'm not certain what they are. We really don't know each other very well. He's a private person and keeps to himself, but he pays his share of the bills on time, and he doesn't cause any trouble for me, so it works." Charlie paused. "You know, there have been a few times where he actually made me nervous. You would think *he'd* be the nervous one, rooming with a vampire." He held up his hand before we could say anything. "Don't sweat it, I know that question had to be back there. But I think I'm more nervous of him than he is of me."

"Why?" Herne set the photo down on the coffee table.

"He's an odd sort. As I said, he keeps to himself, but once in a while, I'll catch him looking at me in a way that makes my skin crawl. And that's not easy to do to a vampire." Charlie's smile vanished as he set the bottle of blood on a coaster. "There's something about him I find...off-putting. But I can't tell you what it is, because I can't pinpoint it."

Charlie was a lot more thoughtful than I had expected.

"Why do you stay? Why not move out?"

"It's hard to find a roommate willing to lodge with a vampire, for one thing. And I can't afford an apartment by myself. Thanks to the college courses I managed to take before I was turned, I have a job coming up with a local credit union run by the Vampire Nation. That should secure me training and allow me to start moving up in *my world*. What's my world *now*, rather. My parents disowned me when they found out I had been turned. They told me never to darken their door again."

"I'm sorry," Herne said. "It must be difficult, your whole life changing like that."

"That's an understatement." Charlie stared at the floor, a misty look crossing his face. "It's a lonely life, being a vampire. I'd give anything to have my old life back, even though I had credit companies coming after me and my girlfriend was a pain in the ass. But now, I don't have anyone, and my sire—who would normally train me and help me make my way—was killed because he was a fucking psycho."

We waited for a moment, then Herne motioned toward Nigel's desk. "Do you mind if we have a look around?"

"Given he hasn't been back in two weeks and I'm worried something might have happened to him, go ahead. If he comes back and pitches a fit about it, I'll kick him out and just figure out a way to pay rent on my own." Charlie stood. "If you don't mind, I'll pop into the kitchen. When you called and asked if you could come over, I decided to make some cookies. I used to do a lot of baking before I was turned. I worked at Doughnut Land, and I was the head baker for the franchise."

The loneliness in his voice was tangible and I found myself feeling sorry for him.

"Would you like any help?" I asked, but he shook his head.

"Thanks, but I'll be right back. Would you like some lemonade? I made it fresh." He looked so hopeful that we all said yes.

"Let's see what we can find," Herne said, sitting himself at Nigel's desk. He handed me a stack of papers. "Here, look through these. Viktor, can you do a quick call to your buddies in the know, to find out if Nigel's been arrested or anything of the sort?"

Viktor nodded, pulling out his phone as I started sorting through the papers. There were a few forms that looked as though Nigel had been filling out requests for credit cards, and a bunch of personal bills, to a car repair shop, a couple department stores, his Paycloud credit card bill, unopened. I hesitated, then slit open the envelope and pulled out the statement. It was for three months, with two in arrears.

It was short, but hefty. He had donated two hundred dollars every four weeks for the past three months to some organization called HLA. I wasn't sure what the acronym stood for.

"Charlie." I looked up as he returned with a tray of glasses filled with lemonade, and a plate of cookies. They smelled wonderful. "Oh, those smell good."

"I hope you like oatmeal raisin." He smiled, then, and I realized I was staring at him. His vampire glamour was in full force, and he didn't even seem to realize he had it.

"Love them," I said, accepting a glass and a cookie. "Listen, do you know what 'HLA' stands for? Nigel donated to them every month for the past three months."

Charlie frowned. "You're shitting me. Seriously, he donated to *them*?"

"Yeah, why? Who are they?" I bit into the cookie, almost swooning from the chewy goodness. "This is great," I said with my mouth full.

He held out his hand. "Can I look at that statement? I still can't believe it."

I handed him the statement and took another cookie. Herne and Viktor followed suit, helping themselves to the lemonade and the sweets as Charlie stared at the piece of paper.

"I'll be damned. I knew he was a little squirrely, but..."

"Is she right? Did he belong to the HLA?" Herne asked, eyeing him closely.

Charlie looked up, his expression bleak. "Apparently so."

Viktor and Herne seemed to know what he was talking about, but I still didn't.

"What's the HLA?"

Charlie glanced at me. "The HLA stands for the Human Liberation Army, a radical hate group out to rid the world of Cryptos. To them, it doesn't matter what race or species or whatever you are, if you're not human, you're better off dead. But why the hell would he room with *me* if he believes in this crap?"

I hesitated. If they were a hate group, and Nigel belonged to them, were they the ones deliberately targeting the Fae?

"Herne, are you thinking what I'm thinking?" I looked over at him, my stomach knotting.

He nodded. "Yeah. I'm going to search his computer, if you don't mind, Charlie?"

Charlie roused himself out of his shock. "Whatever you want. He's not setting foot back in this apartment. I'm hiring a mover to dump his stuff into a storage locker, and I'll give him back his rent for this month, but he's out of here." He slowly sat down between Viktor and me. "So my nervousness was based in reality."

"It seems so." Viktor hesitantly clapped him on the back. "But at least you're okay. He didn't manage to do anything to you."

"No."

A thought occurred to me and I dropped my cookie on the table. "What did you make those from? Were they his ingredients?"

Charlie nodded his head. "Yeah, seeing I don't really eat anymore. Why?" Then he turned a paler shade of white than I would have thought possible. "What did he do?"

"We think he poisoned a group of the Fae with a mutated virus." I began to shake. "What if I ate contaminated food? Nobody survives this virus... no one who is Fae blood."

Herne jumped up and took me by the shoulders, pulling me to my feet. "*Breathe*. I doubt if Nigel cooked the ginger chicken. Whatever he added to it had to be made off-site. The catering staff cooked the food. He probably just doctored it, and I doubt if he'd leave whatever vehicle he used to transfer the virus in the cupboard with the rest of the food. You're okay, Ember." He glanced over at Charlie. "Can we take all the food from the kitchen, in order to test it?"

"Of course." Charlie jumped up, agitated. He rushed into the kitchen and we heard a clanging and a few moments later, he returned with a grocery bag. "I added all the cookies and everything I used in them, along with the lemonade, though that was just lemons, water, and sugar. But the bag of sugar's in there."

Herne braced me up. "You'll be fine, Ember. I promise, you will be all right."

I nodded, trying to calm myself down. "Right. And getting upset isn't going to help, either way.

Go back to searching. We need to know more about this freak."

Herne positioned himself in front of the computer again while Viktor rubbed my shoulder. I leaned back against the half-ogre and he gave me a gentle hug.

Charlie headed over to the door, where he threw the deadbolt and fastened a chain lock. "I'll look through his room, see if he's got anything suspicious in there. As I said, he's not getting back in. I don't want any more surprises from him."

A few moments later, Herne let out a low whistle. "I just hit the jackpot."

We all crossed the room to look over his shoulder, including Charlie, who ran in when he heard the whistle. We were looking at the HLA forum boards. The forum was locked, but Nigel's name was in the log-in bar, and it looked like he had his password set to auto-configure. Herne clicked on it, first making certain that the webcam was turned off.

Nigel had twenty-three unread messages in his in-box, and Herne scanned through them, reading quicker than any of us could.

"He's been missing from the boards for almost two weeks, too. Most of these are questions as to whether he's okay. I'm marking them unread, so that no staff member who might think to look will know whether he's read them."

"Look through his history to see what his last few posts were." I had used a number of forum boards over the years in order to find clients when I was freelancing. Forums had come back in style.

Herne skimmed through the list of links, then paused. He leaned closer, reading the subject line, then clicked on the link to one of the posts. It brought up a local chapter of the forum, and the post was a request for waiters for the FMR Day Labor company. Herne cleared his throat, reading it aloud.

Wanted, one or two wait staff to man booths at local event. Must have experience, be dependable, discreet, and willing to work outside of your comfort zone. This position requires a strong commitment to the tenets of the HLA. Contact FMR Day Labor at 206-555-0134.

"Well, we know how he found the job," I said. "Should we try the number?"

"Ten to one it's a throwaway phone number." Herne pulled out his phone and pressed a button, then entered the number. "I blocked my name."

"That's handy, how did you do that?"

"My father knows a lot of powerful techno-mages. Yep, just as I figured. The number is no longer in use. My guess? A burner phone." He turned to Charlie. "Have you ever heard of FMR Day Labor?"

Charlie shook his head. "Back when I was doing day-labor jobs, I went to Day-Jobs, one of the bigger day labor companies. They're totes legit." A dark look passed over his face. "So, Nigel is trying to hurt the Fae?"

Herne paused, then nodded. "Yeah, we think he is."

"You want to take his computer and shit to look

through? I mean, he's been gone for two weeks. Something had to happen because he's never been gone for more than a day. Plus, if you just leave it, I'm liable to smash it, I'm so pissed right now."

"Then we'll take it, along with all of his papers, if you can bag them up for us. Crap, wait a sec." Herne typed away for a couple moments, then turned off the computer. "I changed the password so we'll be able to get into it when we take it back to the office."

"Good idea," Charlie said. "Listen, whatever he did, I'm sorry. I wish I had never let him move in. I knew there was something wrong with the dude, he was so quiet, but I needed the money and he kept to himself."

He was beginning to spiral. I recognized the emotions. He was blaming himself for what Nigel had done. Guilt by association, and all of that.

"Charlie, it's not your fault. You rented him space because you needed a roommate to make ends meet. That's all. You didn't know he belonged to a hate group." I leaned down, forgetting myself as I patted his shoulder. He jerked back, staring up at me with his fangs fully down. *Oh crap.*

"Sorry, forgive me." He abruptly pulled away. "I wasn't expecting that. Your pulse is beating so loud it's practically playing a symphony in my ears."

I slowly backed away as the light in his eyes died back to normal. Never get too close to a vampire, even if you knew them well. He would have been able to smell my blood right through my skin from that distance.

"Not to sound inhospitable, but I think you'd

better go." He was worrying one lip with his fang, enough so that I thought he might end up putting a hole through it.

Herne quickly closed the laptop and accepted the bag of papers Charlie handed him. "Thank you for all your help, Charlie."

"Listen..." Charlie paused, scuffing the carpet with his sneaker. "Do you think maybe I could come visit your agency sometime? If you're working in the evening?"

Again, the loneliness in his voice was tangible and it was apparent just how desperate the vampire wanted friends. I glanced over at Herne. It wasn't my place to answer.

Herne looked flummoxed, but finally nodded. "Sure, that's fine."

Viktor spoke up. "Hey, maybe we can get together at a bar or something? I have a few free evenings coming up and I wouldn't mind hanging out."

A broad grin spread across Charlie's face. "You would do that? Hang out with me?"

"Sure thing," Viktor said. "I think it would be fun." Whether or not he meant it, the words put a smile on the vamp's face. "I'll call you tomorrow."

"Cool. I don't sleep in the daytime."

Some vampires did, given they couldn't go abroad in the daylight, but a number simply hid out until the night rolled around again. After Viktor and Charlie agreed on a time and date, we headed out, carrying Nigel's computer and the bag of papers from his desk.

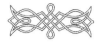

ONCE WE WERE back in Herne's SUV, I pulled out Nigel's little black book.

"I found his planner and address book. I don't know why I didn't tell you in front of Charlie, but it just seemed to be a good thing to keep quiet." I flipped it open as Herne turned on the overhead light. As I skimmed through the pages, I saw an entry for both Fae Day and the night afterward.

"Hey, look, he was scheduled to work on Fae Day at the booth. Then, the next night, he was supposed to attend a party at the Goza Club. There are a few entries after that, but none of them are checked off, and he put a little red tick next to every other event that he didn't cross out."

Herne glanced at it. "So either he never made it to the Goza Club, or that was the last event he attended. You guys have enough energy left to run by there and check it out?"

"All right," I said. "But don't you think we should figure out exactly what the Goza Club is before we go crashing in there?"

"I'll take care of that. Meanwhile, I just found the directions. I'll send them to your GPS, Herne," Viktor said, tapping away on his phone. "It looks like it's in the industrial district. Rough area of town."

As we headed out, Viktor did a quick search on his phone. He let out a sharp whistle.

"The Goza Club...it's definitely the type of place none of us would be welcome in. Humans only.

Segregated. Not overtly—there won't be any 'No SubCults' signs on the doors, but it's apparently known as *the* club to flock to if you're a Xeno. Lot of guys in leather with guns and knives hang out there."

"Great, a bar full of Xenos? I suggest we don't walk in there. There are only three of us, and while Herne can recover from most injuries that come his way, I don't want to test my luck. All right?" I wasn't feeling up to a fight, especially against a lot of angry pitchfork-wielding xenophobic bigots.

"We'll just look around the area. Maybe I can send someone back who can pass to gather information." Herne swung over into the next lane, then turned left. We wound our way through the streets until we pulled up across the street from the Goza Club. It looked jammed, which left me with a sinking feeling in my stomach. It disheartened me to see so many supporting the hate groups.

"What should we do now that we're here? I don't want to go in there." Not only did I not want to face a radical group of zealots, but I didn't want to face the fact that there was so much hate in this world.

"We search around back. We check out the alley. I don't know why I feel we have to do this, but it's the one idea that I think we do. So come on, let's get moving."

We followed Herne across the street into the alleyway. Viktor brought up the rear, keeping a close eye out should the haters find us and decide we were all better off dead.

Noise filtered out from the club, the sound of laughter and hoots, and the clinking of bottles. There were loud voices arguing over the laughter, and I wondered what they were debating. I debated straining to hear, but then again, I wasn't sure I wanted to know.

We slipped into the shadows, silently passing into the alley. The brick building was chipped and worn, like so many buildings from historical Seattle, and the alley was uneven, with potholes everywhere. Weeds grew through the cracks in the concrete, and the dumpsters to the side of the building were full and reeking of decay. The other side of the alley was bounded by yet another brick building, and it, too, had dumpsters and recycling bins that were long overdue to be emptied.

We passed an older streep, a man with a long bushy beard peppered with white and gray, matted hair down to his shoulders. He was leaning against the opposite wall between two dumpsters on a pile of molding cardboard, covered by a ragged blanket. His feet were wrapped in paper bags that had been taped closed, and he stared at us as we passed by, a look of resignation on his face.

I paused, my conscience prodding me. Too many people were living on the side of the freeways and under the bridges and in back alleys. I reached in my pocket and pulled out a twenty-dollar bill as I walked over to him. Herne and Viktor watched from behind me.

"Will you allow me to gift you with this?" I asked, kneeling.

The man stirred, pushing himself to a sitting

position. He stared at the money suspiciously. "Why?"

"Because I want to." It was that simple. I wanted to help him. I wanted him to have a good meal. Or if he wanted a bottle of booze to comfort him during the long nights, I didn't care.

He gazed at my face, then slowly reached out and pressed his fingers against mine. His eyes were misting over and he cleared his throat. "Thank you, miss."

I pressed the money into his hand and folded his fingers over it. "Put that where nobody else finds it till you need it. Peace be with you." It was the best I could do. I couldn't bring myself to say "Good luck" or any other of the inane clichés that were running through my head.

"What can I give you in exchange?" he asked before I straightened back up.

I frowned. I had to give him the chance to offer something in return. He deserved his dignity, even though he was down on his luck. After a moment, I decided to take a chance. I turned to Herne.

"That picture of Nigel—give it to me, please."

Herne silently handed it to me, along with a flashlight.

I held it out, illuminating it with the light. "Have you ever seen this man? We think he used to come around the club there."

The streep leaned forward, squinting. Then, slowly, he pulled back, fear registering on his face. "Yeah, I saw him. He was running from someone. I don't know who. They chased him down to the end of the alley." He pointed toward the opposite end.

"Thanks. You're sure it was him?"

"Yep. I remember thinking how he couldn't run very fast for such a slight boy."

"Do you remember when this happened?"

The streep shrugged. "Week...maybe two weeks ago. The days get lost out here, you see."

"Yeah, I suppose they would," I said, standing up. "Did they see you watching?"

"Oh no, not me. I'm not stupid, even though I do forget things easier now. I hid."

"Well, thank you." I turned to go.

"Good-bye, miss, and I hope you find what you're looking for." And with that, he blended back into the shadows and snoring soon rose from underneath the cardboard.

I returned to Herne and Viktor and, in a low voice, told them what the man had said. We headed toward the end of the alleyway.

The alley ended in a dead end, with a chain link fence covering the exit. Beyond the fence was a lot that looked like it was being used as an impromptu dump. There was no gate leading in, so we could either go the long way around, or climb the fence. I chose the most expedient route, sticking my shoe in one of the open links, and hauling myself up the fence. It rattled as I climbed it, but not loud enough to draw unwanted attention.

Herne and Viktor followed suit, though the fence threatened to topple when the half-ogre began to climb. We dropped over the edge, down to the ground on the other side, and quickly straightened.

The lot we found ourselves in was actually the size of two city lots, and it was overgrown with a tangle of brambles and weeds that were almost as tall as I was. Inroads had been made through the veritable jungle, looking like somebody had come through with a machete and carved a winding path at some point. We slowly began to move forward, Herne insisting on taking the lead. I walked behind Herne, and Viktor brought up the rear. The trail was only wide enough for one person, unless somebody wanted to risk tumbling into the blackberry bushes.

Everywhere, garbage littered the lot, and a dim light filtered down from a street lamp on the other end of the lot. But we were into the wee hours of dusk, and everything was muted in shades of gray. Here and there a wild rose bush pushed its way through the tangle of blackberries, or a cottonwood popped through. The trees were scavengers, growing up where forests had been mowed down.

I grimaced as I stepped on something soft and squishy, and I decided it was better not to look down. Whether it was dog poop, an old slice of pizza, or a banana slug, I really didn't want to know, especially when there wasn't any place I could wipe my shoe off.

We were almost to the center of the lot when the scent of decay grew stronger. I wrinkled my nose at the putrid smell.

"What the fuck is that? It's not skunk, that much I know."

Herne held up his hand, motioning me silent. He held his fingers to his lips. He slowed going forward, almost to a crawl. Then, under the growing darkness, he paused, pointing to the side. There, we saw a feral dog, her eyes glued to us. She began to growl, low and threatening. She had a bone between her feet, one that she had been worrying. The bone looked suspiciously like...

"*Crap*," I whispered. "Is that what I think it is?"

"Yeah, I believe so." Viktor very slowly edged toward the cur. He held out his hand, keeping his voice even and mild. "Come on, girl, let me see what you have. I'm not going to hurt you. I just want to see what you found."

The dog stared at him uncertainly, but then slowly stood and limped her way over to the half-ogre. He brushed her head with his hand and she whimpered, raising her front paw. It looked gnawed on, as though she had been biting it, or perhaps another dog had gotten to her.

"Poor girl, you're hurting, aren't you?" Viktor knelt, scratching behind her ears. He let out a soft curse. "Damned fucking idiots. She's not feral, but she'd be better off. Somebody collared her and it's too tight, it's cut into her neck, like it's grown into her flesh. Either she ran away or they just dumped her."

My blood roiled. I hated people who abused their animals. "Can we help her?"

"We'll help her, yes." Herne crossed to Viktor's side and knelt next to him, running his hand over the dog's head. A moment later, she slumped. "She's just in a deep sleep, don't worry. But move her, if you will, so we can see what she was gnawing on."

As Viktor carefully carried her out of the way, I moved in.

We were right. The bone she had been chewing on was the remains of a human arm, amputated shortly above the elbow joint. The hand and finger bones were still attached, with some flesh still clinging. I shuddered.

Behind where the dog had been resting lay what was left of a human body, gnawed on by what looked like any number of animals. It had been a man, that much we could see, and I saw a wallet next to the body. Ignoring the maggots that swarmed over the rotting flesh, I darted in and grabbed up the tri-fold. After I opened it, Herne shone the flashlight onto the driver's license.

Charlie Darren wouldn't have to worry about his roommate coming home again. We had found the remains of Nigel Henderson.

Chapter 11

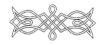

"WELL, WE FOUND him," Viktor said. "Now what? Should we call the police, since he was human?"

"Therein lies the dilemma." Herne squatted next to the body, leaning back on his heels. "I wonder if a Morte Seer could help us speak with him."

"What makes you think Nigel would be willing to help us? Just because he's dead, that doesn't mean he can't lie. And if he's still harboring grudges against all Cryptos, he's likely to ignore our questions." Viktor shook his head. "Besides, I'd say by the looks of him, he's been dead for the two weeks he's been missing. Want to make a bet that party he went to was a setup?"

"Why would the HLA kill him? He was a member in good standing, right?" I wasn't tracking what Viktor was saying.

"That's the thing. Suppose they weren't the ones

who killed him? We're assuming a lot here." Viktor reached down, stroking the dog. She looked like a mutt. She could have been a lab or a retriever or any number of breeds.

Like me, I thought. Like Viktor.

"Herne, what do you want to do with the body?" I stepped to the side as a sudden change in the evening breeze put me downwind of the corpse and the smell washed over me.

"We're going to take care of the cleanup ourselves. There are tactful ways we can reach out to the cops if we need to, but so far, nobody seems to be pounding down doors trying to find Nigel, so I think we're safe." He stood, arching his back as he stretched. Then, pulling out his phone, he punched in a number. "Hey, Akron? We need a cleanup crew. I want any evidence bagged, tagged, and a report on my desk tomorrow. Right... Murdered human, but he's mixed up in a code red case... Yeah, I know." Herne rattled off our location then hung up. "Akron will be here with his crew in twenty minutes."

Over the past few months, I had found out that the Wild Hunt employed a number of contractors. Akron was a shifter—a raven shifter—and he led a clean-up crew that not only took care of crime scenes, but he also ran an underground medical examiner's unit. He was a priest of the Morrígan and was more reliable than Old Faithful. I had never met him, but I knew who he was.

"So we should wait for him?" I glanced around the lot. There didn't seem to be anybody else around.

"Yeah, I'll need to tell him what we're looking for. I think he knows a Morte Seer, so he might be able to convince her to see if she can find out anything." Herne paused, glancing down at the dog. "We can't leave her here. She needs treatment."

"I know," Viktor said. "I thought I might take her, if she's well enough to be adopted." His voice softened. "I can't stand to see critters hurt."

"You already have a menagerie," Herne said, but it was barely a protest. He laughed. "We'll take her to an emergency vet when we leave here. Can you get that collar off her neck?"

"I'm afraid to try. It's embedded too deeply and I think it might be stuck to the skin." He fretted over the pup. "She isn't full grown yet, I'll tell you that."

I walked away from them, looking around the lot. It was a tangle of vegetation and litter, and I wondered how many bodies had gone back to the earth here, beneath the cover of the brambles. And that reminded me of Blackthorn, the King of Thorns. I shuddered, wondering if he ever traveled here, or if there were other Ante-Fae like him. I crossed my arms and turned back to Herne and Viktor.

"I wish they'd get here. I don't like this place."

"Neither do I," Viktor said. "There's something fetid about the energy here. It's tainted."

"We'll be gone soon enough." Herne planted his feet on the ground and, crossing his arms, stared up at the sky. "I feel something coming," he said faintly, a distant look on his face. "I don't know what it is, but there's something in the air, waiting."

I shivered and moved closer to him. "Yeah, I know what that feels like." Then, trying to change the subject, I asked, "How do you think Kipa's doing with Kamaria?"

Herne kept his attention focused on the expanding panorama of stars. They were faint, thanks to the light pollution that radiated out from the city, but the stars were still there, watching down over us, cold and aloof.

"If anybody can reach her, Kipa can. We'll call Talia when we're done here and ask how it's going. She went to the hospital with him."

Just then, a group of men rounded the bend, carrying a number of bags and boxes. They were mere shadows against the dark mounds of brambles and bushes, and they were silent as the grave as they approached us. I was curious as to what Akron would be like.

The front man, a lithe, alabaster-skinned, man with dark stringy hair stopped in front of Herne and knelt, then rose. His features were angular and sharp, and he was wearing a black tunic over camo pants. I nodded to him.

Herne blinked, then said, "Oh, that's right. You haven't met yet. Akron, meet Ember Kearney. Ember—this is Akron."

He stared at me out of beady eyes, his gaze darting over me in a quick appraisal. He neither smiled nor frowned, nor did he reach out to shake my hand. Instead, he bowed precisely, and said, "Well met, Ember."

I wasn't sure what to say, so I just whispered hello back at him. It was an odd thing to meet over a corpse, and somehow shaking hands and being friendly didn't seem proper protocol.

Akron turned to the corpse. "I suppose we're lucky that humans don't decompose on death like the sub-Fae."

I blinked. I hadn't even thought about that. Goblins, along with several other variants of the sub-Fae, decomposed within minutes upon their deaths. They had no cemeteries in their homeland, no mausoleums. It was a trait that seemed to be limited to a few races, and now I wondered what had caused the mutation. I made a note to find out, and turned my attention back to Akron and his crew. They were already busy, bagging and tagging everything around the body.

"We need as much evidence as you can gather," Herne said. "As I mentioned, this is a code red situation. If you have a Morte Seer on hand, it might be useful if we could try to ask Nigel's spirit a few questions."

Akron scanned the body, then shook his head. "No can do, Herne. The body's too ripe. You have a window of about three days, and after that, too late."

"Really? I thought you could use a Morte Seer on old bones?" Herne looked put out.

"Nope. But we'll get you a report on everything we find here. Now scram and give us the room we need to work." He shooed us out, murmuring a good-bye as we left.

Viktor picked up the dog as we turned to go.

"She's skin and bones," he said.

"Come on, we'll find an emergency vet," I started

to say, but Akron came over to see what we were doing.

"What have you got?"

"Dog was chewing on Nigel's finger bones," Viktor said. "She's in need of treatment, I'm afraid." He showed Akron the collar that was effectively choking the pup. "Do you think she's got a chance?"

I wondered why he would ask Akron, but then thought—of course, Akron was a priest of the Morrígan, a goddess who ruled over death. If anybody could tell, he should be able to.

Akron put his hand on the dog's chest and closed his eyes. A moment later he opened them again, smiling. "She can be treated. She's not ready to give up yet. So take her to a vet and get her fixed up. She looks like she's been sorely abused and neglected. She'll need a lot of love and care."

"I can give her that," Viktor said. "Thank you."

"Not a problem. Now, I'll get back to work. By the way, if she's swallowed any of his bones, you know they're gone."

"Right. We're not worried about his skeleton, so much as anything you find around it or on it," Herne said.

And with that, he led us back down the alley, past the sleeping streep, back to his car.

ANGEL WAS WAITING up when I got home. Herne dropped me off, then he and Viktor headed to the emergency vet. I trudged in, feeling covered with dirt and slime. I wasn't, but the whole *hanging out with a rotting corpse* had left me feeling grubby.

"What happened to you?" she asked. "Did you meet the vampire?"

"We not only met the vamp, but we found his roommate dead in a back lot near a supremacy bar. How's that for an evening? And Nigel wasn't just dead, but juicy dead! So we were guarding his corpse until Herne's cleanup crew came in to take over. I need a shower."

"Go on," she said, waving me toward my bedroom. "Are you hungry?"

I shook my head, still feeling somewhat queasy. "That's another thing...but I'll tell you after I've cleaned up." The cookies-and-lemonade incident came flooding back, and now I was back to wondering if somehow I had been infected, thanks to the ingredients Charlie had used.

By the time I showered and then curled up on the sofa with Mr. Rumblebutt on my lap, it was midnight. I told Angel what happened as she fixed me a cup of tea.

"So he was a racist scum, and now he's dead?" She cupped her mug, inhaling the fragrant scent of peppermint. "What's the next step?"

"We see what Akron and his team can find out. It's too late for the Morte Seers to be of any help, but I'm wondering if perhaps someone like Kamaria—a medium—could contact his spirit." I finished my tea. "I'm so tired. I think I'll go to bed. Herne wants us in tomorrow bright and early."

"But tomorrow's Saturday. I thought we could work on the house now that the demon seed thing is gone." She wrinkled her nose. "Not fair."

"Not fair, but the situation in TirNaNog and Navane rate a code red on the emergency scale, so we're going to work."

"Wait, what were you upset about when you came back from talking to Morgana? You never did get a chance to tell me." Angel took my mug, carrying both cups back into the kitchen.

I was too tired to go into it. "I'll tell you tomorrow. Today kind of threw me to the wolves. Or so it feels."

"As long as you don't end up in Kipa's arms, you'll be fine," she said with a laugh.

I tried to smile, but it was hard, given how much had gone down. "Night, Ange," I said, using the nickname I hadn't used since we were in high school.

She stared at me for a moment. "That bad, huh? Well, it will keep till morning. Try to get some sleep."

And with that, we both headed off to bed. As I tried to drift off, though, my mind kept jumping from my grandfather, to the Leannan Sidhe, to the Autumn Stalkers, to Nigel's corpse. Sleep was a long time coming.

MR. RUMBLEBUTT WOKE me up by licking my face. I blinked as he dragged his sandpaper tongue across one eyelid. Seeing I was awake, he settled in on my chest, purring up a storm.

"I'm sorry, Mr. R., but I can't stay in bed today. I know it's Saturday, but I have to go to work." I rolled up to a sitting position, cuddling him to my chest, and sat cross-legged with him in my lap as I grabbed his brush from my nightstand and gave him a good brushing. He rolled over on his back, begging for more.

"You love this, don't you, you little goon?"

Yawning, I glanced at the clock. It was barely eight, and I was still tired, but Herne had given us a nine o'clock start time.

"Okay, time to get up."

Setting him to the side, I slipped out of bed and into the shower for a quick rinse. I braided my hair back and slapped on a quick face of eyeliner, mascara, and lip gloss. A glance out the window told me we were due for a hot day. The sun was already bearing down on the city. I chose a pair of capri pants, a light tank top, and a gauze overshirt. Just in case we had grunge work to take care of, I threw a pair of jeans and a long-sleeve V-neck sweater into a bag to take with me, along with a pair of sneakers. Sliding on my sandals, I buckled them, then headed into the kitchen.

Angel looked just about as tired as I felt. She handed me toast and a latte, and we silently gulped down the bread, followed by a piece of sharp cheddar to give us protein to go on.

Just as we were about to head out, both our work phones beeped. I pulled mine out and saw that Herne had sent everybody a group text.

IF YOU'RE THINKING OF SKIPPING WORK TODAY, DON'T.
GET IN HERE STAT—WE HAVE NEWS.

"Okay, then. Definitely no playing hooky today, it looks like." I shoved my phone back in my pocket and we headed out. I was still wiped out from the night before, so Angel offered to drive and we took her car.

"What do you think the news is about?" Angel asked, sliding on a pair of sunglasses to block the already-glaring rays.

"I dunno. For all I know, they could have found a way to transmute lead into gold." I stared out the window the rest of the way, realizing that this job came with a tremendous amount of stress. No wonder they paid us so well.

By the time we got there, Herne was waiting by the front desk.

"Good, you're here. Everybody else is already gathered. Come on." He gave me an absent-minded peck on the cheek, and we followed him into the break room.

As we entered the room, I saw that both Ferosyn and Kipa were waiting. Ferosyn was eyeing Kipa with distaste, and Kipa was just grinning at him. Talia let out a relieved sigh as we entered the room, and Yutani and Viktor straightened up in their chairs.

"About time," Yutani muttered, but he flashed us a smile.

"What's going on?" I asked as we took our seats.

"Ferosyn has some important news for us regarding the case. And Kipa just returned from a night at the hospital. Let's get that out of the way first. What news do you have for us?" Herne motioned toward Kipa.

Kipa shrugged. "It's not bad. I found her soul and coaxed her back to her body, but she's going to be out of commission for a few weeks at least. That kind of trauma takes time to recover from. However, I can tell you this: You should have your house cleaned professionally. I can do this, but only with both of you present." The way he said it made it sound like an indecent proposal.

I blinked. "Oh?"

Herne let out an exasperated sigh. "Never mind the innuendos, Kipa. If you can clean the house, then good. We'll all be there. But I'm afraid it will have to hold for a few days until we take care of the news Ferosyn brings. I hate to ask, but can you stick around for a while?"

Kipa laughed, a deep resonate laugh that sounded both sultry and frightening. "That's the first time you've asked me to stay, rather than told me to get the hell out, *cousin*. Of course. How can I refuse? But I need a place to stay."

Viktor cleared his throat. "You can stay with me."

Herne blinked, looking at the half-ogre. "That's generous."

"It will keep you from throttling Kipa, won't it?"

I couldn't help it. I nearly snorted my latte through my nose. "Dude, that..."

"Is accurate," Talia finished for me. "It's settled. Kipa will stay with Viktor for the meantime."

Kipa shrugged again. "Fine with me. Do you have an extra key? I had a long, difficult night hunting down Kamaria's soul, and I'd like to rest and meditate."

He ran his hand across his eyes and I could see the fatigue setting in, which surprised me. A part of me had assumed the gods never got tired or ran out of energy; that they slept merely because they enjoyed it. I hadn't really asked Herne about it.

Viktor took a key off his keychain and handed it to Kipa. "Don't lose it. And don't let anybody else in my apartment. Got it?"

"Of course," Kipa murmured. "Your address?"

Viktor wrote it down for him, and Kipa headed out. When he was gone, Herne leaned back in his chair.

"Good, I'm glad he left. I don't want him interfering with this case," he added sternly. "Which means, don't invite comments or suggestions from him. Oh, and Ember? I've given Ferosyn those ingredients we got from Nigel. He'll test them for presence of the virus."

"Good," I murmured.

Ferosyn cleared his throat. "If I might present my findings? I have to get back as soon as I can to my research."

"Of course," Herne said. "I'm sorry for the delay."

"Right." Ferosyn opened a notepad and I could see notes in a language I didn't recognize. I assumed it was Elvish. The healer frowned as he straightened his shoulders and looked around the table at us.

"I have discovered a way to make an antidote to the poison. While it won't kill the actual virus, it will negate the poison's effects, and the only thing left will be a nasty cold. You see, whoever engineered this was able to insert the poison into a virus that attacks the respiratory systems of Fae. First it was ingested, but then it spread through airborne contact. Now, a number of Fae have a natural immunity to the cold virus that the engineer used, so they didn't 'catch' it, and the poison couldn't take hold. So there's a subset of the Fae—both Light and Dark—who are naturally immune to it."

"Can you make a vaccination against it?" Yutani frowned, staring at his computer. "I mean, humans make vaccines against various diseases."

He shook his head. "Not an effective one, at least not fast enough to matter. For the long term, yes, I can probably do so. But at least I can make an antidote to the iron poisoning."

"Then that's a good thing," I said. I paused, because he didn't *look* like it was a good thing. "Isn't it?"

Ferosyn smiled, but faintly. "Yes, it would be except for one thing. Let me explain. I've made more inroads on the meteoric iron. I am wagering that you didn't find any results on sales in this area recently, correct?"

Talia nodded. "How did you know?"

"Because, as I mentioned before, the meteoric iron we're dealing with is ataxite. This makes it extremely rare. And there's more. Not only is it a rare specimen, but I found evidence of bone in the poison. The bone structure is complex and even more rare than the ataxite."

"How's that?" Viktor asked.

"The bone structure is one I've only seen twice before during all the millennia I've been working for Cernunnos. It comes from the Aillén Trechenn." He looked over at Herne, who stiffened.

"The Aillén Trechenn? You can't mean..." Herne stopped, his brow furrowing.

"That's exactly what I *do* mean," Ferosyn said. "For me to make an antidote, we have to find the bones of the creature itself."

The room fell silent, then Angel asked the question that I was thinking. "What's the Aillén Trechenn? I've never heard of it."

"Me either," I said.

"Most people haven't, be they human or Fae." Herne stood. "I'll be back, I need to get my bestiary." He vanished out the door.

Viktor was staring at the table, and by the look on his face, I could tell that whatever we were facing was grave. "Whenever Herne has to get his bestiary, you know we're in for a tough road ahead."

"You can say that again," Yutani muttered.

Talia said nothing, but simply sat there, her attention focused on Ferosyn. The room stayed frozen in the silent tableau until Herne returned, a giant book in his hand. He set it down and even from here, the tome seemed to emanate an aura of times long gone. He flipped through the handwritten pages until he finally found what he was looking for, then he turned the book around so we could all see.

On the page was what had to be a giant creature walking on all fours, though it looked like it could rear up onto its hind legs. It looked almost like a cross between a dinosaur and a komodo dragon, and I could see someone had drawn in measurements as to its length and height.

"Is that...what did you call it?"

"The Aillén Trechenn. Yes, it's a creature out of legend, rarer than unicorns, rarer than dragons. It's also known as 'Iron Bones' because it spawns off meteors come flaming to earth. Its bones include ataxite iron from the meteor. It's only been seen a handful of times by the gods, and can take centuries to spawn off of a fallen meteor. When it dies, the flesh eventually decays but the bones remain. It's anathema to the Fae, due to the iron content, but mostly only the elders of both Courts even remember that it exists."

"Herne is correct," Ferosyn said. "The *bones* are what was used to make this poison. By the relatively small number of cases—and yes, I know there have been a lot—but by the number of cases versus the potential, I am thinking that the engineer of the virus only found one bone of the Aillén Trechenn. The creatures are huge, as large as a full-grown elephant. If they had found all of the bones, they could have wiped out both Fae cities within a matter of a week." Ferosyn let that sink in.

"Then...where are the rest of the bones? And who would have the knowledge to do this?" The thought that one skeleton could end my race—both sides of it—was terrifying.

"That's the question. Probably still out in the

mountains."

Talia rubbed her forehead. "How do we know where it came from?" Then, she stopped, eyes wide. "When did this creature spawn? Is there any way to know?"

"Probably a thousand years ago? Maybe more. So you won't find mention of it online."

"Perhaps not," Talia said. "But we might find mention of it in some of the legends from the Cryptos who have lived here. Let me look on Encyclopedia Mythatopia."

Encyclopedia Mythatopia was an online database of myths and legends from the various Crypto communities throughout the years. Not every story had been entered, but it was a growing site and updated continuously with new information.

She tapped away. "I'm trying both the name as well as a general description of a massive creature. Do you have any characteristics for it, other than it's as big as an elephant?"

"Quadruped capable of standing on its hind legs, belligerent nature, dark fur that almost gleams, long swiping claws on the front paws—it walks on its knuckles like an anteater—and razor sharp teeth." Ferosyn frowned. "Do you really think you have a chance of finding anything?"

Talia nodded. "Yeah, I do...and bingo." She pumped her fist. "Yes. We may have a winner."

"What does it say?" I asked, moving around to look over her shoulder.

"This is from the Rainier Puma Shifters history." She enlarged the text and began to read to us. "About a thousand years ago, a strange light streaked out of the sky, landing in an area now believed to be near Cavanaugh Peak, up on Snoqualmie Pass. The light fell into an area near a small lake. The shifters who inhabited the mountain found the rock that fell from the sky, but it was red hot, and they took it as a sign to leave the area alone. Their legends say that five turns of the sun later, a monstrous beast came out of the belly of the crater, and that they had to leave their lairs and travel to Rainier to find a new, safe home. No other reports of this monster were ever found, and the legend is thought to be a metaphor for some natural disaster that chased them from their lands."

Ferosyn nodded. "That sounds like a meteor. And since the Aillén Trechenn wasn't known in shifter lore, no wonder they had no context for it. So if the meteor fell near Cavanaugh Peak, and the creature lived there, it probably died near there too. The Aillén Trechenn don't usually travel far from their spawning sites."

"Okay, we have a place to go look. But that could a lot of places. What lakes are near Cavanaugh Peak?"

"The closest that you can see from the mountain peak is Hidden Lake," Yutani said, searching an online map. "The trail is similar and not too far from the Snow Lake Trailhead. It will be a good three-hour hike, if not more, to Cavanaugh Peak from Alpental. The going isn't a simple trail through the woods. We'll have a six- or seven-mile jaunt each way, with a lot of rocky terrain. We'd better plan for a night's camping just in case. We don't know how long it will take to search the area, or what we're going to encounter."

I stared at him. "You mean we're going hiking out in the woods, looking for those bones?"

"I need them to make an antidote," Ferosyn said. "If I don't have them, your people will keep on dying."

I groaned but nodded. "Yeah, I get it." The thought of a long hike wasn't exactly the problem. It was coming close to the bones that were contributing to the death of my kind. "What happens if I accidentally touch one of the bones?"

A look of understanding swept over Ferosyn's face. "You won't catch this plague that way. No, you'd burn yourself since they do have meteoric iron in them, but unless you decide to gnaw on one, I don't think you'll have any problem being around them."

"I have a question," Angel said.

"Yes?" Ferosyn turned to her.

"Just who would be able to engineer a virus like this? Surely the Human Liberation Army isn't quite up to speed on the process? And would they go to such extremes? Why not just fire a few bombs into the cities?"

"That's a very good question," I said. "Any ideas?"

Ferosyn hesitated, then said, "Yes, I do. I've had a growing suspicion the longer I've studied this virus. I hope I'm wrong, but I don't think I am. Given all we know, to create such a virus it would require an adept in both magic and alchemy at a level that we rarely see in the world. I'm thinking one of the Force Majeure is behind this."

The Force Majeure? The name sounded familiar, like I had heard it long ago, but I wasn't sure just where.

"Who are they?" Angel asked.

Herne stood, leaning on the table as he stared at Ferosyn. "Are you positive?"

"No, but I'd lay good money on it."

The look that passed between them chilled my blood. Whatever this was, it was powerful and dark. I closed my eyes, thinking back to the monster that I had dreamed about, but then I realized it wasn't the Aillén Trechenn that I had been hiding from. It had been whoever had dug up the creature that I had been running from.

Ferosyn worried his lip before answering Angel. "The Force Majeure are a secret society of magicians, witches, and sorcerers. There are only twenty-one of them in the world at any given time. The only way to join the society is to be hand-chosen by the others. The only way to exit the society is to die."

"To give you an idea of what kind of power is necessary in order to be tapped for membership, one of the members is the Merlin. He's my grandfather—Morgana's father. Another member is Taliesin, one of the ancient Celtic bards. And Väinämöinen, the Finnish bard who rose to become a hero, is yet another." Herne sat down again.

I walked over to the counter to pour myself another cup of coffee. The explosions just kept coming. "Merlin is your grandfather?"

"He is, yes. I have no idea where he is right now. He set out to wander the world some thousand years or so ago."

I digested this bit of information. "Is Morgana one of the Force Majeure?"

Herne shook his head. "She chose deityhood over a life spent with her father's people. She fell in love with Cernunnos, so she stepped into the role of goddess."

"I thought Morgana was originally human," Angel said.

"Human...covers a wide variety of peoples. But no, not in the way you think of it. Her mother was Dark Fae, and her father, Merlin. The Force Majeure are...*human*...if you will, but they are to the magic born, and their life spans and DNA are different because of this. Call them *cousins* to humans. Closer than any of the Fae, or shifters. Hell, I *look* human—at least right now—but I'm a god. Demigod, rather."

Morgana was half-Fae. "How come the Fae accept her as their goddess if she's not full-blooded?" I couldn't imagine how they would kneel before a goddess who contained unwelcome blood.

"Because the Force Majeure are revered by the Fae. So her father's blood is accepted as royal, and since her mother was Fae, she's acceptable to them." Herne shook his head. "Don't get me started on your people's ethics and moral codes."

But I was already onto another thought.

"Who are the other members of the Force Majeure? Do any of them have a strong-enough grudge against the Fae that they would set out to commit genocide?" I wanted desperately to believe that Herne's grandfather wouldn't have partici- pated in an exercise of genocide, but I was quickly learning to hold my belief until it was proven.

Ferosyn wrote something on a piece of paper and showed it to Herne.

A light dawned in his eyes and he nodded. "You're right."

To the rest of us, he said, "There *is* one member of the Force Majeure who would have *every* reason to do this. Her name is Ranna, and she's the mis- tress of the Fomorian King, Elatha."

I sank back down in my chair, almost spilling my drink.

The Fomorians? Even I knew who they were.

"You can't be trying to tell me that Elatha has returned from the mists to destroy the Fae?"

"I believe that this is exactly the case. Cernunnos received word last night from a credible witness that Elatha has indeed returned. Which means, we *must* find the rest of those bones before he sends out a search party to look for them." Ferosyn threw his notepad on the table. "Because I'll guarantee you this: if Ranna finds the rest of the bones, the entire Fae world is in danger of extinction."

Chapter 12

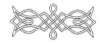

THE FOMORIANS WERE a race of giants who had long been mortal enemies of the Fae. In the past, they went up against the Tuatha de Danann. Elatha, the Prince of Darkness, was not only one of the ancient kings of the giants, he was one of the most crafty, and the most glorious. Unlike the majority of Fomorians, Elatha had shining hair, the color of spun gold, and was rumored to be one of the most beautiful rulers ever to live.

"Elatha...where is he? Do we know?" I leaned forward, clutching the table.

Ferosyn shook his head. "No, I'm afraid not, but he was seen in this area about four months ago. And if he's here, chances are good Ranna is as well. He never went anywhere without her."

"Elatha?" Angel looked confused.

"Yes, he was one of the rulers of the Fomorian giants. They're the mortal enemies of the Fae. They hate each other, almost as much as the Light and the Dark hate each other. They were constantly at war and one of the only forces that could unite both Courts, even if only for the time of the battle."

"Are we talking actual *giant* giants?" She still looked skeptical.

Viktor nodded. "Giants and ogres come from the same family tree, though we diverged at some point. Giants tend to be larger than ogres, but their disposition varies far more than my people. I'm good-natured, but a lot of my father's people aren't so friendly. Giants are a mixed bag."

"How big are we talking here?" Angel asked. "At least, with the Fomorians?"

"Eight to nine feet on average. Some a bit taller, others perhaps a foot shorter." Herne pulled out his phone. "I'm going to text my mother. She may have some information on Ranna's movements, or maybe she can ask my grandfather if he knows anything. Ranna may be one of the Force Majeure but make no mistake, she's loyal to Elatha."

"What else should we know about him? I truly think he was the force in my dreams who was killing the Fae. Either I saw images of the past, or a premonition of the future." I pulled out my tablet and prepared to take notes. No way was I going to be caught off guard. The shadowed force in my dreams had been terrifying, and I had learned what it felt like to be hunted down.

"Elatha's court not only includes giants who are loyal to him, but a number of Fachans, as well as the Bocanach. They're all considered part of the Fomorian kingdom." Ferosyn looked queasy.

"What are they?" I asked, my fingers poised over the keyboard on my tablet.

Talia paled. "I can answer that one. The Fachans are a branch of the Fomorians. Unlike their taller cousins, they stand around five feet tall, and they are one-armed, one-legged, and one-eyed creatures. They're deadly with magic, and they *all* wield forms of elemental magic—although most often earth-based energy in nature. They are loyal to their masters, to a fault."

"They sound horrifying." Angel grimaced. "What about the...what are the others?"

"Bocanach," Herne said. "The Bocanach are a race of goat-headed men. They're the brawn that make up a good share of Elatha's army. Or they did, back when he was at his height of power. They're slaves, but again, loyal and dedicated to whatever their king orders. They usually stand about six feet high, and they prefer to fight with spears and long, razor-sharp scythes."

My stomach lurched. "Fuck. This sounds bad. Do you think Elatha still has them? I mean, his followers? Or is there a chance they've been lost over time? And where has he been hiding out all these centuries?"

"I think we should count on him still having enough followers to cause trouble. As to where he's been, he was last seen over the Great Sea, so he must have returned from there. I'll ask my mother to check into that as well. I can imagine that he might have been ousted from Annwn and driven back here." Herne ran his fingers through his hair, brushing it back away from his face. "If we're right, if this all checks out, then we're sitting on a powder keg. Taking down a Fomorian King? Not so much in my wheelhouse. Even the gods couldn't destroy him."

"If the gods couldn't stop him, how the hell are we supposed to?" Yutani let out a disgruntled sigh. "Well, we have something to go on, at least. What now? If we need the rest of the bones, I guess we should get a move on and figure out how to find them."

"It's simple. We're going camping. Or rather, hiking. We'll hike up to Cavanaugh Peak, and following the hints from that legend, we look for the bones. We'll leave tomorrow, at six A.M. to beat rush hour traffic. Given it will be at least an hour's drive, and then a three- to four-hour hike, we should take camping gear with us in case we need to stay the night. I'm not placing bets on traipsing around and just stumbling over the bones right away." Herne motioned to Yutani. "Is your arm good enough to go?"

Yutani had caught his arm in a trap on Whidbey Island about six weeks before, when he was running in his coyote form, and while it had healed up, it still seemed on the tender side.

"Yeah, I'm good. I don't walk on my arms. Well, at least not in human form." He grinned, then— a rare smile flashing out. It had become a game with Angel and me, trying to make him smile. He played along good-naturedly but, more often than not, all we could cadge out of him was a brief grin.

"What's the weather like up there?" I asked. "I assume hiking boots, jeans, rain ponchos?"

"The elevation on Cavanaugh Peak reaches close to four thousand feet at the top, so it's a steep climb and we could be in for some serious weather." Viktor checked his weather app. "Yeah, potential thunderstorms. Lovely. Well, try to avoid coming dressed as a walking lightning rod."

"Will do." I wrinkled my nose at him, laughing. "I generally don't head into the mountains covered in metal bling."

"All right." Herne pointed to Viktor. "You, please gather camping gear for the four of us. Yutani, figure out the food situation. Given Ember's ability with cooking I have no intention on leaving it up to her."

"Hey, I resent that," I said.

"Can you deny it?" Herne challenged me.

I stared at him a moment longer, then shook my head. "Nope. Not *even* going to try. I barely know my way around a stove, let alone cook over a campfire. What should I do?"

"You and I are going to talk to Marie Shill, the owner of the Constantine Catering Express. I want to ask her about how she came to hire Nigel. Maybe we can uncover a clue where to find Elatha, given my bets are that he placed the advertisement in the HLA forums." He shuffled his papers. "How many of the bones do you need, Ferosyn? To make an antidote?"

Ferosyn shrugged. "At least two good-sized rib bones. But I'll tell you this: you do not want to leave the rest of the skeleton there, because if Elatha returns for it, he could—"

"I know," Herne said. "Wipe out the Fae race. All

right, we'll bag and tag every bone we can find." He looked around. "I guess that wraps it up. Talia, text me the caterer's address? I wrote it down, but I'm not sure where I put the note. Angel, go ahead and contact Rhiannon of the Foam Born Encampment and make arrangements to transfer the savine boys to her. I don't have time to deal with them, but this should give them a decent start."

"Will do," Angel said.

We gathered our things, said good-bye to Fero-syn, and headed to our offices.

"READY?" HERNE PEEKED in my office.

I grabbed my purse and followed him into the elevator. "Where's the catering company located?"

"It's not far from here. Their headquarters are near the Seattle Center. Constantine Catering Express is one of the most prestigious catering companies around, which is no doubt why the Courts Management Organization chose to use them. They have a stellar reputation and are in high demand."

"If Marie Shill owns it, then who's Constantine?" I slid into the passenger seat of Herne's SUV and fastened my seat belt.

"Talia says that he was Marie's husband. He died during a home invasion about five years ago, and Marie kept the company going. She built it from a steady mid-range business to what it is today. I gather Constantine wasn't the best businessman, but Marie has an eagle eye."

He eased away out of the parking garage and we were off. As we navigated through the weekend traffic—which was always rough on a sunny weekend—I watched out the window. Shoppers crowded the streets—some with bags and parcels hanging off their arms, others perusing the window displays. The ever-present streeps were begging for spare change or playing music on the corners, and the entire city had a holiday feel to it.

"What are we going to do if it really is Elatha behind this?"

Herne was silent for a moment as he made a left turn. Then, as we were headed north on Westlake Avenue, he finally answered. "Ember, I don't think there's any doubt that he's behind it. Ferosyn is positive. As to what do we do? I'm stumped at the moment. Cernunnos can't really get involved unless the Fomorians start waging war against the Fae, or vice versa, and the battle spills out into the streets and begins to affect humans. Morgana might be able to dip her toes in the water, but we may just be up the creek on this one. If they begin to wage a covert war, we may just have to let it happen."

I shook my head. "Herne, you know for a fact once Névé and Saílle find out who's behind the iron plague that there isn't a chance in hell they won't retaliate. They'll escalate this. If they can find out where Elatha is staying, they'll be on him like white on rice." One thing I *did* know about my people is that they weren't about to take an attack lying down. "Revenge" was one of the Fae's favorite words.

"I know," Herne said. "Trust me, I know. I'm afraid we may find our business picking up once this all breaks into the open. The Fae will play dirty and they'll play to win."

"I'd say that, given Elatha's opening volley, that gate's already been breeched." I paused. My mind had been running in a dozen different ways over the past couple of days. "Have you ever met him? Elatha?"

Herne shrugged. "No. But my father has. And my mother, I believe, was involved in one of the last wars that was waged before Elatha went across the Great Sea to Annwn."

"I suppose if he's Morgana's enemy, then he's mine as well."

"Sweetheart," Herne said gently, "Elatha is the enemy of *everyone* with a drop of Fae blood in them. If you don't see him as an enemy now, he'll make damned sure you do by the time he's done with you. In the Fomorians' book, the only good Fae is a dead one." Herne swung left onto Denny Way. Shortly before the Seattle Center, we turned onto Taylor and parked. "Here we are."

To my right, I saw the CONSTANTINE CATERING EXPRESS sign hanging in a window, paired with a sign that read BRENDA'S BAKERY. I shouldered my purse as Herne joined me on the sidewalk and we headed into the building.

The catering company reminded me of a bridal store, probably because of all the wedding cakes that were on display. Two tables, with two chairs each, sat to our right. To the left, benches lined the walls, a waiting area by the display case, which offered up a host of baked goods, all looking so good I wanted to buy every single one.

"Brenda must be one hell of a baker." I glanced around as a woman entered from the back, behind the case.

"May I help you?" she asked.

"We'd like to talk to Marie. Please tell her Herne's here, from the Wild Hunt." Herne didn't wait for an invitation, but walked over to one of the tables and sat down, motioning for me to follow him. I joined him, settling into the chair.

Two binders sat on the table, one for the bakery and one for the catering company. I opened the bakery binder, to see page after page of wedding cakes, birthday cakes, and just about any other occasion you could think of, along with prices and the number of servings. After the cakes were a couple pages offering bulk deals on doughnuts, pastries, and other goodies.

"I think we should buy a cake," I muttered.

Herne snorted. "You planning on proposing to me?"

"Wipe that grin off your face before I do it for you," I said, blushing. "And no, for your information, I am *not* proposing to you. They just all look so good."

"We'll buy a box of doughnuts to take back to the office before we leave," he promised.

At that moment, a short blond woman wearing an apron came bouncing out of the back. She wiped her hands on a dishtowel as she joined us at the table and sat down on the opposite side.

"Hello welcome to Constantine Catering Express—I'm Marie Shill the owner—you called this morning right?" The words came out in a stream and I swear, the woman wouldn't know a comma if she met one. She thrust out her hand.

"Right. I'm Herne, owner of the Wild Hunt Agency. This is Ember, one of our investigators." Herne shook her hand, and then she offered it to me.

After the pleasantries were out of the way, Marie cleared her throat. "What can I do for you? You said it was urgent, about one of our waiters who served at Fae Day."

"Do you remember Nigel Henderson?" Herne pulled out his tablet and opened it.

Marie squinted for a moment, then nodded. "Yes, I do. We tried to find him to pay him afterward, but couldn't get hold of him. Is that what this is about? Because I have his check in the back, if he wants it." She seemed worried, and I realized that she must think he had sent someone to put the arm on her for his money.

Herne picked up on it, too. "No, no—we're not here on his behalf. We just have some questions about how you came to hire him. Did the recommendation come from your usual staffing service? How does the hiring process work with your company?"

Marie stared at us for a moment. "I never hire anyone who isn't legally capable of working in this country."

Another concern. I smiled at her. "We're not from immigration. Who recommended him? And what happened to your usual waiter? We understand he had an accident shortly before you hired Nigel?"

She still looked confused, but seemed to relax. "Yes, John is one of my usual contractors. You see, I keep a list of twenty wait staff on hand. When I need someone for a job, I start with the next name on the list. I may need two waiters, or fifteen, so I cycle through to be fair. For Fae Day, I needed everybody on board. John called the day before and told me he had been hit by a hit and run driver, and he was laid up in the hospital with a broken leg."

"What did you do next?"

"Well, everybody was already working who was on my list, so I normally would call a day labor company. Oddly enough, not even an hour before John contacted me, someone from FMR Day Labor called asking if I had any positions open. I said no, and they left their number. When John called, it seemed like fate had stepped in to save my ass. I called FMR back and hired Nigel. I thought I could add him to my roster if he was good enough. I told FMR where he should show up and what he'd be doing." She was worrying her lip. "Did I make a mistake?

I stared at the table. How could we tell her that, by allowing Nigel to work at Fae Day, she had given him access to kill dozens of people? It would devastate her.

"What did he do?" She tensed, hands clutching the table as she leaned forward.

Herne paused for a moment, then said, "Something you're better off not knowing. If you could just answer our questions, it would be best." He kept his voice low, and turned around to make certain nobody else was in the shop. "You say you tried to contact FMR Day Labor about him after Fae Day?"

Marie paled. "Yes. I normally give paychecks the next day, but he didn't come in to pick up his. I had planned on getting his information then. So I called FMR, but their number was disconnected."

"Thank you, that's all." Herne stood. "Next time, go through already vetted contracting companies. And you might as well just tear up that check. Nigel won't ever be coming in for it."

She looked confused, but nodded. "All right, though I wish you would tell me what he did."

"No, trust me. You don't want to know." I pushed to my feet. "Thank you for your time."

"Is there anything else I can do for you? I feel like I haven't been any help at all." She was still looking at loose ends.

"You can box us up a couple dozen assorted doughnuts and pastries," I said, pulling out my wallet and giving her a smile. "My mouth's been watering since we walked in."

Marie moved over to the counter. "They're on the house. I have a feeling you're sparing me from something that I wouldn't be able to shake off."

She quickly boxed up two dozen decadent pastries. As she handed us the boxes, she caught my gaze, and I could tell she was trying to get a better read on the situation, but I merely smiled, thanked her for the pastries, and followed Herne out to the car.

"I feel bad, leaving her confused like that," I said as we pulled away from the curb.

"Better than having her beat herself up for allowing a murderer to poison her ginger chicken and kill dozens of people." Herne switched lanes as we headed back to the office. "Something like that can destroy a person's confidence for good. She would probably blame herself, and what good would that do? She didn't know what Nigel was up to."

"True. And that would just be allowing Nigel to ruin one more life."

BACK AT THE office, I called Marilee and rescheduled my appointment for that evening. Given we were going to be out of town the next day, and Morgana wanted me to start right in working with her, I didn't want to wait much longer before having my first session.

"I can see you this afternoon. Can you come over now?"

"Let me check with Herne." I darted into his office. "Hey, Marilee can move my appointment to today, but I need to go now. Can I duck out early, given it's Saturday?"

He waved me on. "Sure. Be ready and downstairs by five-thirty tomorrow morning. I'll pick you up at your place. We're taking my SUV."

I blew him a kiss, then called Marilee back and

told her I'd be right over.

Angel was gathering her things, and Talia was talking to her.

"I'm off to meet with Marilee now." I realized that I still hadn't told Angel about my parentage. I also realized that we had come together in my car and I would be leaving her stranded. "Crap. Talia, can you run Angel home? I need my car and don't have time to go back to the condo right now."

"Sure, but who's Marilee?" Talia squinted. "What's up? You're hiding something."

I glanced at the clock. "I'm not trying to hide anything. Can you come over tonight for dinner? After I get home, I'll tell you both what's going on. Right now, I have to run."

Talia agreed, and I waved and took off.

Marilee lived near the arboretum on Boyer Avenue, before it merged with Lake Washington Boulevard. I had spent a fair amount of time in the two hundred–acre preserve.

Home to an incredible array of plants and trees, some of them exotic and rare, the arboretum was a mutual endeavor between the University of Washington and the city of Seattle proper. Over the years, the staff to maintain it had changed and was now mainly composed of Fae. The gardens were bigger and more beautiful than ever, and the arboretum was spectacular.

I had a momentary impulse to take a side trip through one of the trails nearest to Marilee's house, but shook it off. She was expecting me, for one thing, and for another, tomorrow would bring a long hike and I didn't want to wear myself out before we got there.

Marilee's house reminded me oddly of a Japanese pagoda. At least the roof did, with a slight curve up on the edges and a steep slope up to a point at its apex. The house itself was a lovely shade of green, with manicured herb and flower gardens that almost overflowed their borders.

I parked in the driveway and jogged up the porch steps. I had barely rung the bell when she opened the door.

"Ember? Come in."

Marilee looked nothing like I had expected. I didn't even know *what* I had expected. Around five-four and petite, she looked to be around her mid-sixties to early seventies. She was human, or at least she looked it, and her hair was pulled back into a shocking silver braid. Her eyes were pale blue, and she both looked her age and yet didn't. She was wearing a pair of jeans and a neatly tucked-in polo shirt.

"Hi, Marilee?" I walked into her living room and was hit with a tranquil, Zen energy that flowed through the house. Everything seemed in its perfect place. A water fountain sat in one corner, trickling water over bamboo shoots and rocks. The walls were painted a misty gray with a blush of pink spreading through it. The polished wood of the tables and bookshelves had a soft glow to it. The living room opened right into the kitchen and dining area, flowing smoothly, and everywhere, the house seemed thoughtfully arranged, yet not so rigid that it felt untouchable.

"Morgana told me about your predicament.

We'll get you situated." She motioned for me to follow her. "Please come this way."

"How long have you been one of Morgana's priestesses?" I found myself breathing easier as she led me through the living room. The worries of the day seemed to fade into the background.

"All of my life. My mother served her, and her mother before that. I was brought up to be her priestess."

Marilee led me into a hallway with five doors— two to the left, two to the right, and one on the end. As we passed the first door on the right, she pointed to it.

"There's the restroom, if you need it."

We entered the room at the end of the hall and I caught my breath. The energy practically sang here, reverberating through the air, ricocheting off the walls. The room was filled with crystals. They were on shelves, on four altars spaced evenly around the room. A few even hung from the ceiling, cradled in wire woven hangers that gently cupped the spheres and eggs.

A round table sat in the center of the room, a black and silver cloth stretched over it. In the center of the table was a clear bowl filled with water and a variety of small crystals and seashells. A small bucket rested to one side of the bowl. Two chairs sat on opposite sides of the table.

"Please, sit down. I'm going to cast a Circle so no wayward energies will be attracted to our work."

Marilee walked over to the altar in the west, which looked dedicated to water, and picked up a sharp blade. The dagger was long and narrow and the hilt looked to be made of mother-of-pearl. It was wrapped with silver wire, and glimmered in the afternoon light. The window just above the altar looked over a wooded expanse, right into the arboretum.

"If you'll sit down at the table, please."

I sat, placing my hands on the table as she began to circle the room, blade pointing toward the walls. She began to chant:

Circle of power, Circle of might,
Strengthen the wards, lock them tight.
From Earth to Air, From Water to Fire,
Strengthen these rites, may they soar higher.
From Star to Sun, from Earth to Moon,
Morgana's will, become our boon.

Marilee joined me at the table as the energy settled around us like a warm blanket. "We're ready to begin. Hold out your left hand, palm up, please."

I did as she asked. With her left hand, she took hold of my fingers, bending them back over the bowl of water. With her right, she raised her dagger and I realized she was going to slash my hand.

I looked at her. "What—"

"Hush. This will not harm you."

I closed my mouth. Morgana had given me over to her. It was my place to trust that everything was going the way it should. I waited, nervously. Marilee slid the tip of the dagger along the surface of my palm. It was razor sharp—so much that I didn't even feel it as it pierced my skin. A thin wheal of blood rose along the cut. Marilee squeezed my palm, and the blood began to run along the skin. She nodded to the bowl.

"Place your hand in the water for a moment."

I did, wondering what she was doing. The moment my hand met the water, it reminded me of a paraffin dip. Something warm and viscous encased my palm, like some invisible glove, or amoebic creature. A second later, what felt like a tongue began to lick the blood off my hand. Thoroughly creeped out, I almost pulled away my hand but Marilee hadn't given me permission yet.

"What's happening?"

"The Veni-noir is tasting your blood so it can help me see into your nature. Now, please, remove your hand and remain silent until I tell you to speak."

I zipped my lip.

Marilee dipped a ladle into the water and waited. Then, as I watched, something mostly translucent crawled into it—it looked like a tiny octopus. She poured it into a goblet and stared at the crystal glass for a moment before cupping it in her hands. She held it up in front of her, closing her eyes.

Vein to vein, blood to blood,
Life force moves, visions flood.
Bind with me, I bind with you.
To thy nature, sight be true.

Then, without opening her eyes, she lifted the goblet to her lips and upended it, chugging down the contents. I grimaced as the creature's tentacles disappeared between her lips. Marilee shuddered, wincing as she swallowed. I wanted to ask if she was okay, and what the hell was she doing, but I didn't want to disturb whatever spell she was casting. I had no idea what would happen if it went wrong and I didn't want to be responsible for any backlashes or glitches.

One moment passed, and then another, and finally Marilee opened her eyes. As she held my gaze, I realized I wasn't looking into *Marilee's* soul, but the soul of someone else, someone far more ancient and cunning.

She spoke, and the voice seemed to be coming from a distance, from somewhere in the back of her throat—it was raspy, like the wind streaming through a dried cornfield. As far as I could tell the voice was female.

"Ember Kearney, I have tasted your blood. I feel the autumn nights that run through your veins. I sense the hunger that lurks deep inside, waiting to be free. I see the dark skies that give you blessed cover, and the spiral that waits to unfold."

I wasn't sure what to say, or if I should say anything, so I just listened. Whoever was speaking to me, their words were setting off an explosion of sparks inside, and it felt like I was waking up. With each word, another explosion of recognition flared. I knew this creature, even though I didn't yet recognize it. But I knew it as sure as I knew my own name.

"You are nearing the Cruharach, as it comes spiraling into your life. You must prepare. You are not ready for it and it will rise and swallow you into the darkness if you remain closed to yourself. I see the bloodlines."

And then, before I could respond, Marilee grabbed up the bucket, groaning, and leaned to the side. She gagged, and although I couldn't see what she was doing, I heard a splash and realized she had vomited into the bucket. A moment later, she sat up again, groaning, and placed the bucket on the table.

"Excuse me. I'll be back—don't worry, this is normal." She stood and, carrying the bucket, exited the room.

I stared at the bowl. The water remaining in it was clear. There was no sign of my blood—no sign that *anything* was in there beyond the water and crystals. I was feeling a little queasy, given what had just happened, but I was more curious than anything.

Marilee returned, bucket in one hand and a glass of water in the other. Inside the glass, I could see the tiny creature that she had swallowed. The tentacles were waving, so it was still alive. She poured the water and creature into the bowl and sat down, placing the bucket back in its place.

"You can speak now." She looked a little worn.

"What the hell just happened? What is that thing? Who was speaking through you?"

"One question at a time. I'll answer them all, but before that, you need to know that the Cruharach is dawning in you. Within a couple months at most, it will be on you, and we have to make certain you're ready for it."

"What happens if I'm not ready?"

She remained impassive, but a look of compassion filled her eyes. "With your bloodlines? Ember, you could die."

Chapter 13

"HOW WILL I know when I'm..." I wasn't even sure what I was asking.

"You're already in the beginning stages. The Cruharach usually takes a couple of months to fully manifest, and then a couple more to end. I've seen this before, so I know the signs." Marilee held my gaze and I suddenly had the feeling she was far older than she looked.

"*What* are you?" I asked, aware that it was a rude question, but wanting to know just who I was dealing with.

She arched her eyebrows. "Not exactly diplomatic, but given that you're fast-tracking on a path you know little about, I forgive the tactlessness. I'm one of the magic-born."

That made sense. The magic-born were those who weren't quite human, but were born into magical families. They were usually quite long-lived, and they tended to blend in with the rest of human society until you looked below the surface. They aged slowly, though not as slowly as the Fae, so Marilee must be ancient, given she looked in her seventies.

"You said you've served Morgana since you were young?"

"I've been her priestess since the day I was born. My mother gave me into her service when I was barely two years old. As to what you're *really* asking, I'm over a thousand years old. I've lived dozens of lifetimes in dozens of places, moving on when it became apparent I wasn't aging like my friends. Now, of course, it doesn't matter. I remember when everyone first emerged from the shadows. It was well before your time. The turmoil that ran through the world...but in the end, it brought relief to the SubCult, and to those humans who had discovered the truth and weren't believed." Marilee smiled and her eyes sparkled. She suddenly looked dazzling and beautiful.

"You said, while you were in trance, that you could see my bloodlines?"

She nodded, the smile slipping away. "Yes. Morgana is correct. You have the blood of the Leannan Sidhe in you, and also of the Autumn Stalkers. Both are strong, and their natures fight one another. The resulting mix will be fascinating to watch. I cannot tell you if one will win over the other, or if they'll blend into some kind of mutant strain, but make no mistake: this is going to make the Cruharach more difficult for you."

"How so? Don't most Fae have different strains,

though they're usually from the same Court?"

"Not as much as you would think. And usually matches are engineered to produce the least resistance and trouble. I think our first step should be to introduce you to your lineage in the truest fashion. I intend to introduce you to your potential, should either side win out and negate the other."

I was beginning to have flashbacks of my grandfather, wanting to root out and eradicate my mother's bloodline. "I won't become fully Dark or Light, will I?"

She shook her head. "Not to worry there. That never happens, but in cases like yours, usually one side will become dominant. When the races are similar, it doesn't create much conflict, but in your case, the battle could tear you apart. Which is why you can't be allowed to go through the Cruharach without help."

"How comforting." I shivered, suddenly growing cold. Actually, I just wanted the Cruharach to go away and leave me alone. I liked myself the way I was.

"How much will this change me? Will I be the same person?" I gave her a pleading look.

Marilee searched my face. Then she knelt beside me, taking my hands.

"Ember, don't worry. You'll be who you are. It's just that your burgeoning powers will lean—or generally *should* lean—more toward one side than the other. While you might find some aspects of your nature will change, this won't erase who you are. It won't erase your passions and joys, your memories or your desires. No worries over that."

She smiled then, a kindly grandmother-like smile.

I tried to believe her. Tried to accept that everything was shifting around me as it should, but I just wanted to feel settled again. "All right. What do I do? Tell me what I need to do."

"I'm going to give you a tincture. Then I'll guide you to meet yourself. Or rather, one side of yourself. We won't know which until you take it, but I should be able to identify which lineage is coming to the surface first. We'll work on the other side later." She walked over to a cabinet that sat against one wall and pulled out a bottle. "This compound is safe, but it will send you into a deep trance. You need to let it do its work and not fight it. Do you understand?"

I nodded. "Got it. All right. What do I do?"

"Hold out your tongue and I'll drop the tincture on it. Then just let it absorb inside your mouth, and you'll find yourself turning inward. Don't be worried if it seems like you're hallucinating—this is a vision quest. However, your body will be here with me, even if your mind goes wandering, and I'll be watching over you the entire time. I'll be able to bring you out of it, should the experience become too intense."

"Is there anything else I should do to prepare? Can I go to the restroom first?" I realized that I did not want to be caught in the middle of a ritual needing to pee.

She laughed. "Of course."

In the restroom, I peed, then washed my hands. As I stared at myself in the mirror, I realized I was afraid. I was afraid that I'd go in as *me*, and come out of the trance as somebody else.

"That's silly," I told myself. "You're not in the midst of the Cruharach yet. You've got a little time left. At least, I hope so." Finally, I had no excuse left. I returned to the ritual room.

Marilee was waiting. She had changed into an indigo gown, off the shoulders, and belted at the waist. She was wearing a circlet around her head, with a sparkling sapphire in the center of a crescent moon, tines pointed up.

I stared at her. "This is for real, isn't it? We're not just doing a simple meditation."

She held my gaze. "*Everything* is a ritual when you're pledged to the gods, Ember. Every sneeze, every movement, every thought is a prayer. Life is a ritual, when you think about it. We're seeking important knowledge about your future. The quest deserves a little formality, don't you agree?"

Her words echoed in my heart. "I need to sit down." I sank down onto the floor, staring at the hardwood.

"What's wrong?"

"It just hit me that...I'm bound to a goddess. I'm pledged to Morgana. This isn't a game or lip service or like signing up for a gym membership. This is for *life*."

I felt stupid saying it—it should have been obvious, but I had been taking it lightly and now, I was beginning to understand just where I stood.

Morgana owned me, heart and soul. I reeled from the realization that, no matter what, she would always be with me. No matter where I was, what danger I was in, or how alone I felt, she would always be there. She might not speak to me all the time, but she was in my heart and in my life for good. I looked up at Marilee. She had a knowing look on her face.

"You begin to understand what it means to belong to a goddess. This is part of the journey, Ember."

I nodded. "I'm ready, I think. Whatever this brings, I'm ready to face it." I swallowed hard. "What should I do?"

"Stay on the floor and give me your weapons and any electronics you may have. You are to lie down and spread your arms to the sides and your legs wide to form the points of a pentacle. I will draw another circle around you so that nothing can get in...or *out*." The last, she said so softly I almost didn't hear it.

After handing her my dagger and a pocket pen-knife, and my purse with my phones and tablet in it, I lay down while she took them outside of the room. When she returned, she was carrying three bowls on a tray. She sat them on the table and picked up the first.

"I put your things away for their safekeeping. And for our safety."

She spread a ring of salt around me, an inch wide, making certain every bit of the floor surface was covered. Then, from the second bowl, she added another ring, this one I recognized as frank-incense. And the third, she lay a ring of something that made my body tingle from where I was lying.

I flashed back to the first vision I had had at my house. "Is that *iron*?"

She inclined her head. "For my protection, should your nature give way and you decide to attack me. It's not likely to happen, but it's not out of the range of possibility either."

I didn't want to think about the iron there on the floor, or the idea that I might try to assault her. "Won't those sides of me, both the Leannan Sidhe and Autumn's Bane, recognize that they, too, are bound to Morgana?"

"One would hope. Most likely, yes. But I've always taught my students to be prepared. Assume nothing. Expect nothing. Be open to what happens."

She finished the circle and whispered a few words. I had the sensation that an invisible barrier rose between us. I knew that if I stood to leave the circle now, I wouldn't be able to cross it without getting a sharp burn from the iron.

"We're ready. I'll get the tincture. You breathe deeply and try to relax. This won't hurt."

She hustled over to the cabinet to the side and I tried to will my body into as relaxed a state as it could get. I opened my mouth and closed my eyes, and three drops that tasted somewhere between sweet and spicy landed on my tongue.

The liquid absorbed and I waited. I wasn't sure how long it would take, or what to expect.

I flashed back to the time when Angel and I swiped a bottle of wine from Mama J.'s stash and snuck out of our bedroom, climbing the fire escape to the top of the roof. We drank the whole bottle, got drunk, and watched the stars come out as we talked about our plans for the future. We were sixteen, and I had been living with them for about eight months. We had been *so* full of plans—places we'd travel, and things we'd see.

"I'm going to be a big-time newscaster," Angel said. "My name will be in all of the magazines and I'll travel all over and write about the places I see."

"I'll go with you. I can take photographs, and scope out crimes to solve," I had proclaimed. "I'm good at figuring out when something's wrong."

Angel and I had spent most of the night on the roof, talking about one dream after another until Mama J. called Angel on her cell phone and told us to get our asses home. We somehow managed to climb down the fire escape without killing ourselves, but even though we ate an entire package of mints, Mama J. could smell the booze on us and she grounded us for a month. She made me trade places with DJ so that he had to sleep in his sister's room. We weren't allowed to talk together except at school and during meals, and Mama J. had taken away our TV privileges. That was the first and last time we drank until we were eighteen and in college.

I blinked, wondering why the memory had suddenly flashed through my head so strongly, but then, like a rainbow, it shimmered, and vanished.

I started to ask Marilee if the tincture was working, but my words came out garbled and I wasn't entirely sure if I had spoken aloud. I tried to sit up, but a wave of dizziness shot through me and so I lay down again. My tongue felt too big for my mouth, and for a moment I was terrified that maybe I was allergic to something in the tincture and had gone into anaphylaxis, but I forced myself to calm down. When I paid attention to my chest, I realized that I was breathing just fine. My tongue just felt clumsy and thick.

I drifted further out, feeling like I was at sea. The room around me shifted, and I was in the ocean, surrounded by massive rolling breakers that crashed over me. I welcomed them in, embracing their energy as they swallowed me. As I sank in slow motion, giving in to the depths, they tugged me down. Bubbles streamed from my mouth, and I let the waves lull me into the half-light. My arms lazily drifted over my head as I sank, my hair streaming in the water, and yet I wasn't gasping for air. I didn't even know if I was breathing, but that didn't frighten me either. I turned in the water, rotating slowly as the sea-green depths welcomed me in.

I don't know how long I drifted, but then a soft breeze washed over me and I began to realize that I was sitting on a shoreline. I dragged my fingers through the water that crashed along the dunes.

Someone was walking toward me and I rose to my feet. My clothes were gone, and I was standing there in a ribbon of gossamer silk, which wound around me in a gravity-defying swirl, covering my breasts and groin.

The woman who approached looked like me, only she seemed more vibrant, her skin a fairer shade of pale with a translucent bluish cast. Her hair was wrapped in intricate knotwork, the strands looping around and through each other. She was wearing a thin shift, translucent and filmy, and the gown floated from her shoulders, barely touching her skin.

"Who are you?" I mustered up the question, but the words didn't come. Yet I felt she understood me.

"Take my hands and find out," she whispered, holding out her hands.

I stared at her fingers for a moment, then took them in my own. There was a pause, a fraction of a second where the thought *I shouldn't have done that* ran through my mind, but then it was too late, and she had hold of me.

She swept me into a dance, and we were whirling, spinning through a downpour that began the moment our fingers touched. The clouds had broken open, the storm had come. All around me, the lightning forked through the heavens, striking down to touch the water and sand. The storm both repelled and attracted me, and I reached for its core, longing to become part of it.

The waves grew fractious, cresting across the sand, as the downpour—stirred by the wind—created a vortex of rain. We were right in its path. The rain slashed against us, cutting and cold, as the sky darkened even further.

Yet still she held my hands fast, spinning on the beach, whirling me around in a dizzying blur. Yet still she held me firmly and I couldn't let go. The storm grew louder, the rain thundering down. Lightning broke the sky again, and we were caught up by the gale, dancing among the forks that lit up the sky.

She drew me closer, pulling me in, until we were

spinning in a lover's embrace, at the center of a waterspout. Dizzy, I closed my eyes, letting go of my thoughts. I couldn't focus—my equilibrium had been stripped away—and I finally gave in to the dance, letting it encompass me as my mysterious partner pulled me even closer. There was no distinction between our bodies, and as she pressed against me, we began to merge.

I fought my fear, wanting to keep myself separate, but then I realized that I couldn't resist her, and under the rain and lightning and thunder, the boundaries came down and she flowed into me, and I allowed her to enter my thoughts.

HUNGER. I WAS *so hungry,* but not for food. I wanted *more.* I wanted sex. I wanted someone to run his hands across my skin, to touch me in those places that I kept sacred. I wanted to open myself to him, to feel him enter me even as he became my servant. I wanted to sing to him, whisper in his ears in the night when he slept, drive him mad with visions of beauty.

Hear my song. Come to me. Touch me. Taste me. Let me delight your soul. Let me inspire you and send you reeling into the passion that stems from that sacred mix of creativity and the drive to mate. I will be your muse. I will give you the world of dreams, and I will feed you delights untold, and you will be mine. To own. To pos-

sess. To sing you to sleep, and finally, to feed off of your hopes and dreams and your very life essence. And when you fall into that final slumber, far ahead of your years, you will remember me with blood and pain and passion...and you will die a husk, burned to a crisp for your vision and lust. And I will find another to inspire.

I ran my hands down my body, moaning as my fingers darted over my nipples, along my hips, down my stomach toward my thighs. Everything felt like it was crisped and burned and yet it was the fire that did not burn, the heat that did not char. But still it scorched, like sunlight on ice, the rays giving no heat but still blinding in their brilliance.

I opened my eyes, reaching out, searching for someone near enough to entice in, to call my own. I would bestow upon them the revelations to make them a tortured genius, a brilliant visionary, but they would never be satiated, not until they held me in their arms, and they would love me. And I would feed until they had no more to give.

Sitting up, I looked around. There was a woman, and part of me recognized her. *Marilee*. She watched me cautiously from outside the Circle. I knew I couldn't pass the borders. I could feel the iron encircling me, and the promise of pain kept me from crossing the barrier.

"Ember?" She was wary, I could hear it in her voice.

"Let me out of the Circle." I held her gaze, willing her obedience, but she kept where she was, shaking her head.

"No. You are confined for a good reason. Do you know who I am?"

I nodded. "Marilee. My *keeper*." I laughed. "But I need no one to handle me. I need no one to guard my conscience."

"Do you know what's happening?"

Something about her question struck a chord in me, and the whisper would not be ignored. There was something we were supposed to be doing. Something we had been searching for. I didn't want to pay attention, but in the back of my mind, I knew that I had to listen. I blinked, and for just a moment, I split in two, and found myself looking at the Leannan Sidhe, realizing that she was part of me. She looked back, eyes narrowing.

"Give into me. Give yourself over to me, and we will be everything we were meant to be." Her whisper was enticing, and I thought about how easy it would be to accept her, to let her take over and become the power and force she was.

Marilee's voice echoed through the room. "Ember, listen to me. You cannot totally resist this part of yourself, but you must find a way to keep her under control. She would destroy your friends. She would destroy Angel if you don't learn how to harness her energy."

At Angel's name, a vision arose of my friend burned out and tortured by the hunger that I could too easily visit on her.

"Back. Your time has not come yet," I said, turning to the Leannan Sidhe. "I will find a way to allow you into my life. But not yet, and you will not be in control."

"That's it. Ember, remember, she is only *part* of who you are."

My alter-self turned, hissing viciously at Marilee. "Old hag, keep out of this. You do not make the decision."

"Neither do you," Marilee said. "Ember makes the final decision, not you."

With a cunning gaze, the Leannan Sidhe turned to me. "Don't deny me. Do not cast me out, for you will be a pale shadow of yourself without me. Give me control and we rule the world."

"Go back. *Now*," I said, trying to shield myself from her lure.

Her eyes sparkled with a sea-green fire and she started to rise up, but I forced all my will to shove her back. She let out a shriek, but then a wave crashed through the circle, and she leaped on what looked like a wild horse and rode off, into the water, laughing.

"I'll return soon, and you will not deny me my rightful place," she called over her shoulder. As I watched, a wall of water crashed down and swallowed her under.

I blinked, and in that fraction of a second, the tincture drained out of my body and I was lying in the Circle again, every muscle in my body aching. I waited for a moment, but she was gone, so I sat up, groaning. I squinted, glancing around, but everything looked normal.

"She's gone," I whispered.

"Who's gone?" Marilee was sitting on the floor next to the Circle.

"You know, the Leannan Sidhe. You talked to her. She talked to you."

Marilee shook her head. "No, Ember, whatever occurred happened inside your own thoughts."

I stared at her. "Are you sure? I could have sworn..." I paused, glancing around. The air within the Circle felt moist and damp, as though I had just walked out of the ocean into the salt-sea air. The enormity of what I had felt and experienced hit me. "I want out of this Circle. Let me out?" I began to shake as the tears rose in my throat.

Marilee held up her hand. "Hold on, I'll open the gate. Just hold on." She swept away a patch of the iron and held her hand out to guide me out of the Circle. As I cleared the gate, my head felt like I had suddenly had a bucket of cold water poured over me.

"Crap. What the fuck happened in there?" I stared at her, my stomach queasy.

"You need to tell me everything. But first, let's go out into the kitchen and get some tea and something to eat. You expended a great deal of energy, and whatever was happening in that Circle was forcing me to keep a tight hold on the power. Something was trying to break through the gates and I had a hard time controlling them."

"Yeah," I whispered. "And that something...was me."

I TOLD MARILEE about everything, including

what I thought the Leannan Sidhe had said to her. "This is my mother's blood waking up, isn't it?"

Marilee slid a plate of crackers and cheese over to me, along with a glass of orange juice. "You need the energy. Eat up." She waited until I was halfway through my third cracker and slice of cheese to answer. "Yes, you have just met your mother's bloodline."

"But I don't remember her ever being that way." I frowned, picking up another cracker. I hadn't thought I was hungry but now I was ravenous and felt like I could eat a full three-course dinner and have room for more.

"That's because your mother went through the Cruharach and she, too, was faced with a choice of whether to give in to the full nature of her blood or to rein it in. She obviously chose to rein in her tendencies."

"If that's what I could become, I'm scared spitless." I stared at my plate. "I don't want to do that to people. I don't want to feed on them."

"I'm afraid you'll have to accept at least part of your mother's blood. To deny your essential self will not only put limits on your abilities, but the energy can back up like a clogged sink. When the clog breaks, you don't want to be in the way. If you can integrate the best qualities, you can use them to become a strong, vibrant, well-rounded woman. But we haven't even touched on your father's nature yet—you still have to face that part of yourself, and then we work on finding a way to integrate both parts into your life."

I pressed my lips together. I didn't want to integrate *anything* right now, but Morgana had sent me to Marilee for a reason, and when I faced the seriousness of the situation, I knew I didn't have any choice. I didn't want to end up dead or out of control. Just touching the Leannan Sidhe's nature, feeling her become part of me, had been intoxicating.

"All right. So what's the next step? When do we go in search of my connection to the Autumn Stalkers?" I was sincerely hoping she wouldn't say today, because I was exhausted and needed to process everything that had happened.

"Not for a while. You can't take the tincture more than once every few weeks, or it could tumble you into a realm from which you might not be able to return."

"Thanks for telling me now." I gave her a long look.

Marilee faced me squarely. "Truth? You must give up control to me, Ember. You have neither the experience nor knowledge to navigate this journey by yourself. If you try, you'll end up dead, mad, or worse. The power radiating off of you when you walked out of that circle was incredibly strong."

"Great, so it's like I'm stuck with three personalities, only we all know about each other, and we all want control." I was joking, but she didn't laugh.

"No, it's *not* like that. These sides of yourself are part of you even now, but they haven't manifested fully. They're as much Ember as you are, but you're afraid of them so you try to push them away. I can't wait to see the woman you become once you pass through the transformation, lose your fear, and learn how to control your nature."

"What do I do in the meantime? What if, now that she's awake, my Leannan Sidhe side tries to take over?" I had visions of her creeping out of my dreams at night and taking over.

"I'll give you an herbal powder. It won't hurt you, but will help you keep things under control. It will also ease you into the Cruharach and smooth the way for the coming changes."

"All right. I'll take it. When should I return?"

"We'll have to meet twice a week for the next few weeks. You have a lot to catch up on. Most families would have long ago prepared their children, so we're rushing against time." She hesitated a moment, then took my hand.

"I'm afraid," I said, not wanting to voice my thoughts. "I know you say we'll make this work, but I'm afraid."

"You'd be a fool not to be afraid, Ember. But I guarantee I'll do everything possible to help you through this. You're not the first tralaeth I've guided through the Cruharach, and I doubt you'll be the last." Her eyes twinkled. "You thought, perhaps, you were the only one?"

I nodded. "I know that my kind—tralaeths—are rare."

"Yes, rare, but not entirely unheard of. I've met a few others along the way, and Morgana has had me help them, as well." She motioned to the box of crackers. "Eat as many as you need. I'll get your herbs."

When she returned, she handed me a couple bottles of herbal powders, complete with instructions on how to use them.

"Don't forget to take them on schedule. They should prevent any slipups until we can see you through to the ritual itself." She paused. "Do you have any questions?"

I had a million questions, but none she could effectively answer at this point.

"No, I guess not right now. I'm not sure how long it will take us to...well, we're going out on a search for something, but we should be back by Sunday at the latest. When should you and I meet again?" I pulled out my calendar.

"Let's say Wednesday nights and Saturday nights. If we need to reschedule, so be it. Around six-thirty?"

I marked the appointments down for the next few weeks. "How long do you think it will be before this is all over? The Cruharach?"

"From what I've seen in the past, I'd say you're about six to eight weeks away from fully entering into it. So I'd estimate sometime near the equinox in September. If things go as usual, you should be done by Samhain—November."

She guided me to the door. "Next time, we'll start working on some magical exercises for you to do. And then, at the end of the month, we'll go in search of your father's bloodline, because I guarantee, you may have a strong tendency toward the Leannan Sidhe, but the Autumn's Bane blood is no slouch. Now, have a good evening and try not to worry."

I murmured good-bye, but as to not worrying? That was more to ask than I was capable of. As

I headed home, I wondered how I was going to explain to Angel and Talia what was happening. They had to know, and the sooner the better, but it wasn't something I was looking forward to.

Chapter 14

ANGEL AND TALIA were waiting dinner for me. The table was covered with takeout Chinese, pizza, and fried chicken. By the expansive feast, I knew something must be up.

"All right, I've had a rough afternoon. What's going on?" I glanced at Angel, then at Talia.

Angel started to say something, then glanced at Talia. "Why don't we talk after dinner?"

Yeah, something was up. "Spill it."

"I'll tell you," Herne said, swinging around the corner from the living room. "I decided you'd be exhausted after your meeting so I filled them in on the situation." He ran his gaze over me. "You look beat."

I felt a surge of irritation. I had wanted to break it to them. *Gently*, in *my own* way.

"Thanks, but you might have let *me* decide how to tell them." I felt grumpy and hung over, probably a side effect of the tincture and of stirring up the Leannan Sidhe that I had locked away inside me.

"I'm sorry. I was trying to help, but you're right." By the look on Herne's face, I realized I had hurt his feelings. I struggled between wanting to be right and just wanting to eat dinner.

"I didn't mean to snap, but I like to do things like this in my own manner. It doesn't really matter, I guess." I turned to Angel. "Well, now that you know *what* I am, how do you feel? Do you still want to live with me now that you know I carry dangerous blood in my veins?"

Angel smiled, though beyond the smile I could see concern in her eyes. "You've always carried dangerous blood in your veins, Ember. We just have a name for it now."

I let out a deep sigh. "You may not feel that way after I tell you about my visit with Marilee. But first, I need food. It's been a long, long day."

I piled a plate high and carried it into the living room. "I'm too tired to eat at the table. Let's eat in here, if you don't mind." I just wanted to curl up on the sofa and rest. Mr. Rumblebutt was sprawled across the cushions, but he took one look at me and jumped up on the back of the couch, making room. "Thanks, Mr. R. You're a sweetie."

He let out a *purp* and went back to sleep.

As we settled in with our food, I could tell they were all on edge, and I finally set my plate down and wiped my hands on a napkin. "All right, I'll get to it. I met..." I paused, trying to think of how to explain exactly what had happened. "I'm near the

Cruharach. Very near. Marilee estimates another two months at most before it fully overtakes me. Today, I met the Leannan Sidhe part of myself. And she scared the hell out of me."

They listened without commenting as I filled them in on everything that had happened. Finally, when I finished, the room felt heavier and I felt near tears. I picked up my plate again, more to fill the awkward silence than out of hunger.

Angel was the first to speak. "Marilee thinks you can control the hunger, though?"

"Yes," I said, finishing off another egg roll. "She says I can learn how to blend both sides, though we'll have to see which one will win out in terms of dominance. It could be my father's side. Right now, I'm not hedging bets on either of them—I have no idea which is the most ruthless and dangerous. I can tell you, my mother's bloodline is seductive. It was tempting to just give in, to let the hunger swallow me up."

"You had no idea your mother was a Leannan Sidhe?" Herne asked, refilling his plate.

I shook my head. "That alone gives me hope. My parents were caring. They were good people. If they were true to their Fae natures, I don't think I ever saw it. Or maybe, I just remember them that way because I was young."

Angel carried her plate to the kitchen. On her return, she brought a platter of cupcakes. "Dessert, because sugar always makes everything seem brighter." She handed me a dessert plate with two cupcakes on it. They smelled like rich chocolate, with a swirl of peppermint icing on them. "Ember,

your parents were always kind to me. I think...
there *was* an edge there to them, but I never saw it
in action. Mostly, they seemed wary and cautious,
probably because they knew that your grandparents weren't happy."

"Oh, it wasn't just my grandparents. Both
families were fairly well placed in their respective
Courts. Thinking about it now, I'm not surprised
they were killed. Well, I was then, but after the
shock wore off, I realized that I had always har-
bored a secret fear that somebody would make
them pay for their choices." I licked the top of the
icing swirl, blinking as the sharp mint hit my taste
buds. "I think...I think that I should spend some
time digging into their lives, if I can find a way.
Now, I'm curious. Did they reject their natures? Or
did they just hide them from me?"

Herne looked at me warily. "I'd be cautious going down that road. You may find out more than
you really want to know."

I caught his gaze. "Do you know any more
about this than you're telling me? I realize that
your mother and father may have told you to keep
quiet, but I'm tired of the secrets and of following a
labyrinth just to find out who I *really* am. If there's
more baggage back there, I want to know. I want it
all upfront, so I can deal with it."

He frowned, biting his lower lip. "I'll be honest.
Did I know your mother was Leannan Sidhe? No. I
didn't. Morgana didn't tell me. Did I know your father was descended from the Autumn's Bane? Yes,
actually, but I never thought much of it, because
most of the original clan are over the Great Sea.

Their descendants here tend to be on the roguish side, but the truly dangerous members are few and far between nowadays."

"Why didn't you tell me, though?"

"I thought you had been through the Cruharach and that everything had been sorted out already. I didn't know that you hadn't faced the transformation yet, so I thought you'd talk about it when you were ready. If you ever wanted to." He shook his head. "My mother and father chose not to confide in me. I think they didn't want to chance me opening my mouth. I'm good at keeping secrets, but not that good."

I still wasn't happy about the fact that he had known that I was descended from the Autumn Stalkers and had chosen to say nothing, but I understood his reasoning. And I understood why Morgana and Cernunnos had remained silent. If I had learned about the Cruharach a few months ago, I wouldn't have been able to cope with the knowledge—or at least, not well. The truth was, I had grown a lot, and I didn't realize how much until now.

"It's okay, truly. I get it." I paused, then glanced over at Angel. "You still okay with living with me? There's a part of me that's terrified I'll somehow hurt you."

Angel smiled. "I'm not afraid, Ember. We've been best friends since we were in grade school, since we were eight years old. I'm an empath—you know how good I am. And I have no worries about living with you, other than I'm going to be stuck cooking all the meals because...well...I'm a good cook and you suck."

Talia laughed. "She's got you there. Angel's right, though. You won't hurt her. When I had my full powers and was fully dedicated to my nature, I had a best friend who wasn't a harpy. She wasn't human, but she wasn't one of us. And while my nature is to hunt and lure people in with my song, I never once tried with her, because the hunger you're talking about—it discriminates. It's not like being a succubus, not fully. You aren't at the nature of your libido, and the Leannan Sidhe don't require life force in order to live."

"I guess you're right," I said, relaxing. "It's not like I'll be driven by necessity to feed off people."

"There's another facet you aren't thinking about," Herne said. "What I do know of the Leannan Sidhe—they prefer men. All the Leannan Sidhe are women, and when they give birth, there's a fifty-fifty chance their child will be born fully immersed in the bloodline. So your grandfather on your mother's side had to be different blood."

"Great. I wonder what *he* was. Morgana didn't mention anything about him. Is there a third bloodline I'll have to watch for? And what about the Autumn Stalkers? Are they all male?"

Herne shook his head. "No. They aren't. There's a good chance Farthing's wife is also from that line, because they tend to stick to their own, whereas the Leannan Sidhe don't have much of a choice if they want a mate. They have to look outside their race."

"This is getting to be more complex than I can handle for one day." I brushed my hand over my eyes, suddenly so tired I could barely move. "Can we just table this discussion for tonight? We have to get up early tomorrow to leave for Cavanaugh Peak, and I'm exhausted."

"Of course." Angel began to carry dishes into the kitchen. "Herne, why don't you help Ember to bed?"

Herne laughed. "I'm afraid it won't be as much fun as it usually is, but yeah, I'll help her." He wriggled his eyebrows at me and winked.

I laughed. I needed silly right now. Silly and lighthearted and something far away from talk of Leannan Sidhe and the hunger and how I had suddenly become a powder keg just waiting to go off. I handed Talia my cupcake plate as she passed by, helping Angel to clear, and pulled Mr. Rumblebutt into my arms.

"Hey, little guy...I'm going to be gone for a couple of days so you need to be good for Angel. Okay?" I nuzzled the top of his head.

He let out a *purp*, then began to purr, kneading my shoulder. He was a Norwegian Forest cat, and he was big and gorgeous, with shiny black fur that waved when he walked. I finally set him on the sofa.

"I'm going to bathe and then go to sleep. Herne, I love you, but go home. If you stay, I'll want to talk and frankly, I'm about talked out for the night."

"Got it." He stood, leaning down to plant a kiss on my forehead. "I'll see you on the curb around five-thirty. And you two," he said, turning to address Angel and Talia. "Tomorrow's Sunday, so enjoy the day. Got it?" He gave them a stern look, but I could see the smile creeping beneath it.

"Yes, sir!" Angel saluted him, then stuck out her tongue. "While the stag's away..."

"What? The bunnies will play?"

"Bunnies, my ass," Talia said. "I used to eat rabbits for breakfast. Come on, I'll walk you to the elevator, and you can escort me to my car."

As they left, Angel locked the door behind them. She dropped into the rocking chair next to me. "I didn't want to mention this while Herne was here, because I figured we could do without the drama, but you got another call from Ray."

I groaned. "When?"

"He left three messages this afternoon. I guess he's back in town."

Ray and I had dated for a brief time, a year or so back, and then when he had interrupted me while I was on the job—I had been hunting down a goblin for a client—he had almost ended up dead. He had a long scar on his leg from where the sub-Fae had tried to take a good-sized bite out of him. I realized that he was in danger, and since I had already lost two boyfriends, although Leland's death had been a heart attack while we were making love, I opted not to see Ray anymore. But somehow, I always felt I had been at fault. Robert had died while trying to help me put a stop to an infestation of will-o'-the-wisps. They had managed to lure him away and drain him.

So when I found myself falling for Ray and realized how fragile he was, I had ended the relationship. All seemed to be well until I had met up with him again in March, when his store was vandalized. That one meeting had set him off and he had been stalking me ever since.

"I thought maybe he finally got the message," I said, glumly. "I haven't heard from him for a couple of weeks."

"I did a little poking around after I got the message this evening," Angel admitted. "I've still got a good foothold in the grapevine around here. Ray was out of town at an uncle's funeral. He just got back last night."

"And he's right back on my ass." I sighed. "What did he say?"

"I kept the messages. You might want to turn them over to the police. As I said, I was tempted to tell Herne about them, but I thought you didn't need the drama tonight. But when you're well rested, you need to talk to someone. We have to do something about him before he shows up again." She shook her head, grabbing the landline when I reached for it. "No. Not tonight. You don't need to listen to what he said tonight. Go to sleep, Ember. Rest up for tomorrow."

I stared at the phone, but finally nodded. "I wonder why he didn't call my cell this time."

"Because he knows you blocked his number. He said so. We forgot to block him on the landline." She pulled me off the sofa, turning me around to face the hallway. "Go to bed. Sleep deep. Don't have nightmares." With a little shove, she pushed me toward my bedroom.

Impulsively, I turned to give her a hug. "Thank you. Thank you for being you."

Angel gave me a squeeze. "I love you too, Ember.

Now go."

I dragged myself into the bedroom. I managed to take off my makeup but decided I was far too tired to take a bath. I'd catch a shower in the morning instead. So, wearing an oversized shirt I had stolen from Herne, I climbed into bed. I had barely turned out the light and rested my head on my pillow before I fell asleep. Luckily, my dreams were mute, and I slept through the night without stirring.

MORNING ARRIVED AND I was showered and waiting on the curb by five-twenty-five. Angel had dragged herself out of her room while I was making a quick sandwich to take with me for breakfast. She fixed me an iced quad-shot latte to go, and I gave her a quick hug and kissed Mr. Rumblebutt on the head before heading downstairs to meet Herne.

He was good to his word, pulling up in his sleek, black Ford Expedition at precisely five-thirty. Viktor and Yutani were in the back. They had left the front seat for me. I tossed my pack in the SUV and climbed in, fastening my seatbelt. As soon as I was strapped in and my drink was in the cup holder, next to Herne's mocha, we took off.

"How are you doing this morning?" he asked me.

"Better than last night." I glanced over my shoulder. "Did you tell them?"

"Yeah. They had to know." He navigated toward

the freeway. "We're taking I-90 across the lake, over to the summit of Snoqualmie Pass. There, we turn onto Erste Strasse Road, and follow that to Alpental. We'll park and head out on the trailhead. It's near the Chair Peak trail."

"And then a three- to four-hour hike in?" I glanced out the window. The day was overcast, threatening rain. "Looks like we might have some weather today."

"Eighty percent chance of rain, but the snow level's at over seven thousand feet so we shouldn't see any new snow up there. I doubt if there are any patches left from winter, either, so I wouldn't worry too much about that," Yutani said. "We're going in at the perfect time. August is the best month to avoid getting slammed by bad weather."

"A three- to four-hour hike, yes, though if it pours, that will probably add a good hour or two to the hike. I think we really do need to plan on staying the night, given we don't know where to hunt for the bones of the Aillén Trechenn." Herne frowned as we headed onto the freeway. The ramp was metered, and the traffic was beginning to bog down. "Damn it, I had hoped to miss rush hour. I guess we should have left another hour earlier."

"Speaking for myself, I'm glad you didn't think of that." Viktor snorted. "Oh, I decided to have a drink with Charlie Darren last night. That vamp is actually a pretty good egg, from what I can tell, but he's definitely got some social anxiety issues going. I ended up drinking more than I usually do, just to get through the evening. It was awkward."

"How so?" Yutani asked.

"He got into a crying jag over the life he left behind. I guess he had a girlfriend who dumped him, and parents who really didn't want to claim a vampire for a son, and one thing after another until I wanted to take him by the shoulders and give him a good shake and tell him to pull himself out of it—to move on. I think he's trying, but he's so angst-ridden that by the time I left, I was three sheets to the wind, just trying to blot out the endless drone of complaints."

I was trying not to laugh, but the thought of Viktor playing Dr. Phil to an emo-vampire was just too funny. "You had a better evening than me, I'll bet. Now for the million-dollar question: did you agree to go out with him again?"

"It's not like I'm dating him, woman." Viktor was sounding surprisingly grumpy.

"Well, did you?"

"I don't want to talk about it anymore," the half-ogre said.

"You did. You agreed to get together again, didn't you?" I turned around in my seat, staring at Viktor. "Why didn't you just say you were busy for the next few weeks and stop it at that?"

Viktor let out a huff. "Because it's obvious the boy is hurting. He lost his entire way of life, and was turned into something that seems to go against his nature. He's doing everything he can to cope, but he doesn't know how. He might say he wants to work his way up in the vampire community but I know that's a lie. He doesn't like vampires, and is dealing with some pretty severe self-loathing right now." He paused. "I get the impression he's been thinking a lot about walking into the sun."

"Walking into the sun" was one of the most common ways vampires had of committing suicide. Not much else killed them, except a stake through the heart and prolonged exposure to fire. But the easiest way was to walk into direct sunlight. Within less than two minutes, intense contact with sunlight would crisp them to ashes.

I stopped laughing. "I didn't realize he was so unhappy. He seemed awfully eager to maintain contact, though."

Viktor nodded. "Yeah. That's because the dude is pretty much alone in the world. As uncommunicative as Nigel was, I think he was one of the only lifelines Charlie had to the outside world. The only thing he has to hold onto is that job he has coming up with the credit union. He's got so many hopes riding on it that I'm worried it won't work out." It was obvious that Charlie had tugged on Viktor's heartstrings enough to engage the half-ogre.

Herne glanced in the rearview mirror. "First Angel drags in the savines, and now you're bringing home a pet vampire. Honestly, are we running an adoption agency for strays?" But he laughed, a good-natured smile on his face.

"Hey, I'm entitled to my share of the feels, you know?" Viktor shrugged. "I just think that when we can offer a lifeline to somebody who's basically a good-hearted person, maybe we shouldn't be so quick to turn away."

Something had set off his empathy meter, that was for certain. But even though I wasn't all that sympathetic, I understood the impulse. When you were considered a stray or a misfit yourself, it was hard to turn away from others who were in the same boat.

"Tell you what," I said. "When we're done with this case, you and I can take him out bowling, or something he might enjoy. I'm pretty good at pool."

Yutani brightened up. "Pool? You play pool? I didn't know that."

"Yeah, I learned when I was in college. Angel and I used to hustle some of the jocks. She'd bring them in, I'd play the ditz, and we'd end up with extra spending money." I laughed. "I remember this one guy. He was six-five, basketball player, a real smooth-talker, if you know what I mean. Love 'em and leave 'em, and macho as hell. He couldn't believe that a woman would ever beat him. He wasn't happy when he realized that I was a pool shark and that Angel had reeled him in. But he paid up and we were two hundred dollars richer by the time I finished three games."

"That sounds like you, but *Angel* was in on it?" Yutani sounded skeptical.

"Oh, don't let her mild demeanor fool you. That woman is a chameleon when need be. Though she'd never take advantage of someone who couldn't afford it or didn't deserve it."

We were over the I-90 bridge and onto the eastbound freeway. Luckily, we were going against traffic now, and zipping along at a decent clip. We were almost through Issaquah, and heading southeast. Down here, the shifters really had taken over.

Tiger Mountain State Forest was a prime destination for shifters of all sorts to run freely in their animal forms, and hunting was strictly forbidden inside of the park and around the outskirts.

I fell silent again, watching out the window as the miles sped by. Before long, we were passing through Preston—a town just big enough to have a name, a school, and a cemetery. The rain had started to come down and was drenching the asphalt. The clouds were hanging low and dark, and the foothills around us, misty. Maybe it was better for hiking. Too much climbing under the sun could be awfully uncomfortable, and it was easier to put on layers than to take them off after a certain point.

The road bent further east, jogging north just a bit, and we passed Snoqualmie Parkway. We wouldn't be able to see the Falls today, I thought sadly. I had always loved coming over to the towering waterfalls that roared into the river below. The road made another bend to the southeast, and we were through Snoqualmie and nearing North Bend, another stop in which to buy gas and grab a bite to eat.

By six-forty-five we had passed through Tanner, the next town, and were coming up on Twin Falls. The road continued, falling beneath the wheels of Herne's SUV, and we lapsed into a comfortable silence as the rain continued to splatter down around us. The road was beginning to ascend at a gradual pace, and Herne moved to the inner lane. The right-hand lane was for semis, the big rigs having to churn their way up the hills at a slower pace. To either side of the road, the forest was thickening, and the guardrails became more apparent. Overhead, the cloud cover darkened and a brief blast of hail slowed our speed to a crawl, but it didn't last long.

Near the Granite Mountain Trailhead, the east- and westbound sections of I-90 diverged, the eastbound lane that we were in winding its way up toward the summit. At an elevation of just over three thousand feet, Snoqualmie Pass was open all year round, and was the primary connector from the east side of the state to the west. In winter, it often closed for avalanche control, but was usually passable with chains or snow tires. It was decidedly cooler up at the summit, but the mountain passes could get crazy warm during the peak months of July and August. I was grateful we were running a steady sixty degrees today.

As the foothills to either side steepened, the rock faces became more exposed, and the restraining walls became more necessary. Washington's Cascade Range was an impressive array of towering peaks, born from the molten fire lurking below the surface. The volcanoes that watched over the land in brooding silence were sleeping for the most part, but they could awaken at any time. St. Helens had done so with a massive fury back in 1980, and the other volcanoes were just biding their time. During the birth of the Cascades, the fires from the earth had pushed the mountains up, the tectonic plates below fracturing and shifting and reforming again and again.

We were approaching the exit for the summit,

and Herne eased over onto the off-ramp. Another few minutes and we parked in the lot near the Snoqualmie Pass Visitors' Center.

"Make use of the restrooms if you need them," Herne said. "This is a good place to get out and stretch. Afterward, we head out on NF 9041, then onto Erste Strasse Road, which will take us to Alpental."

"What's the NF stand for?" Yutani asked.

"National Forest, I think," Herne said.

We scrambled out of the car. I winced as my back groaned a little. Sitting so long in a car—even a comfortable one—wasn't conducive to good back care. But we'd be moving around soon enough.

We headed into the visitor center. I made use of the women's room to freshen up, then stopped at the concession stand to pick up a rain poncho. I didn't own one, but I had the feeling it might be a good investment, given it was pouring outside, and it wasn't going to stop anytime soon. I also grabbed a couple extra chocolate bars. I knew that Yutani had brought food, but I wasn't sure what he had decided on and it couldn't hurt to take a little extra sugar along.

As we met back at the car, it struck me how clear the air felt. It was cool and damp, and we wouldn't want to get soaked—that was a recipe for disaster—but the scent of wet firs and moss cushioned me, lulling me into a calm that soothed my frayed nerves from the day before.

We settled in again and headed into the last leg of the drive. Ten minutes later, we were pulling into the parking lot, off the Alpental Access Road.

We parked near the trailhead.

Herne turned off the ignition. Yutani and Viktor began unloading the back of the SUV. I walked over to the massive sign that had maps on it. Made from debarked timber the sign was rustic, and yet would probably stand through a major quake. The tree trunks that the posts had been made from were a good sixteen inches in diameter.

Next to the Cavanaugh Peak Trail sign was a staircasing path, the sides of the steps formed from eight-inch timbers. The steps were filled in with gravel and dirt to offer hikers an easier climb up the beginning of the trail. They reminded me of an old children's toy—Lincoln Logs—and I wondered how long it had taken to create the trail itself.

The forest closed in quickly on either side with tall firs that towered over the land, low-running vine maple and massive ferns that spread out wider than a car. Red cedar and alder trees filled in the gaps, and salmonberry and huckleberry. I spotted several patches of stinging nettle, and quickly pulled out my gloves from my pack. I didn't want any welts from the blistering plants. I had dressed in jeans, a long-sleeve V-neck sweater, and had brought a windbreaker, which I tied to my pack. I pulled on the rain poncho, and adjusted the hook.

The others were dividing up the extra weight, including the food and the tents. Viktor handed me a large empty pack.

"Here, for the bones. Knock wood we find them. And here's an extra water bottle. We'll need to stay hydrated, even though it's raining."

"Thanks. I think I'm set. Everybody else ready?"

If I had forgotten anything, it was too late now, but I thought I had brought everything I might need.

"Ready to go. Let's go find those bones." And with that, Herne double-checked the SUV, making certain it was locked.

With one last look at the parking lot, we started up the trail.

Chapter 15

THE FIRST BIT of the hike was a good ascent. We started up the rock-and-dirt staircase, and I promptly stopped, looking for a walking stick.

"What are you looking for?" Herne asked as I poked around in the bushes.

"A staff. I have no problem with the climb, but it just makes things that much easier."

Viktor joined me. "Here, let me help." He pointed to a downed log. "Will that branch do?"

The nurse log was covered with moss, but there was one limb, about four feet long, that had been stripped of bark. It was fairly straight and thin enough so my hand would wrap around it, but looked sturdy enough to manage the trip. But it was still attached to the tree.

"That would be perfect." I started over to it, but Viktor motioned me back. He leaned down, bracing one foot against the tree and the other on the ground. Then, with a mighty heave, he leveraged the branch till it bent upward, then splintered off the base of the tree. He handed it to me and I gratefully accepted. I would have had to either jump up and down on it, which would have been a feat in itself, or I would have had to borrow Yutani's hatchet that he had strapped to his belt in order to manage it.

Yutani had been watching. "Here, let me see it," he said, unstrapping the hand-ax. I handed him the stick and he laid it across a stump, then gave a good whack to the end, taking off most of the splinters so that it was fairly even on the bottom.

"Thanks so much," I said, testing my weight against it. "This is perfect. It's dried out, so it's light enough, but it's also sturdy."

We headed off again, Herne in the lead with me behind him. Yutani and Viktor brought up the rear. We didn't talk much, letting the hum of the insects and the chirping of the birds fill the silence. Instead, we focused on the ascent.

Unlike Snow Lake Trail, which was heavily used, Cavanaugh Peak Trail wasn't nearly as trafficked and today there was a dearth of hikers, for which I was relieved. I didn't feel like hunting around for the bones while others asked what we were doing.

We continued through the morning drizzle, and I quickly decided that sun would have been better than rain, even if we had chanced getting overly heated. The rain made the trail slippery, and going up a muddy slope wasn't exactly a barrel of laughs. I was glad I wore hiking boots, and the walking stick helped, but it was still slick work.

We spent a good hour on the first mile, which after about three hundred yards of steps turned into a fairly steep trail. The forest closed in around us on our right as we ascended. To our left, the slope was growing steeper and rockier. I could see through the trees that a ravine led down into a deep gash, and I crowded toward the right, not wanted to trip and go tumbling down the hill. The trees would have stopped my fall, but there were a lot of rocks and fist-sized boulders littering the ground—perfect for bruising the body.

Ahead of me, Herne climbed like a mountain goat, sure-footed and without any discernible effort. He kept one hand to the right, holding on to the now-vertical slope, and used it to brace his climb.

We had been hiking for about twenty minutes when I suddenly got the feeling we were being followed. I mentioned it, in low tones, to Herne.

"We may well be. Do you have any clue of what it might be?"

I shook my head. "I don't know. I just feel like we're being watched."

"There are so many sentinels in these woods that you're probably right. The guardians who patrol these mountains are ancient, and they are found deep within stone and cave and rock and shadow." Herne glanced over my head at Viktor. "Have you sensed anything?"

Viktor squinted, then shook his head. "No, but that means nothing. I'm used to the earth elementals in the mountains, so much so that if it were one of them, I probably wouldn't even notice.

They're as much a part of my world as the water is for Ember."

"Well, let's get moving again, but everybody keep on your guard," Herne said.

We set out again and about half an hour later, the rain began to slack off and breaks in the clouds let sunlight beam through. The temperature was starting to rise, and wherever the light hit, swirls of mist rose up from where the heat evaporated the rain.

We suddenly broke through the trees just as the sun burned off the clouds. The slope to our right towered straight up, the rock face covered with clefts and fractures. To our left, the trees gave way to a steep slope, covered with low-growing vegetation that stretched toward a curve leading to the right. The ferns and low-growing shrubs covered the sides of the ravine, and down below, a stream wound along the forest floor. The valley below swept out in a wide swath of foliage across the bottom, then up toward another peak covered with trees.

I stopped, shading my eyes as I looked across the valley toward the next hill. In some parts of the country, these would be considered towering mountains, but here, they were the children of the Cascades, the young blood.

"This is incredible." I couldn't look away. The valley was dotted with wildflowers—larkspur and lupine, foxglove and Indian paintbrush. The entire meadow was abuzz with fat, sassy bumblebees and honeybees, darting from blossom to blossom now that the sun had come out. The birds were starting to sing, and everywhere, the sun glinted off the raindrops, scattering hundreds of tiny prism rainbows through the steep lea.

"It is," Yutani said from behind me. He, too, had stopped to stare down into the valley. "I'd love to go running through there in my coyote form."

As he spoke, I spotted a movement in the meadow below. Then, the form of what looked like a large dog leaped up on a boulder, staring up at us. Beside me, Yutani froze, staring at the animal. I caught a sudden flare of energy between the two.

Herne edged back toward us, his gaze locked on the meadow below. "Is that..."

"Yeah," Yutani said. "Coyote. I can sense him from here."

"Shifter?"

"No. Messenger." Yutani slowly slid his pack off his back. "He's stalking me."

I stepped away to give Yutani some room. He inched forward to the edge of the trail, where the slope immediately began to descend. Once there, he crouched, squatting on his toes, one hand bracing himself against the muddy pathway as he reached out with his other. His hair was caught back in a braid that fell to mid-back, and his skin gleamed with a golden tint in the flare of sun that was overtaking the clouds, sending them packing.

Viktor glanced at Herne, who gave him a shake of the head. I wasn't sure what they were thinking, but the magic around us was heavy, and I could feel the conversation flowing between Yutani and the coyote, though I had no clue what the exchange was about.

A few minutes later, the coyote turned and bounded away, vanishing into the undergrowth. Yutani sighed, pushing himself to his feet again. He was still staring over the meadow, a wary look on his face.

"What did he say, or can you tell us?" Herne asked, his voice low.

"I don't know. He was warning me, but I couldn't get a clear message." Yutani opened his mouth, about to say more, but abruptly shook his head. "I can't tell you what he said because I'm not sure what it was. I suggest we just keep going."

"Do you think that you were sensing Coyote earlier, Ember?" Herne turned to me.

I thought for a moment, trying to piece together my feeling that something was following us with Coyote, but it was all a blur.

"I don't know. Like Yutani, I'm not getting anything clearly. Let's move on. I'd like to get there before too late."

We started off again, and before long, we were nearing the bend that curved right around the mountain. As we swung around the towering cliff, a massive rock field spread out below to our left. A glacial deposit, countless boulders—some as big as a car—stretched down into the valley floor.

I glanced to the right. Upslope, the grade had mellowed some, but the same fan of rocks spread out above us, the bottom boulders held back by a restraining wall that had been built along the two-hundred-yard wide field of debris.

As we began to make our way across the boulder field, my nerves scrambled into high gear. All it would take was a small quake, or a loud noise, to send those rocks tumbling down the mountain at us, and no three-foot-tall restraining wall would hold them.

Herne was moving quickly, and I had the feeling he was feeling the same fear as me. He moved decisively and quietly, and I did my best to follow suit. It was eerie, staring up at the massive rock field, know that the boulders had been left behind when the ice retreated so many thousands of years ago. They were a silent testament to the march of time, and the power of earth's forces.

Finally, we were past the field. It hadn't taken long, really, but the awareness of just what *could* happen had made it seem like it was taking forever.

Beyond the field, we came to the turnoff leading to Cavanaugh Peak and Hidden Lake. The other direction would take us to the Snow Lake trail.

We had been hiking for over two hours by now, and it was going on eleven-thirty. I was getting hungry and wondering when we'd be stopping for lunch when I remembered the candy bars in my pocket. I slipped one out and began to munch on the chocolate and coconut as we finally reached a part where the trail evened out.

Herne saw me eating and held up his hand. "Lunch break. We're over halfway to Cavanaugh Peak, so a break won't hurt us."

Grateful, I slipped off my pack and sat it on the ground, sitting on a chair-sized boulder next to it. Yutani was scouting around and he came jogging back to us.

"There's the remains of an old cabin just through the trees over there. Part of the chimney and fireplace are still there, and you can tell where the foundation of the cabin used to be."

"People actually lived up here?" While we were only an hour and a half away from the city, it was hard to imagine *anybody* living out here. They'd have to live sans electricity and running water, that much was for certain.

"Well, the Puma shifters did, until the Aillén Trechenn rousted them from their homes. And I imagine some of the native tribes lived here, too." Viktor stretched. "But my bet is that Yutani found an old mining cabin. I'll come with you and take a look at it." He followed Yutani across the open glade and ducked into the tree cover with him.

Herne sat down beside me. "How are you doing?"

"All right. Sweaty now that the sun is out, but that's not a problem. You say we have another hour or so to go till we reach Hidden Lake?"

He nodded. "Hopefully we'll make up some time that we lost due to the rain." He pulled out a sandwich and offered me half.

"You too cheap to give me my own sandwich, dude?" I laughed as he rolled his eyes and handed me a roast beef sub. "Thank you. Unlike you, I need to eat in order to manage."

"Yeah, well, never say I didn't do anything for you." He pursed his lips and blew me a kiss, then bit into his ham and Swiss.

"What's the rest of the trail like?"

"We start ascending again in about a quarter

mile, and then it's through a small pass and down into the valley in the center of Cavanaugh Peak, where Hidden Lake is." He wiped his hands on a paper napkin after polishing off his sandwich.

Yutani and Viktor returned and settled down, immediately plowing through the food.

"So, was it what you thought?" Herne asked.

Viktor nodded. "Pretty sure it's the remains of an old mining cabin. Found the head of a pickaxe there, rusted to hell. The miners were through these woods like carpenter ants. There's a lot of ore still up in the hills here."

"Gold?" I asked.

"Some, yes. There was a rush in the 1850s but it didn't last long. The main discovery came around 1873 and it never rivaled the gold rushes in California. There's still gold in the mountains, and other ores, but only the dwarves really have a handle on where it is, and they keep the knowledge secret." Viktor shrugged. At my questioning look, he added, "You learn a lot when you hang out with the right people."

"When you're done eating, we should shove off," Herne said, dusting his hands on the legs of his jeans as he stood. "Ready?"

Viktor and Yutani finished their sandwiches as I excused myself to use the bushes. I kept one eye on what I was doing, the other on making sure no animals or anybody else meandered up to startle me. When I returned, after washing my hands in a small puddle of water nearby, we set out again.

We came to a ridge leading across to another upward climb. I caught sight of a sign that read CA-

VANAUGH'S PEAK & HIDDEN LAKE. The slope would turn into a steep climb after the ridge, but thankfully the sun had dried out the dirt so we didn't have to slog through the mud.

"It's not that the heights are so terrible," I said, staring across the narrow ridge, "but there's nothing to fall onto but rocks."

"True, but this is the last leg. Once over the ridge, we climb up to the saddle, and then we are in sight of the lake. The descent is tricky, but then we'll be in the valley." Herne glanced at the sun. "What time is it?"

"Quarter to one," Viktor said. "We're running later than we hoped, but we should be there by one-thirty or two at the latest."

Herne set foot onto the ridge. The top had been worn relatively flat over the years, but was only about two feet wide. He quickly passed over the surface, light on his feet. I was slower, trying not to look down, but afraid that if I stared up at the clouds I'd get dizzy. About two-thirds of the way there, I took a deep breath and raced forward, leaping off onto the other side beside Herne. Yutani and Viktor followed, neither one looking particularly nervous.

We crossed to the bottom of the ascent, and I stared at the steep rock wall. Hand-and-footholds had been gouged into the side of the rock, and I nervously glanced around at the field of sharp rocks that were scattered everywhere.

"I don't know if I can make that. I'm good at climbing, but that looks daunting."

"You'll be fine. You won't fall," Herne said, trying to encourage me.

"I'm not afraid of *falling*. It's the landing I don't look forward to."

"I'll tell you what," Herne said. He unwrapped a coil of rope from around his waist. "Here, keep hold of the end. Once I get up there, I'll secure myself and then you can tie the rope around your waist and that way, if you fall, I'll be able to catch you."

Grateful, I did as he said. When he reached the top—the man's agility seriously rivaled that of a monkey—he straddled the saddle, bracing himself back against the rock. He motioned for me to start up.

"Let me strap you into that," Yutani said. "We should probably work up a quick, makeshift harness to avoid hurting your ribs if you fall."

"How do I do that?"

He quickly began threading the rope around me, between my legs, around my waist, in a complicated pattern that I couldn't follow. But a moment later, I was firmly wedged into a rope harness that reminded me of the ropes holding a hot air balloon.

"Thanks," I said. "When did you get so proficient with tying knots?"

He stared at me, then a slow smile crossed his face. "I'm a student of kinbaku."

I blinked, about to say something but then Herne tugged on the rope. I quickly turned around so that Yutani wouldn't see how flustered I was, and began my ascent, using the hand- and foot-holds as best as I could. On the way up, though, it gave me something to think about rather than focusing on how steep the slope was.

I knew that kinbaku was also known in some circles as shibari—though I wasn't clear on the difference. Japanese rope bondage was an erotic art that was also a discipline, and I hadn't had a *clue* that Yutani was into that. I decided that I wouldn't pursue the questions running through my mind, unless he brought it up again.

By the time I neared the top, I was having trouble managing the handholds. My fingers were aching, and I dreaded trying to manage the last few feet.

"Herne? Can you help me? I'm having trouble holding on." I didn't try to look up, but stayed where I was, desperately trying to hold on.

"I'm here." His voice echoed down, and I suddenly felt the rope go taut. "Let go of the handholds, but keep your feet against the rock and use them to brace yourself as I pull you up."

I was sweating by now, and the thought of letting go terrified me, but I put my trust in him. I had seen his strength before and logically, I knew he could easily pull me up. I braced my feet against the rock, and took hold of the rope. My feet almost slipped, but Herne was keeping a tight grip and I was able to walk my way up the side of the rock as he leveraged me up. Another minute and I was at the top and he pulled me onto the saddle.

Scooting away from the edge, I scrambled out of the harness, shaking. "I'm not afraid of heights, but damn, that was scary. And damn it, I forgot my walking stick down there." I didn't want to think about the return trip.

"The descent to Hidden Lake is pretty steep, but it's not quite the same pitch and it's not as far down," Herne said. He scooted to the edge, and waved for Yutani to come next. I lay down on my stomach to watch over the side because sitting there, looking down, made me dizzy.

Yutani, apparently, had noticed my stick on the ground and fastened it to his back, then began to climb the wall like a spider. As I watched him, I wondered what other secrets he had tucked away. He was an enigma to me, silent and with a bare sense of humor, and apparently into some hard-core fetishes. He scrambled up, as though he were immune to the effects of gravity. After he joined us, Viktor started up. The half-ogre was slower but sure-footed, like a mountain goat. He, too, had no problem, and within minutes, we were all sitting on the saddle of the pass.

The other side of the saddle was, indeed, a steep descent, but there were trees and bushes along the way to help. Yutani handed me my stick, and unknotted the rope, coiling it and returning it to Herne, who accepted it without a word.

As I looked at the land spreading out below, I realized that Hidden Lake was cradled in what look like a bowl.

"Was this a volcano? I thought there were only about seven volcanoes in the area?"

Viktor shook his head. "Perhaps active, but as far as I remember my geology, there were over twenty major volcanoes in the Cascades, and thousands of vents, fissures, and so forth. This looks like it was a small caldera, and the lake seems to have formed at the lowest point."

The rock fields leading down through the trees were rough and sharp, and the footing was treacherous, but after the initial start, we came to a path that had been smoothed out. The compacted soil meant easier walking, though the pitch of the grade was steep enough to cause its own issues. But another twenty minutes saw us to the bottom, where we were able to drop our packs and sit on the boulders near the lake.

Hidden Lake was a deep blue, and the forest covered the sides of the rounded lake, their brilliant greens providing a striking color contrast. It was gorgeous, but now I understood why Herne had been adamant about bringing camping gear. My legs ached from the climb, and we wouldn't have time to search and still safely get back to the trailhead before dark.

"I suppose we should start hunting for the bones," I said, reluctant to stand. I just wanted to sit and listen to the gentle lapping of the waves. They were singing to me and I wanted to tune into them, to let them whisper to me.

"Not quite yet. First, we make camp. We set up the tents, get a fire going—safely—and sort out what we have. That way, we can search until dark and not have to worry about trying to set up our gear." Herne motioned to Viktor. "Go ahead and get started. I'll put up the tent Ember and I'll be using."

Viktor and Yutani began to erect their tent, while I helped Herne with ours. They were easy enough—pop-up tents that were extremely light-weight. The tents were generously sized, and tall enough so that Viktor barely had to duck to get in-side. After rolling out our bedrolls, I helped Yutani sort through the food, and then we rigged it in a backpack, hanging over a tree limb away from the tents to avoid bears tearing up the campground. Meanwhile, Viktor gathered rocks to build a fire ring and Herne started the fire with a quick spell. When the blaze was tidily burning, we were ready to head out to look for the bones.

"Do you think I should see if there are any water elementals in the lake that might help us?" I asked, not certain of where to look first.

"I guess it can't hurt," Herne said.

We wandered down to the edge of the lake. A flurry of wings caught my attention as a gray jay bird whisked away from a nearby bush, scolding us for intruding. I let out a long breath, relaxing as we came to the edge of the lake. Overhead, a hawk soared by, hunting prey among the debris, and then I saw another—albeit smaller—following closely behind. The parents must be teaching the young to hunt.

Hidden Lake was small. It could have been mistaken for a pond, but I could feel how deep it was, through my entire body. The depths of the lake resonated in my bones, and it occurred to me that I was becoming more and more attuned to the water.

"It's beautiful." Yutani shaded his eyes, looking across the lake. "What's on the other side?"

"More rocks, leading up to bigger and more

dangerous foothills. And from there, the Cascades just take over in a massive sprawl of jagged peaks and high timber." Herne shook his head. "I've lived a long time, and I've visited a number of places in my life, but I've never seen anything quite so beautiful and yet as treacherous as the Cascade Range. There are places in these mountains that have never been touched by human hands."

I knelt by the water's edge and lowered my hand into the lake. It was surprisingly cold, considering it was summer, and I paused for a moment to let the shock wear off. As the chill from the water faded, I began to feel the energies running through the lake. There were several elementals here, playing, and then, in the depths of the lake, something else. I sent out a call, asking for guidance, and shortly, I felt something licking my hand. I looked down and saw that the water was swirling around my fingers. I recognized the shape—it was an elemental.

I formed a question surrounding the image of bones. Metal bones. There wasn't a way to stipulate iron—and I doubted the water elementals would make much of a distinction—but visualizing metal should do the trick. I waited for a moment, and then a flurry of images began to flood into my head, so fast I couldn't take them all in.

A tall stack of rocks high on the opposite hill...a hole behind them, leading into a shallow cave... an explosion and the rocks began to fall, tumbling down into the lake...screams from behind the cloud of dust and debris...and then...silence.

I was about to break off contact when the elemental abruptly cut ties and something else grabbed my hand and pulled me into the lake. Startled, I found myself struggling to keep afloat as something wrapped around me, attempting to drag me down. I swallowed a mouthful of water, coughing, and then, everything began to waver.

Hungry...the hunger raced through my veins like an icy fire, burning...yearning to feed. I ached. *How long had it been since I last fed?* I gazed at the three men on the shore. I wanted someone I could feed from, whom I could drain dry.

As I rose, standing hip-deep in the lake, the men were watching me. One was staring at me with narrowed eyes, and I realized I'd have no chance with him. He was too powerful. The half-ogre tugged on his collar, looking uncomfortable. But the third—the shifter...I could feel his arousal. I held out my hands and began to sing. He started in my direction as I wove my charm around him, summoning the glamour that would transfix him to me.

"Yutani, stop!" the strong one called, and my prey froze.

Damn it. I pushed all my will into my charm.

"I have come for you," I whispered. "Come to me." I began to sing again, trying to lure him forward. The hunger was ricocheting through my body, coloring my thoughts, coloring everything as it exploded through me.

"I can't let you take him." The other man waded into the water, grabbing my wrist as he shook me and the half-ogre restrained my quarry. "Ember, snap out of it."

Furious, I struggled, but he was stronger than I was. I tried to drag him down into the water, and he caught hold of my other wrist. I leaned down and bit his hand. Startled, he let go, cursing, and I dove into the icy water, swimming toward the middle of the lake. But he was right behind me, and he caught me again, dragging me toward the shore. I fought, thrashing, but he tossed me on the ground, landing beside me to grab my wrists. As he held them together, the half-ogre bound them with a rope. I kicked at both of them, but they tied my feet as well, and I began to shriek, calling for help. There were those who would come to me, who would help me escape.

"Shut up!" The gorgeous man clapped a hand over my mouth. "She's calling for reinforcements and I don't want to see who shows up!"

The half-ogre brought over a strip of cloth and they gagged me. I tried to break away but I was trussed like a fish in a net.

"What's going on?" A fourth man stepped out from behind a large boulder. He looked familiar but I couldn't place him through the haze of hunger that swirled in mists through my thoughts.

"Kipa! What the hell are *you* doing here?" The man who had bound me stood, hands on his hips, staring at the wild one who had emerged from behind the boulder.

I immediately realized that I'd never be able to charm either one. They were of a kind, the pair, though as different as day and night.

"I followed you—I have my reasons, but leave them for now. It's a good thing I did because you need my help."

"This is probably one of the only times I'm glad to see you," his lighter counterpart said. "I think Ember's possessed by something and we need help freeing her."

The feral man looked down at me, and I found myself transfixed. I couldn't look away as he leaned down and brushed my hair away from my face. His hand felt smooth, and he felt ancient, and I fell into the lull as he began to whisper in a language I couldn't understand.

"*Kuule minua*, Ember. *Palatkaa minulle.*" And then, he pressed his hand on my forehead, and the world exploded.

Chapter 16

A WHITE HEAT as brilliant as sunrise blinded me as his fingers brushed my forehead. I could feel him pressing his hands to either side of my head and I tried to shake him off but I couldn't move, couldn't think, couldn't see. The world began to grow dark.

Ember...

The voice was seductive and rich, deep and earthy, and it reached through the fog that was swallowing me up. I started, looking around. I was lying in a pool surrounded by tall reeds, curled in a fetal position, and I realized that I had been sleeping. Or maybe not *sleeping*, but...drifting. I had a moment of panic when I realized that I wasn't in my body. I sat up, wondering how the hell I was able to breathe when I was clearly underwater, but then logic soothed me.

I might be underwater, but since I'm not in my

body, I don't have to worry about breathing. The thought calmed me down as I tried to make heads or tails out of what was going on.

Ember...can you hear me?

Behind the voice, I could hear the howling of wolves. They echoed around me, a haunting refrain, and I wanted to follow their call, to let them lead me into the cold winter night.

Who are you?

You can hear me, then. Good. I need you to follow me. I need you to follow the thread of my voice, back to your body.

The words wrapped around me, caressing my mind. I realized that I was in pain, but as the words showered around me, cascading over my form, the pain began to lessen its grip.

I looked around, still caught within the pool. Then, I remembered. I had been shoved here when the kelpie took over my body. I had been tossed into the depths, and it wasn't ever planning on returning for me. That brought images flashing to mind, faces...Herne, and Viktor and...*Yutani.* Crap! The kelpie had been going to feast on Yutani.

Yutani? Is he okay?

Yes. But you must follow me now. And you need to hurry.

At that moment, I knew who was talking to me. *Kipa? All right, I'll follow.*

I wasn't sure how he had come to be there, or where I was or how he had found me, but when he told me to follow him it felt absolutely vital that I obey. I swam through the mire of a pond, realizing that the reeds had been trying to hold me down.

Kipa began to sing, so I could pinpoint his voice. I started in his direction, walking through the water, dodging this way and that to avoid the numerous logs and whirlpools that tried to block my way. As I broke the surface, I was facing the endless vista of an ocean, the breakers rolling in toward me.

What do I do now?

You must have faith. Dive into the ocean. Let it pull you down. I'll be there to catch you.

I hesitated, but the urgency to act outweighed my trepidation and so I dove into the ocean. Immediately, I began to spiral down, and it was all I could do to keep conscious. A few moments later, I began to black out, and I wondered if I had made a mistake. As the vortex began to spin faster, I realized that I couldn't stop it if I wanted. I closed my eyes, trying to hang on. My last thoughts were of Herne, and of Kipa, and of wondering if I would ever see anybody I loved again.

"EMBER? CAN YOU hear me?" Herne's voice cut through the fog that clouded my senses. He sounded worried.

"Her eyes are fluttering. I think she can hear us, but can't yet respond." Kipa's voice, all right. I felt a flood of warmth and security when I heard it, which startled me. "Ember, it's time to wake up. You're back. It's time to get up."

I managed a groan, and my eyes began to respond. When I tried to open them, it felt like my lashes had been glued shut. They protested before finally I was able to pry them open. I was staring up at Herne and Kipa, who were hovering over me with concerned looks on their faces.

"Ember?" Kipa asked. His question was a command, and I felt no option but to answer.

"Yes," I croaked out. "It's me."

Herne let out a long sigh and relief swept over his face. "Thank all the stars in the sky, you're back. Are you all right?" He knelt beside Kipa, who gave him an odd look, then moved out of the way. Herne slid his arm under my back and helped me to slowly sit up.

I was shivering, and the sun looked to be lower in the sky than it had been. "What happened?" I couldn't remember much, just fuzzy images of trying to...*Yutani.* I frantically looked around for the coyote shifter. "Yutani? Is he all right?"

"He's okay. He's sitting back by the campfire. We couldn't take you there until Kipa called your soul out of the lake." Herne looked crestfallen now. "I'm sorry. I failed you. I should have stopped you from trying to commune with the water."

"Kelpie." I swallowed hard. "There was a kelpie."

"Yeah, there was a kelpie and it targeted you and sucked you in. It controlled the water elemental you tried to contact about the bones." Kipa gave me a stern look. "Until that teacher of yours helps you transition, you need to quit doing that."

I blinked. "How do you know all this?"

"Because Herne asked me to retrieve your soul and fight off whatever had hold of you."

Kipa's eyes flashed and there was a soft tug inside me, as though I recognized him more than I felt I had any reason to. He hesitated, tilting his head, and I felt the desire to reach out, to stroke that long, flowing hair. It wasn't sexual, the feeling, but a desire for connection. An *understanding*, if you will. Nonplussed, I turned my head but not before Kipa winked at me.

He stood and walked away, leaving me to Herne.

Herne helped me stand, gathering me to his chest, holding me tight. "I was so afraid, Ember. I was afraid we were going to lose you."

"I couldn't fight it off. I didn't even know *what* it was for a while." I shivered. "What if it had gotten hold of Yutani? I could have killed him."

"Yes, you probably could have, though we would have fought you off. We *did* fight you off." He kissed me very gently, as though I was a fragile piece of porcelain.

Truth was, I did feel fragile, and vulnerable, and terribly uncertain. I struggled to keep back a flood of tears. I rested my head on his shoulder.

"What do we do now?"

"We keep you away from the water, for one thing. There are some dark spirits that live in the depths, and you're too open to them right now. We'll eat and give you a time to rest, then start hunting for the bones."

His arm around my shoulders, he turned me back toward camp and we started walking. My knees were weak, but I was starting to feel more grounded. As we left the edge of the lake, I could feel the kelpie out there, watching, but there was nothing she could do if I didn't focus on her, and didn't give her an opening.

"I know where to look. Or at least, what to look for. I managed to get that much information before the kelpie caught hold of me."

We were back at the campfire by now. I glanced at Yutani, both embarrassed about what had happened, yet grateful that he was all right.

"It's okay," he said without prompting. "I'm fine and you're back, and no worries."

Grateful that he had approached the subject first, I nodded, silent. Viktor made room for Herne and me to sit down. Kipa was standing by the fire, staring into it. I blinked as I saw several shadow forms surrounding him. They looked like wolves.

"Am I imagining things?" I started to say.

He looked over at us. "No. My pack always runs with me wherever I go. They stay out of sight in cities and buildings, for the most part, but we are in the wild and this is their territory. They are my children and I am their Packmaster."

As I watched him, then looked at Herne, I began to understand. Kipa was the chaotic side of the forest, the deeper, darker woods. Herne might be Lord of the Hunt, but Kipa was lord of the pack that ran under the moon. They were both part of the Wild Hunt—the *actual* hunt—but played very different parts.

The wolves swirled around him, their shapes misty in the afternoon sunlight, but they were there and I felt more secure knowing they were.

"Before the kelpie got hold of me, I learned what to look for in order to find the bones."

"Good, then at least we are ahead of the game." Viktor handed me a grilled cheese sandwich and an enamel cup filled with tomato soup. I saw the pans sitting on the edge of the fire and realized that either he or Yutani had been cooking while Kipa was retrieving me.

Hungrier than I had expected to feel, I dove into the food and polished it off before any of the men managed to finish theirs. As Viktor poured me another mug of soup, I let out a long sigh, feeling mostly back to myself.

"The hill across the lake, there's a tall stack of rocks over there, and behind them, there's a hole that will lead into a shallow cave. I think that there was a cave-in or something, leading to a landslide down to the lake, but the bones should be around that area."

Herne glanced at the sun. "As soon as we're finished eating, we should get over there and start looking. It's nearing three-thirty. We lost a good two hours thanks to the kelpie. And we may be smack in the middle of summer, but the light fades in the mountains early, and dusk will settle here in a few hours."

We finished our lunch, and then, putting out the fire until we returned, began to circle the lake. Kipa joined us and I glanced at Herne, but he merely shrugged and said nothing.

IT DIDN'T TAKE long to navigate around the

lake, and as we came to the opposite side, my gaze immediately fastened on a tall stack of rocks about a third of the way up the cliff.

"There—those are the rocks we're looking for." I began to scramble toward them, but Herne grabbed my arm.

"Nope. *You're* not going anywhere alone, or first. Not up here, not when we know that Elatha is the one who came after the bones in the first place, and that one of the Force Majeure is by his side. Ranna is a powerful sorceress and she's loyal to the core." He didn't say it, but I got the sense that Herne was worried I'd end up in another jam like the kelpie.

"All right." I stepped back.

Herne took the lead, followed by Yutani, then me, then Viktor, and Kipa brought up the rear. We scrambled our way up the rockslide, cautious to avoid sending debris scuttling down the hill. None of us said anything—we all knew how dangerous loud noises could be. They could set off not only avalanches, but debris slides as well.

An hour after we started, we were standing at the tall heap of stones. They had been weathered by the wind and water till they were smooth, and they had been stacked into a towering obelisk. How long they had stood there, I didn't know, but I was amazed they hadn't come crashing down. As we cautiously skirted around the back of them, I caught the glimpse of a hole in the ground.

"There it is," I said, keeping my voice low.

Kipa murmured something and one of the shadow shapes of his wolves went darting inside. He returned a moment later. Kipa held out his hand and the wolf placed his muzzle in it.

"There's a cave-in in the hole," he said. "The path is blocked."

"That must be why the Fomorians only ended up with a few bones," I said, looking around. "Ten to one, there are more bones scattered through this rock field that they didn't find."

As if to answer me, I felt a tingle coming from under me, an uncomfortable sensation prickling through my shoe. I cautiously stepped to the side and knelt, hoisting aside the rock I had been standing on. There was something gleaming beneath it, sparkling like hematite. I reached for it, but the minute my fingers touched it, they began to burn and I quickly pulled my hand back.

"There, there's one." I stepped back.

Kipa glanced at the rocks on the slope above us, then cautiously began to shift the boulders where I had been standing to the side. Viktor joined him as the rest of us stood back, out of the way. A few moments later, Herne held up what looked like a long rib bone made out of iron.

"The creature must have been huge," I whispered, staring at the bone that was almost as long as Herne's torso.

"The Aillén Trechenn is a huge beast." Herne set the bone to the side. "We need at least one more of these in order for Ferosyn to concoct an antidote. Spread out, look for any sign of any other bones, but be cautious."

"I'm a good litmus test," I said. "If you think there may be a bone under a rock, call me over and

I should be able to tell."

We began to hunt, combing the hillside. Viktor was the first to find another bone—this one a great claw attached to what looked like a finger bone. Another search of the immediate area uncovered two more. The light was beginning to fade when Yutani stumbled over two more rib bones. He piled them with the others.

"We should probably get back to camp for the night. It would be easy to break an ankle heading down to the camp in the dark." Herne bagged up the bones. "We'll hunt again early morning. I wish we could find the entire skeleton so we don't end up leaving any for Elatha, should he decide to pull this same stunt again."

"We'll figure out something," Kipa said. "Here, let me carry those while you lead the way." He slung the bag of bones over his back as if it were a bag of feathers.

Herne paused, gazing at the rock field. "I'm unsettled. Something feels off."

"Worry about it when we get back to camp," Viktor said, glancing at the sky. "I'm uneasy too, and I want to get that fire built up again before it gets much later. We're only an hour away from dusk."

We began to descend back into the crater. The going was tougher than the climb, because it was harder to keep balanced on the rocks as we edged down the hill. I almost fell twice and Viktor, behind me, steadied me. Finally, we reached the bottom, and headed back to our camp on the other side of the lake.

"What time is it?" I looked over at Viktor.

He stopped building the fire back up to consult his watch. "Nearly six."

I nodded, handing him sticks of wood as he arranged the kindling and began stacking the firewood around it. Yutani had retrieved our food and was sorting out what we would need for dinner. Kipa and Herne were in some sort of deep conversation over by the tents. At least they didn't look like they were arguing.

Within minutes, the blaze had flared up and our campfire was going again. Viktor brought out a handful of metal pipes, which fit end to end to form an arch over the campfire, sturdy enough to hold a hanging soup pot.

Yutani glanced down at the lake. "We need water for the pot," he said, hesitating.

Viktor glanced over at Herne. "Better let one of those two get it. After what happened to Ember today, and the fact that you were responding to the kelpie, I don't trust any of the three of us near that lake."

"Did someone mention me?" Herne said, looking our way.

"Yeah. We need some water, boss. And I think either you or Kipa ought to get it." Viktor pointed to Yutani's cooking pot.

Kipa jogged over, grabbed the pot, and headed down to the shore.

I turned to Herne. "Why did he follow us?"

Herne shook his head. "I asked him, but he just said that he felt like it. There must have been some reason, though, but he won't tell me and I refuse to play Twenty Questions with him."

We gathered around the campfire as Yutani brought the water to boil. He poured the noodles into the pan when the water started to bubble and moved it so it wasn't directly over the fire.

"This will take a little longer than usual, given the higher altitude. I don't want it to burn, so I had to move it a little ways off the main heat." He began to skewer hot dogs onto sticks and handed them around. "You can each cook your own. Buns and condiments are on that rock over there," he said as he motioned to a relatively flat boulder near us. "The mac 'n cheese will be ready in a while."

"You bring marshmallows too?" I asked, hoping he had.

He held up two bags of the fluffy white candy. "Also chocolate and graham crackers. Can't go camping without s'mores. I also brought some popcorn."

Herne laughed. "I guess if we're out in the woods, we might as well do it right." He accepted a skewer with a couple hot dogs on it and held it over the fire.

We fell into a comfortable silence, the only sounds the crackle of the fire, the sizzling hot dogs, and the sound of birds who were out too late and hurrying back to their hiding spots. A low *hoooo hoooo...hoo hoo hoo* echoed through the growing dusk, and then a loud screech followed, as we looked up to see a dark silhouette gliding overhead.

The owl's wingspan had to be almost four feet wide, and I caught my breath, rapt as it circled over us, then flew up toward the rockslide. As we watched, the great horned owl plummeted at an angle, wings sweeping back as it swung its legs to the front, catching up some small creature who had come out onto the rocks. As it pulled up barely before it hit the ground, it screeched again and then, circling once, flew back to the tree line.

"You have to admire the skill," Herne said in a hushed tone.

I nodded, thinking that this was where life truly happened—out here in the woods and forests, between prey and predator. Something stirred within that made me want to jump up and join the owl in its hunt. I froze. Could it be the Autumn Stalker nature within me coming to the surface? Not wanting to be sucked into another situation like I had encountered with the Leannan Sidhe, at least not without Marilee here, I forced my attention back to the hot dogs on my stick, turning them and focusing on my stomach, which was clamoring for something to eat.

My hot dogs were charred and bursting, and I slid them onto buns with ketchup. I didn't care for mustard all that much, preferring the tang of the tomato with the char of the meat and the soft bread. As I bit into the first one, the flavor exploded in my mouth—an orgasm of beef and smoke and bun all coming together in the perfect bite.

Yutani was stirring the noodles and now he used a heavy-duty glove to grasp the handle of the pan and pour the noodles into a colander, taking care not to burn himself in the process. He added what looked like a buttload of preshredded cheese, and poured a little milk out of a single-serve vacuum box into it, then added half a stick of butter and began to stir.

"Dinner's ready." He spooned the mac 'n cheese into plastic bowls and handed them around. My stomach was already doing a happy dance, and I eagerly dug into the creamy noodles. After everybody was deep into their food, we finally relaxed enough to begin talking.

"So, alarm set for six A.M.? We go up and search for more bones? Then head out around elevenish?" I asked.

"Sounds good to me," Herne said. "We should have plenty of time to make it back to the car before dusk. As soon as we're done eating, I recommend we turn in to get as much sleep as we can. I think, though, we should keep watch."

"Why?" I asked, but then stopped. "Oh, right. Cougars, bears, and coyotes, oh my."

"That, yes, along with kelpie in the lake, and who knows what else out here. And *nobody* go toward the lake, especially Ember, Viktor, and Yutani. We have enough water right here, and if you need to go to the bathroom, behind that rock over there is private enough." Herne looked at me. "If you hear anything during the night, any singing or anything, you wake me up."

"Be sure to bag your waste, though—there's a carry-in, carry-out rule in these mountains. You'll find plastic bags and gloves over there on that rock, with toilet paper and hand sanitizer." Yutani pointed over to one of the rocks near the campfire. It was the size of a small end table, with a flat top.

The gloves, toilet paper, and blue plastic bags were inside of a larger, clear bag, along with a battery-operated light.

Lovely. But I understood the need. The hiking trails around here were heavily used and the forest service did their best to keep them clean.

I finished one s'more and fixed another. I thought about a third, but decided to leave some room for a snack later if I wanted it. Kipa offered to take the dishes down to the lake to rinse them out. After a quick argument with Herne, he wandered off toward the water.

I suddenly had a thought. "Where's he going to sleep? There's not enough room in either tent, is there?"

Herne snorted. "Well, he's not sleeping with us." He paused, then gave me a stern look. "Don't even think of offering, no matter how much you feel you owe him for today. Viktor and Yutani have room. They have an oversized tent to accommodate Viktor's stature."

"I'm going to turn in," I said, yawning. Even though it was early, the day had been long and arduous, and my encounter with the kelpie had left me drained. "Coming to bed?"

Herne shook his head. "I'll take the first watch and Kipa can keep second watch. The three of you get some sleep."

He stretched out his legs, leaning back against the rock he was propped against. Against the glow of the firelight, he truly looked like what he was: the son of a god, the lord of the hunt, wild and wonderful and absolutely stunning.

I thought about cajoling him into sneaking off for a little backwood nookie. The thought of sex on a summer night out in the middle of the forest turned me on, but then I realized I really *was* exhausted, and decided we could come back here later. Or find another park to canoodle in that was easier to get to.

I crawled inside the tent and stripped off my jeans and shirt, slipping into a pair of pajama bottoms and a sleep shirt before using the flashlight to make sure nothing had managed to crawl inside my sleeping bag. Satisfied that I wouldn't be sharing it with anything too wild and unwelcome, I thrust my feet into the bag, arranged my backpack as a pillow, and drifted off to sleep, lulled by the sound of the lake lapping in the distance, and the owl who was singing to the forest.

I WAS STANDING in a wide meadow, under an unending stretch of blue sky. The meadow was ringed by mountains and I couldn't see beyond the peaks that rose to protect the valley. As I shaded my eyes against the brilliance of the sun, I suddenly became aware of how vulnerable I was and I felt far too exposed. Looking around for something to shelter me, I saw a shadow pass by on the ground. It was a massive winged creature, and I glanced up to see an owl circling overhead. It must have had a twenty-foot wingspan and the giant raptor was focused on me.

As it came hurtling toward me, I started to run, trying to find something to hide behind, but there was nothing save the gentle concave bowl of the valley. I raced for one of the peaks, but as I ran, the hill began to recede into the distance. Panicking, I swerved to the side. Every time I switched directions, the mountains would fade into the distance, and the valley seemed to keep getting wider and wider.

The owl circled around me, and with each revolution it kept descending. I met its gaze, and the chill in its eyes paralyzed me as I fell to my knees, sobbing. It was coming for me and there was nowhere I could go, nowhere to hide.

As its wings gusted through the flowers and grass around me, I leaned forward, not wanting to watch as it caught me. I prayed for an easy end. Let it break my neck, or stab me through the heart. *Just don't eat me while I'm alive*, I prayed.

And then, the talons grazed my back as the earth fell away from beneath my feet, and I knew that this was the end.

"EMBER, GET UP! Arm yourself!" The voice broke through the dream and I startled awake, blinking in the dark tent. Herne was beside me, dragging me out of the sleeping bag. He thrust my dagger into my hands as he pulled me out of the tent.

"What—what the hell—" I shut up as we exited the tent. All around us, the camp was filled with feral-looking creatures, all wielding massive scythes and axes and spears. There were too many to count, at least in my sleep-befuddled state. They were goat men, with the heads of goats and the torsos and legs of men. There must have been at least ten of them. Kipa was fighting with one, and I could see two packs of wolves attacking two others. Viktor was swinging a hammer at one, while a coyote was leading another away from the camp. It had to be Yutani, on the run.

Herne pushed me toward the nearest boulder. "Keep out of range!" he shouted before diving into the fray. He brought up his pistol crossbow and aimed at one, narrowing his eyes as he let the arrow fly. It lodged dead in the center of the creature, who wavered a moment before it dropped to his knees.

I tried to make out what the fuck was happening. We were being attacked, that I knew. But by what? And then, as the fog from sleep lifted, I knew what we were facing. The *Bocanach*—the goat men who were aligned with the Fomorians! And if they were near...

I jumped up on top of the nearest boulder, trying to make out the forms in the light of the campfire. They were hard to discern, but I needed to see if what I feared might happen, had happened. Contingents of the Bocanach were usually accompanied by at least one Fachan—the monstrous one-armed, one-legged, cyclopean sorcerers.

I squinted, scanning the chaos. The Bocanach we could probably win out over, but if...*oh crap.*

There he was—staring right at me. *A Fachan.*

The creature was about five feet tall, and he was like a pillar, with one arm coming off from his left side, balancing firmly on his foot. One eye rested in the center of his bulbous head, and he was wearing no clothing, which left nothing to the imagination given his gender.

I wanted to summon up a water elemental to help but quickly quenched the thought.

What else could I do? I was good with a dagger, but not nearly as adept as Viktor or Herne or Kipa. Besides which, the Bocanach looked tough. *Tougher* than tough. And I couldn't shapeshift like Yutani.

The flickering campfire flared up, and a thought hit me. I leaped down and grabbed one of the sticks of burning wood—the longest one I could see. I darted forward toward one of the Bocanach and smashed him with the burning wood. The flames caught hold in the hair of his chin, catching at the stringy goatee faster than he could put it out. He slapped at it, screaming in some tongue I didn't understand, then went running for the lake. I silently wished the kelpie a good feed. To bad I couldn't enlist her help, but again, not such a good idea.

I looked around for another goat man to smack with the makeshift torch and froze. The Fachan had moved—silently and swiftly—and now he was standing right in front of me. I stumbled back, then caught myself. He only had one eye, but it was a big one. As he held up his hand, I could see sparks surrounding his fingers. He was preparing a spell, mostly likely to my detriment.

Holding the flaming branch straight out in front of me, I charged, heading directly toward him. Startled, he stopped. I took advantage, pushing extra steam into my legs as I aimed the torch at that one massive eye.

The Fachan suddenly seemed to be aware of what I was planning and he lurched to one side, but too late. The flame hit the center of his eye and I shoved the stick extra hard, knocking the creature over onto his back. I lifted the branch, which was still alight, and brought it crashing down at the exact moment the Fachan barked out a curse. As I crushed his skull, I felt my legs go numb, and then my hands. I dropped the branch, toppling over to land face first on the ground.

Chapter 17

"MOTHER PUS BUCKET," I croaked, unable to move for a moment. At least I could still speak. I struggled, but it felt like there was barbed wire around my legs. And it was digging in tighter the longer I lay there. "Herne!"

But Herne was engaged with one of the Bocanach. He appeared to be winning, from what I could see at this angle, but he couldn't just drop everything and come to my rescue.

After much effort, I managed to sit up, wincing as the magical wire tightened even further. "Cripes, does everything I end up fighting want to punch a bunch of holes in me?"

I stared at my legs in horror as I realized it wasn't just a spell. There actually was some sort of barbed snake wrapped around my legs. Looking like a neon-colored boa with thorns sticking out of it, it was doing its best to constrict around me.

"Fuck you, too!"

I raised my dagger and brought the edge slicing down across the body of the snake. The moment the silver blade hit the snake's body, it let out an echoing hiss and turned its head toward me, coiling for a strike. I twisted, trying to hide my face from its wicked-looking fangs.

But before it could strike, there was a loud howl and one of the shadow wolves came leaping over to me, grabbing the snake in its jaws. It shook it, dragging it away from my body, and I screamed as the barbs raked their way out of my skin. The wolf gave the snake another good shake and the snake vanished in a puff of bright light.

My legs were bleeding, saturating the legs of my PJs, but at least I was able to stand. The wounds burned like hell, but I ignored them, trying to take stock of what was happening now. The Fachan was dead on the ground, the branch from the fire protruding from his giant eye. The sight seemed even more hideous given the branch was still burning.

Herne was just finishing off his opponent, and Kipa had killed yet another. There were two more of the Bocanach in the camp, but Viktor had one on the run. Herne turned to the other and aimed his pistol bow, and the arrow went singing through the air to land dead center in the goat man's chest. Slowly, the creature toppled over. At that moment, Viktor landed a blow on the last one. Long hair flying, Yutani came leaping over one of the boulders to skewer it in the back. He and Viktor both twisted their blades and the Bocanach fell over, silent.

I was breathing hard, the pain of the snake's

barbs burning brighter on my skin. I limped over to the campfire and, shaking, sat on one of the boulders ringing it. My pajamas were saturated with blood—at least the bottoms—and I could only stare at the creeping crimson that spread across the material.

Herne and Kipa spread out to check out the perimeters of the camp as Viktor and Yutani joined me.

"You're hurt," Viktor said.

I nodded, unable to speak. I was exhausted, but the adrenaline was rushing so hard through my system that I felt like I was flying. The camp was littered with blood and bodies and the smell of death hovered over us like a cloud.

"They must have followed us, hoping we would lead them to the rest of the bones," Yutani said. He motioned to my PJs. "Take off the bottoms. You don't want the material to stick to the wounds."

I blushed. "I don't have underwear on."

"Do you think I really care?" the coyote shifter asked, giving me a blank stare. "Get them off now or you're going to regret it. I'll go get the first-aid kit." He ducked into his tent.

I slowly peeled off my pajama bottoms, pausing as the cotton began to yank at the wounds that had already started to clot. "Fuck. He's right."

Viktor offered me his shoulder and he helped me work the material away from my flesh. He glanced up at me as I winced. "Trust me, I'm not enjoying this. I don't like hurting friends."

Finally, we got them off as Yutani returned with the kit. Viktor headed toward my tent.

Yutani frowned. "I'm going to assume you only wore jeans."

"I have underwear in my pack, dude. Going commando while hiking isn't my idea of comfort. I just took them off for bedtime." I was beginning to get irritated with his haughty tone.

"That's not what I was asking. I meant...your jeans are going to rub against the wounds and hurt like hell. We'd better rig you up a skirt, even though it makes hiking harder. You're going to need help anyway, by the time tomorrow morning comes. The wounds will start to stop bleeding and you're going to be in quite a bit of pain, I'm afraid."

"Oh. All right, then." I thought for a moment. "I suppose we can cut open the lower legs of my jeans...sort of make bellbottoms."

"Here," Viktor said, returning with a unused pair of my panties, and he had also brought a microfiber blanket—the kind that folds up small and compact, but does a good job of keeping the chill away. "Put these on and then wrap the blanket around your shoulders."

With their help, I stepped into my underwear and they helped me pull it up over the punctures on my legs without scraping them.

"What's going on?" Herne's voice echoed from across the campfire. He and Kipa had returned.

"We're fixing Ember up. She got attacked by the Fachan. She also did a damned good job of bringing him down," Yutani said.

I glanced at him and he smiled. I gave him a weary smile in return.

"Crap, those look nasty. I can see I'm going to be

carrying you out of here on my back tomorrow," Herne said, kneeling to examine my legs. "Fix her up, Yutani."

"Anything else out there?" Viktor asked.

"We didn't see anything, but at first light, we need to destroy that rock field up there and then get the hell out of here. Elatha will no doubt send another contingent in to search for the first group. We have to bury the bones if we can't get to them ourselves." Herne handed Kipa one of the pans. "Can you bring water so we can heat it and clean up Ember's wounds?"

"My pleasure," Kipa said, his gaze catching mine. Once again, I felt a feeling of recognition and it unsettled me.

As the water heated, Herne and Kipa set up a ring of makeshift torches around the camp, just in case there was anything else waiting in the wings. Yutani and Viktor bathed my legs, counting the puncture wounds.

"Thirty-five total. Seventeen on one leg, eighteen on the other. Yeah, you're going to have scars, I'm afraid," Yutani said.

"War wounds," Viktor added. "I'm still amazed by how you took down the Fachan. I doubt if he was expecting anything like that attack."

"I learned early that you have to make do with what you have. You learn to fight dirty when you're constantly a target."

I flashed back to my high school days. Angel and I had managed to stave off most of the bullies when we were together, but they learned to wait for when I was alone, then ganged up on me. I was strong, but it was hard to fight off a half-dozen jocks and cheerleaders. And the hayseed types were worse.

They had left me bruised up and bleeding several times, had jammed me in my locker, had thrown me in the dumpsters, and everything else they could think of. All this urged on by some of the other Fae students who taught them to chant "tralaeth" over and over as they beat on me.

A couple of the jocks had set out to rape me, but I always managed to get away, once crushing one of the boy's nuts so hard that he ended up in the hospital. He couldn't exactly confess to what he was trying to do, so he said he had landed hard on a railing while trying out a skateboarding move. After that, the guys stuck to beating me up. And I kept my mouth shut, not telling my parents, not wanting to burden them with the knowledge.

Kipa suddenly knelt beside me. I glanced at him and realized he had caught a flash of what I was thinking. I prayed he'd keep quiet. I had talked about some of it to Herne and the others, but I didn't feel like dissecting the abuse I had taken. He gave me a soft smile and stood, turning away to whistle for his shadow-pack.

After Yutani doctored up my wounds, Herne carried me back to our tent. He lay beside me, stroking my hair.

"Who's keeping watch?"

"Kipa and his wolves."

I wondered how to approach the question that was running through my mind. Finally, I decided that being direct was the best choice. "About Kipa.

Something odd happened during the time he was retrieving my soul from wherever the kelpie took me."

"What was it?" Herne asked, his fingers tracing my cheek.

"There seems to be some sort of connection—not sexual," I hurried to add. "But, it's like he can sense what I'm thinking. At least I think he can."

"He's been inside your mind, Ember. He's seen your memories and your thoughts." Herne almost sounded jealous. "It comes with being a shaman. You will always have some sort of connection with him because of that." He closed his eyes, and in the soft light of the battery-operated light that rested by our heads, he almost looked ready to cry.

I reached out, pressed my fingers to his lips. "Herne, I love *you*. Kipa? Yes, there is a connection, but it only makes me curious about him as a person. And I think your background might color your perception of him. I see how that would be, but I feel we can trust him. I didn't sense any deceit. He can sense my feelings or thoughts, I suppose, but I think I can sense his, as well."

"I don't know if I can ever trust him," Herne said. "I try, as much as I can, but he wounded me so deeply that I don't know if there's any coming back from that." He paused, then added, "When we were young, we ran through the forests together. He would show up in my father's realm for months at a time, and we would chase through the woods and hunt, and play. But as we grew older, he grew more chaotic while I...while I grew up."

"What was she like, the woman he stole away

from you?" I suddenly wanted to know just who the woman was who had broken Herne's heart. Reilly, his last girlfriend, had hurt him, but I had the feeling it was in no way to the same degree.

Herne rolled onto his back and crossed an arm over his eyes, blocking out the light. "Do you really want to know?"

"Yes. Please, tell me. I want to understand you. And to understand you, I need to know more about you." I caught my breath. If what he said hurt, I had only myself to blame.

"She was a dryad. Golden as the morning sun, as beautiful as a falling star. She lived in the woods outside my father's palace, and it was there we met. Her name was Nya, and she was about as free a spirit as I have ever known. We fell in love, and I was convinced that she would be my princess." His voice had taken on a drifting quality and I felt a stab in my heart. He still loved her—I could hear it in the broken tone.

"What happened?" I wished I hadn't started the line of questioning, but I couldn't stop now. He would wonder why.

"Kipa came to visit. We were...well, the equivalent of teenagers. I introduced them, and they seemed to hit it off. I was happy, because I wanted my best friend and the love of my life to get along. And then, a few weeks later, I got done with an errand early. My father had asked me to deliver something to the Morrígan. I decided to surprise Nya, so I slipped down to her home in the woodland and, instead of knocking, I walked right in. And that's when I caught them."

His voice grew darker and he let out a sigh. "They were fucking. Nya was calling out Kipa's name over and over. When they realized I was there, Kipa glanced up at me, but he didn't quit. He just kept moving inside of her, with that damned smile on his face. She held out her hand, inviting me to join them. I turned and walked out. And that was the last time I willingly talked to Kipa until now. If I had tried to say a word at that moment, I would have killed him. And her."

His tone took a dark turn, and he lowered his arm, pushing himself to a sitting position. He reached out, taking my chin in his hands. His touch was gentle, but I could feel the power behind it as he held my gaze.

"Ember, if you ever want to leave me, just say so. I won't try to keep you. But *never* betray me like that while we're still together. When I realized I was going to have to call Kipa in to help Kamaria, it tore me up because all I could think about was that he would try to lure you away. He's seductive, and magnetic. I do understand this."

"And now, because he had to help me, there's a connection..." I tried to get on my knees, to gather him in my arms, but the pain of my shins made me cry out and I abruptly sat back down. But I took his hand in mine.

"Kipa's handsome, yes, more than any man has a right to be—but so are you. But Herne, I have had my fill of chaos. I love your stability. I love that you're there for me. I still can't believe you chose me. I love being with you. You make me smile. You make me feel safe."

He stared at me for a moment, and then pulled me into his arms, his lips finding mine. As he kissed me, long, deep and demanding, I felt him weaving magic around us. I didn't know what it was, but it felt like gentle vines surrounding us, coiling around us as a protective barrier. My hunger for him grew.

"I want you," I whispered. "Now. Here."

"You're hurt. It would hurt you."

"My legs hurt, but the part of me that matters right now is perfectly fine. Fuck me, Herne. Make me yours. I want you inside me." My breath was coming in ragged pants, and I realized I was cold, but that didn't matter.

Herne shrugged out of his jeans and he sat up, straightening his legs in front of him. "Straddle me, that way it won't hurt your legs as much." He helped me take off my panties, and the light in his eyes reassured me that he wasn't thinking about Nya now.

With his help, I slowly lowered myself onto his lap, straddling him and resting my legs in back of him. We were facing one another, and his erection rested against my sex, hard as a rock. I reached down to stroke him and he leaned back, resting his weight on his elbows, as I slid my hand down between my legs to moisten my fingers. Then, slippery with my own juices, I clenched his cock, firmly sliding up and down his magnificent shaft. I began to breathe harder, watching his face as he let out a low growl. Pumping faster, I squeezed hard—not enough to hurt, but enough to make him know I had hold of him.

"You're mine," I whispered. "You're the only one I want. Do you hear me?"

He moaned again, then, he sat back up, his eyes wide and wild. He leaned down, taking my right nipple in his mouth, sucking hard as he slid his hand into the cleft between us to finger my sex. I lost my grip on him then, as the pleasure of his touch shot through me like hard liquor. He was gasoline and I was the fire, and I was hungry to burn bright.

He rolled my clit between his fingers, then stepped up the pace and I suddenly found myself shrieking as I tumbled over the edge, coming so hard that everything went gray and I found myself in a field of ferns and wildflowers. The vibrant energy of the forest rocked me, stroking me higher, and then I saw the King Stag standing there, silver and brilliant, waiting for me.

"I need to ride you," I whispered, coming back to myself.

He lifted my ass up, sliding me forward as I guided his cock to my cleft. As he slid inside of me, filling me full, I felt like we were dancing in the rain, spinning together in a whirling gyre until it felt like our bodies were blending together. He began to slowly move inside me, and I leaned back, resting on my hands, to give him the freedom to move.

Without warning, he grabbed me around the ass and sprang to his feet. He pulled out of me, then dragged me to the door of the tent. As we staggered out into the camp, I was relieved to see that Viktor and Yutani had gone to bed, and Kipa was nowhere in sight. Staying by the campfire, Herne bent me over one of the taller boulders and I groaned as he slid back inside me from the rear, thrusting so hard that I could barely keep up. He howled in delight, and in the distance, I heard someone howl in return. And then, I forgot all about where we were, or who might be watching, because the full impact of his passion hit me, sweeping me under into a haze of lust and desire.

I began to whimper, and then let out a shriek of my own as Herne thrust one last time and held me tight by the waist as he grunted and, in a rough voice, whispered, "Mine. You're mine, do you hear me?"

With the stars whirling overhead, I came, matching his passion with my own. We continued on in the night, making love until the beginning of dawn. Then, in the faint light of the approaching sunrise, he led me back into the tent, where we slept for the last few hours until Viktor woke us up by peeking in the tent to rouse us.

WHEN I WOKE, I realized that as passionate as the night had been, I had made a terrible mistake. I was sore from the top of my head to my toes, inside and out. Every muscle in my body hurt—including my cooch. I winced as I tried to stand up.

"You're going to have to help me." I held my hand up to Herne. "Damn, post-battle sex really has something going for it, but I wish to hell that I didn't hurt so bad."

He laughed, pulling me to my feet and draping an arm around my shoulders, leaning down to kiss me. "You're my love. You'll survive." He glanced around. "What are you going to wear?"

"Yutani was mentioning it might be a good idea to fashion a skirt so that my jeans don't rub against my wounds." I glanced down at my legs, grimacing at the red puncture wounds. Nothing looked infected—at least not yet—but my skin looked like I had lost the war with a rose bush. I flashed back to our last big battle with a bunch of thorn bushes and my stomach lurched.

"I think he's on to something." Herne pulled out a pair of my jeans. "How should we do this?"

"First, help me get my underwear back on." I realized that I was partially stiff because I had gotten chilled as we were sleeping. "And hand me that microfiber blanket."

He held my panties for me as I stepped into them, then inched them up over my legs. After he helped me into my bra, I held up the blanket and stared at it. It wasn't full size—it was a throw, really—and it might just work as a makeshift skirt.

"Hand me my sweater. Then, see if Yutani has a pair of scissors. I'll also need a length of rope or a sash to keep it tied up." I paused, then glared at him. "And nobody better take any pictures of me because this is going to be an epic fashion fail."

Herne returned with scissors and I folded the blanket and cut a small circle out of it, big enough for me to shimmy into. I held it snug around my waist as Herne tied the rope around it, looping it through a couple of impromptu belt loops that I also cut with the scissors. Finally, I was ready to go. I leaned over to put on my hiking boots but cringed as my socks brushed the lower punctures.

"Fuck. I can't wear my boots without socks. How the hell am I going to get down the mountain?"

"We'll find a way. Come on, the dirt's fairly even around the camp." He led me out of the tent.

Viktor glanced at me, letting out a snort, but he said nothing, returning to the breakfast he was making. It appeared we were having lake trout.

"Kipa caught us a string of fish and gutted them. Breakfast is almost ready," he said.

Yutani pulled out his phone when he saw me but I stomped over and shook my finger in his face. "One picture and I break your phone."

His eyes glinted, and he let out a laugh. "All right. But you tempt me, you know that? I could use it for leverage in the future."

I grabbed for the phone but he quickly stowed it away in his pocket. At that moment, Kipa returned and we gathered around the fire for breakfast.

"What are we going to do with the bones up there? If we leave them, you know they'll be back for more." I licked my fingers. The fish was delicious and I could easily have eaten a second one.

"We have to bring down the mountainside. Bury the cave under tons of rocks that nobody will ever be able to get through." Herne looked at Kipa. "You know what we need to do."

Kipa nodded. "Yeah, but we have to make certain everybody is up the other side first."

"What are you going to do? Set off an explosion?" Viktor asked.

"Something like that. We also need to bury these bodies. We don't want Elatha to know that we wiped out his raiding party. He'll be suspicious, but there won't be anything that he can use as proof." Herne sighed. "That means we have to carry them up to the slope and lay them out so that the rocks will cover them as well."

"What do we do about them? The Fomorians? Elatha?" I asked.

"Nothing. At least for now. The Wild Hunt can't go after them, because this is between the Fae and the giants. But we have to keep an eye on where this is leading. Elatha is smart, though. He'll know better than to start something that directly affects the human world. The Fae? Not so much." Herne set his dish down. "We better get ready. We have the bones we found?"

Yutani nodded. "I made certain they were secure. If we can find one or two more before we leave, it would be a good idea. Because I have a feeling that once you two are done with that slope, there won't be any way to dig up what's left of the Aillén Trechenn."

And so we set to work. Viktor, Yutani, and I packed up camp while Herne and Kipa began carrying the bodies up the other mountain slope to lay them out for their final resting place. When they were finished, we had removed every speck of evidence that we had been here.

I stood, staring at the lake as we waited for them to finish with the last of the Bocanach corpses. The kelpie was out there. She was singing again, but this time I kept a tight rein on myself, keeping my guard up. I looked around the area. It was beautiful and still, and the hike was hard enough that few hikers tried it so there was plenty of solitude. In some ways, I envied her. She could live within her womb-like chamber, waiting for victims, at peace except when someone roused her.

There was a part of the kelpie I understood, now that I had met the Leannan Sidhe side of myself. We were different, but we were both bound to the water on an elemental level, and we both had that eternal hunger, though I hadn't yet fully faced mine. The kelpie was what she was, and she took pride in her existence. I wondered, would I ever be able to feel that way? Would I ever be able to embrace my Fae nature with joy, rather than trying to distance myself from it?

From somewhere deep within the lake, I thought I heard a whisper.

If you refuse to face yourself in the mirror, you'll never be able to be true about who you are, and you'll never find your true self. And then, a deep resonant laughter echoed from the depths of the water, and vanished as quickly as it had come.

WE WERE STANDING on the saddle of the pass. Herne had brought me to the top on his back, and now I stood there beside Viktor and Yutani, watching across the lake at the opposite cliff.

"Why do we have to wait here?" I asked.

"Because if the rockslide is too great, it might spur on a slide on the descending side and we could be caught in it. This way, we should be fairly stable." Viktor shaded his eyes, watching. "I just wonder how they're going to do this."

"You and me both," Yutani said.

I leaned against the wall of the saddle, bracing myself.

In the distance, we could see them, two specks on the opposite wall, climbing fully to the top. They stood there, talking for a moment, and then Herne raised his hands just as Kipa knelt beside him, hands firmly on the ground. There was a slow echo that rolled across the valley, rippling with power, and as it swept past us, it nearly knocked me off my feet. Startled, I slid into a squatting position, bracing myself.

The next moment, a great roar filled the air as the entire mountainside below them began to slip. It was gradual at first, almost in slow motion, as the rocks began a slow tumble. Then, like a pyrochlastic flow, it picked up speed, and tons of rocks—some the size of cars—began to rumble and roar as they raced down the hillside. A great plume of dust filled the air, rolling our way on the wind. I turned away my face, lifting the hem of my blanket-skirt to cover my eyes and nose. I could hear Viktor and Yutani coughing.

Finally, as the roar settled into a dull trickle, I lowered my skirt, blinking as the dust settled around us. Viktor and Yutani and I were all covered with a fine layer of the dust, and as we turned, we saw that the landslide had filled half the valley, and every sign of the Fomorian goat men were gone. The rest of the Aillén Trechenn was buried under tons of rock and debris, effectively gone forever.

"Are they okay?" I asked anxiously.

"I hope so," Viktor said, scanning the horizon.

I shaded my eyes, trying to find Herne and Kipa in the valley that had suddenly become a desolate moonscape. I held my breath, waiting, and still no sign of them. Fretting, I began to run through a dozen dire scenarios in my mind, each one worse than the last. I was about to head back down into the valley, regardless of what Viktor or Yutani said, when Yutani let out a cry. He pointed to the eastern side of the lake, and there, we saw the pair running toward the area where we had made camp.

"They're okay," Viktor said. "At least, they look it."

Within minutes, Herne and Kipa had climbed up the side of the cliff, joining us.

"You're okay," I whispered, latching onto Herne, not wanting to let go.

"We're fine," he reassured me. "We realized it wouldn't be entirely safe to come down a fresh rockslide, so we made our way over to another part of the ridge where the descent was safer. We would have just kept going, but there was a treacherous part that would have been difficult even for us, so we decided to cross the valley floor."

"Explanations are fine, but we'd better get out of here. You know the park service is going to send somebody out to find out what set off their seismometers. They have them everywhere in these mountains." Kipa nodded toward the wall. "Time to go."

And so, the men hoisted me down in a harness chair and once at the bottom, Herne turned into his stag self. I marveled at him. Every time he transformed I was struck by the sheer beauty of his form. As he knelt so that I could climb on his back, I caught sight of Kipa. He was staring at us with a peculiar look on his face that unsettled me. I stared back at him for a moment, then quickly looked away and swung onto Herne's back. Yutani turned into his coyote form, and we traveled swiftly back over the miles to the parking lot, Kipa carrying our bag of bones.

Chapter 18

THAT EVENING, ONCE we had gotten home, showered and changed, Herne and I found ourselves standing in Cernunnos's throne room. Only this time, Morgana had joined us as well as Kipa. Well, Herne and Kipa were standing. The moment he saw the wounds on my legs, Cernunnos had called for a soft chair and insisted I sit down.

"When Ferosyn gets here, I will make certain he looks over your wounds." The Lord of the Forest paused, tilting his head as he gave me a cunning smile. "You throw yourself into your work, that much I'll say for you."

"Oh shush," Morgana said, giving him what I could only identify as the stink-eye. "Don't tease her. You know what she's been through these past few months."

Cernunnos reached out to stroke Morgana's face, still grinning. "Of course I do. That's why I tease her, my sweet one. She needs to smile."

"She needs to rest. She's facing the Cruharach—" Morgana started to say, but Cernunnos leaned over and planted a long, slow kiss on her lips. I could almost see the steam rising between them and, blushing, I looked away. Apparently they had engendered Herne in passion, not just in a dalliance.

"Get a room," Herne muttered, but he, too, was smiling.

"Watch your tongue." Cernunnos turned to Kipa. "So, you are once again welcome in my court, it seems. Behave yourself this time." The words took on a very different tone than the ones he had aimed at Morgana and at me. I had the feeling he could easily wring Kipa's neck if he wanted to. But then again, Kipa was an elemental spirit—perhaps stronger than the gods. I wasn't clear on what the relationship was between gods and elemental spirits.

"As always, Lord of the Wood and Water." Kipa gave him a stately bow that verged on the edge of mockery, but after that, everybody seemed to relax. Although I wondered if things could ever truly be relaxed in the company of the gods.

There was a noise from behind the throne and Ferosyn entered the room. Herne strode over to hand him the bag of bones.

The healer grimaced. "This is all you were able to find? Where are the others?"

"Buried under tons of rock, now. Kipa and I brought the mountain down to cover them since we couldn't gather all of them. But I hope these are

enough for you to make an antidote for the Fae."
Herne sounded uncharacteristically nervous.

Ferosyn frowned, but nodded. "These will do,
with some left to spare, but I really don't like to
think that the rest of that skeleton is out there and
that Elatha knows it's there."

"Speaking of Elatha...we had visitors while we
were on the mountain that prove we're facing the
Fomorian King." Herne told them about the Bocanach and the Fachan, including how I had managed to kill the sorcerer. "They have to know we'll
have the antidote. They won't know how many of
the bones we found, however. Perhaps they'll think
we found the whole skeleton. And it will take them
some time to sort through matters, because we
killed the entire party and buried them under the
rockslide."

"There's no question, then." Morgana cleared
her throat. "Matters are clear. We must inform
TirNaNog and Navane about the Fomorians. And
yes, Herne, in answer to your questions, Elatha
was ejected from Annwn some time ago, and they
do believe he sailed back over the Great Sea."

"Do we have to tell them? Won't that just stir
things up even more?" I asked.

Morgana gave me a long look, then said, "They
deserve to know. They're my people—and yours.
And they have to prepare in case Elatha strikes
again."

A silence fell through the room then.

Ferosyn guided me back to his office, where he
examined my legs and gave me a salve for them.
"While we're alone, I think we should talk about

something. It might be embarrassing, but it's something you need to think about." He paused, staring at his medical chart.

"What?" I wasn't ready for any more unpleasant surprises.

He cleared his throat. "I'll be direct. If you don't want a child, you're going to need to think about birth control."

I blinked. "Holy crap, I hadn't even thought of that. Herne's a god. A demigod, but still...I thought he could just..." I stammered.

"Just magically tell his penis not to shoot out some very potent sperm?" Ferosyn laughed. "It doesn't work that way, not even for the gods. No, you've been lucky until now. But if you don't want a child, you're going to have to take action. I can tell by the way he acts that Lord Herne is..." He paused.

"He's in love with me," I whispered. "And I love him. But I'm not ready for a child. I don't know if I'll ever be, but I know right now, definitely not. Especially since we have no idea where the relationship is going."

Ferosyn nodded. "I thought as much. But you see, the lords of the forest...part of their power lies in their virility, and that includes fertility. If you don't want to end up pregnant, you need to start using birth control and I'm not talking about condoms. I wouldn't trust them to last through..." Again, he paused, tugging on his collar.

"Herne's very...active."

"Right. So you see what I'm getting at." He walked over to one of his cupboards, rummaging through it. "Here. This is an herbal mix that works for the Fae, and it's very strong. It will suppress your ovulation until you're ready. Then, you just have to stop using it for three months and your fertility should return. It will take one cycle to take effect."

I peeked in at the powder. "How do I use it?"

"Once a month, you take two teaspoons' worth in a cup of hot water. Drink it all down. That's it."

I nodded. "What should I do until then? I don't think Herne will want to wait a month and..." Again, I blushed. "I don't know if I can, either. Being around him drives me crazy."

"Again, for those who are touched by the energy of the Hunt, the gods of the wild play havoc with your senses. It's like the perfect storm of passion and lust. And you, my dear, have the blood of hunters in your veins. Morgana told me what you found out about your heritage."

I let out a long breath. "Yeah. It's like my life decided to just turn on end and shake me around. I feel like I'm in a snow globe. I don't know where this will take me, but I guess I don't have a choice except to follow the path that destiny has set out for me."

"Tell Herne why you need to wait. There are other methods of pleasuring, and I'm sure you both have good-enough imaginations to figure them out." He grinned. "Take heart, Ember. Too many people lead lives of boredom or pain. You have a hard road ahead of you, but it's definitely not boring, and the journey is what counts. Make the most of it. Explore the unknown. Security offers safety, but true joy lies in freedom. And sometimes, freedom comes at a hefty cost."

With that bit of wisdom, he began to work on the antidote, sending me back to the throne room, where we finished up our talk and then, went home.

TWO WEEKS LATER...

Kamaria was still in the hospital, though on the mend, so Kipa had cleared the house from any remaining spirits. We had then thrown one massive painting party that lasted three days. Herne had closed the agency for the week to give us all a break and Viktor, Yutani, Talia, and Kipa had joined us to finish pulling our house together.

Now, bringing in the last of our boxes and furniture, and bringing Mr. Rumblebutt over, Angel and I were in our new home, lock, stock, and barrel.

She and I walked out into the tangled yard, finding a neglected bench to sit on.

"I'm so glad that the Fae are beginning to respond to the antidote. So, there's enough to go around?"

"Ferosyn said yeah, there will be plenty with some left over. But he's still worried about the bones buried out there. Morgana has informed Saílle and Névé about Elatha. I'm afraid that we're going to be caught smack in the middle of the war between the Fae and the Fomorians. You know my people aren't subtle."

"What about your grandfather?" Angel asked, picking a wild rose from one of the sprawling bushes that wound its way through the yard.

"I have no idea. But Morgana also informed the United Coalition about the existence of that ritual and they're debating whether or not to ban its use. The magical guilds will be against the ban, of course. They hate regulation, but...I hope they do illegalize it." I caught a deep breath, holding it for a moment before slowly letting it out. "What do you want to do tomorrow?"

Angel leaned back, staring up at the cloudless sky. "Do you want to go down to the docks and ride the Ferris wheel?"

The Seattle Amusement Park was located by the docks and included a variety of rides and booths. It was usually jammed but given tomorrow was a Friday, most people would still be at work during the middle of the day.

I nodded. "Let's spend the day shopping. We can stop at the fish market and bring home a feast to thank everybody for their help."

As we sat in silence, a flutter of wings filled the air and I opened my eyes to see a murder of crows landing in the trees of our yard. There was something about them that I couldn't pinpoint, but they made me nervous, and as I listened to their raucous cawing, the breeze wafted by, and I could feel the first tang of autumn on it, filtering in to surround us.

Something inside me flared, and I wanted to run off to the woods again, to go on a hunting spree.

The colors of the yard grew more intense, and I stood, holding my arms out to the crows. They flew up from their trees, circling overhead, and then began to land on the ground, surrounding us in a circle.

Angel stiffened. "The crows know something. Can you feel it? Thunder echoing?"

"The sky's clear," I said, but even as I spoke, the clouds gathered in the distance, rushing in on a sudden gust of wind. I turned to the birds and they fell silent, staring at me.

"They're here to gather the harvest," Angel said softly.

I nodded. I wasn't sure what they wanted, but they were here, and they spoke to my blood. They spoke the autumn, and all things that walked its leaf-strewn paths. They spoke of bonfires flaring in the nights, of hay and apples and cinnamon. They spoke to the harvest of meat, and the sacrifice of the grain god.

A bright flash lit up the sky, and as it ripped through the air, I caught a flash of a massive bronze cauldron. Behind it stood a woman dressed in black, and her eyes were the color of stars. She stirred the cauldron, and as I watched, a crow landed on her shoulder. She gestured toward the vessel.

"Are you ready?" she asked. "Rebirth awaits."

And then, the clouds broke open and the rain started to pour. The crows went winging off, and Angel and I sat there in the drizzle, feeling the turn of the wheel as the season began to shift around us, sweeping us along on the journey that never ends.

"I don't know where I'm headed, Angel," I whispered. "But my blood is stirring, and I can only answer its call."

She wrapped her arm around my shoulders. "I'll be by your side, girlfriend. I feel change coming too. A storm is rising, but we'll meet it together."

And, hand in hand, we headed back to the house, drenched, but ready to face the future.

If you enjoyed this book and haven't read the first two, check out THE SILVER STAG and OAK & THORNS. Book 4—A SHADOW OF CROWS—will be out later this year. And more to come after that.

Meanwhile, I invite you to visit Fury's world. Bound to Hecate, Fury is a minor goddess, taking care of the Abominations who come off the World Tree. The first story arc of the Fury Unbound Series is complete with: FURY RISING, FURY'S MAGIC, FURY AWAKENED, and FURY CALLING. The second story arc will begin later this year with FURY'S MANTLE.

For a dark, gritty, steamy series, try my world of the Indigo Court, where the long winter has come, and the Vampiric Fae are on the rise. NIGHT MYST, NIGHT VEIL, NIGHT SEEKER, NIGHT VISION, NIGHT'S END, and NIGHT SHIVERS are all available now.

If you prefer a lighter-hearted but still steamy paranormal romance, meet the wild and magical residents of Bedlam in my Bewitching Bedlam Series. Fun-loving witch Maddy Gallowglass, her smoking-hot vampire lover Aegis, and their crazed cjinn Bubba (part djinn, all cat) rock it out in Bedlam, a magical town on a magical island. BLOOD MUSIC, BEWITCHING BEDLAM, MAUDLIN'S MAYHEM, SIREN'S SONG, WITCHES WILD, BLOOD VENGEANCE and TIGER TAILS are available. Look for CASTING CURSES in September!

If you like cozies with teeth, try my Chintz 'n China paranormal mysteries. The series is complete with: GHOST OF A CHANCE, LEGEND OF THE JADE DRAGON, MURDER UNDER A MYSTIC MOON, A HARVEST OF BONES, ONE HEX OF A WEDDING, and a wrap-up novella: HOLIDAY SPIRITS.

The newest Otherworld book—HARVEST SONG—is available now, and the next, BLOOD BONDS, will be available in May 2019.

For all of my work, both published and upcoming releases, see the Bibliography at the end of this book, or check out my website at Galenorn.com and be sure and sign up for my newsletter to receive news about all my new releases.

Cast of Characters

THE WILD HUNT

Ember Kearney: Caught between the world of Light and Dark Fae, and pledged to Morgana, Goddess of the Fae and the Sea, Ember Kearney was born with the mark of the Silver Stag. Rejected by both her bloodlines, she now works for the Wild Hunt as an investigator.

Herne the Hunter: Herne is the son of the Lord of the Hunt, Cernunnos, and Morgana, Goddess of the Fae and the Sea. A demigod—given his mother's mortal beginnings—he's a lusty, protective god and one hell of a good boss. Owner of the Wild Hunt Agency, he helps keep the squabbles between the world of Light and Dark Fae from spilling over into the mortal realms.

Angel Jackson: Ember's best friend, a human empath, Angel is the newest member of the Wild Hunt. A whiz in both the office and the kitchen, and loyal to the core, Angel is an integral part of Ember's life, and a vital member of the team.

Viktor: Viktor is half-ogre, half-human. Rejected by his father's people (the ogres), he came to work for Herne some decades back.

Yutani: A coyote shifter who is dogged by the Great Coyote, Yutani was driven out of his village over two hundred years before. He walks in the shadow of the trickster, and is the IT specialist for the company.

Talia: A harpy who long ago lost her powers, Talia is a top-notch researcher for the agency, and a longtime friend of Herne's.

DJ Jackson: Angel's little stepbrother, DJ is half Wulfine—wolf shifter. He now lives with a foster family for his own protection.

THE GODS, THE ELEMENTAL SPIRITS, & THEIR COURTS

Cerridwen: Goddess of the Cauldron of Rebirth. Dark harvest mother goddess.

Cernunnos: Lord of the Hunt, god of the Forest and King Stag of the Woods. Together with Morgana, Cernunnos originated the Wild Hunt and negotiated the covenant treaty with both the Light and the Dark Fae. Herne's father.

Coyote, (also: Great Coyote): Native American trickster spirit/god.

Danu: Mother of the Pantheon. Leader of the Tuatha de Danaan.

Ferosyn: Chief healer in Cernunnos's Court

Kuippana (also: Kipa): Lord of the Wolves. Elemental forest spirit; Herne's distant cousin. Trickster.

Morgana: Goddess of the Fae and the Sea, she was originally human but Cernunnos lifted her to deityhood. She agreed to watch over the Fae who did not return across the Great Sea. Torn by her loyalty to her people, and her loyalty to Cernunnos, she at times finds herself conflicted about the Wild Hunt. Herne's mother.

THE FAE COURTS

Navane: The court of the Light Fae, both across the Great Sea and on the east side of Seattle, the latter ruled by Névé.

TirNaNog: The court of the Dark Fae, both across the Great Sea and on the east side of Seattle, the latter ruled by Saílle.

THE ANTE-FAE

Creatures predating the Fae. The wellspring from which all Fae descended. Unique beings who rule their own realms. All Ante-Fae are dangerous, but some are more deadly than others.

Blackthorn, the King of Thorns: Ruler of the blackthorn trees and all thorn-bearing plants. Cunning and wily, he feeds on pain and desire.

Straff: Blackthorn's son, who suffers from a wasting disease requiring him to feed off others' life energies and blood.

THE FORCE MAJEURE

A group of legendary magicians, sorcerers, and witches. They are not human, but magic-born. There are twenty-one at any given time and the only way into the group is to be hand chosen, and the only exit from the group is death.

Merlin: Morgana's father. Magician of ancient Celtic fame.

Taliesin: The first Celtic bard. Son of Cerridwen, originally a servant who underwent magical transformation and finally, was reborn through Cerridwen as the first bard.

Ranna: Powerful sorceress. Elatha's mistress.

Väinämöinen: The most famous Finnish bard.

FRIENDS & ENEMIES

Aoife: A priestess of Morgana who guards the Seattle portal to the goddess's realm.

Charlie Darren: Vampire who has latched on to Viktor. Emo-boy.

Elatha: Fomorian King; enemy of the Fae race.

Marilee: A priestess of Morgana, Ember's mentor. Possibly human—unknown.

Playlist

I often write to music, and IRON BONES was no exception. Here's the playlist I used for this book. I consider three songs to be "theme songs" for *Iron Bones*: *We Travel* (Marconi Union), *The Low Spark of High Heeled Boys* (Traffic), *And the Rain* (Shriekback).

AC/DC: Back in Black
AJ Roach: Devil May Dance
Alice Cooper: Go To Hell; Welcome to My Nightmare
Alice in Chains: Man in the Box; Sunshine
Android Lust: Here and Now; Dragonfly; Stained; Saint Over
Arch Leaves: Nowhere to Go
AWOLnation: Sail
Band of Skulls: I Know What I Am
The Black Angels: You on the Run; Never/Ever; Indigo Meadow; Don't Play With Guns; Holland; Black isn't Black; Young Men Dead; Phosphene Dream
Black Mountain: Queens Will Play; Roller Coaster
Black Rebel Motorcycle Club: Feel It Now; Fault Line
Black Sabbath: Lady Evil; Paranoid
Blue Oyster Cult: Godzilla; Don't Fear the Reap-

er

Bon Jovi: Wanted Dead or Alive
Broken Bells: The Ghost Inside
Camouflage Nights: (It Could Be) Love
Clannad: Newgrange
Cobra Verde: Play with Fire
Colin Foulke: Emergence, Caravella
Crazy Town: Butterfly
Creedence Clearwater Revival: Green River; Run Through the Jungle
Damh the Bard: The January Man; Spirit of Albion; Land, Sky and Sea; The Cauldron Born; Obsession; The Wicker Man; Spirit of Albion; Iron From Stone
Dizzi: Dizzi Jig; Dance of the Unicorns
Eastern Sun: Beautiful Being (Original Edit)
Eivør: Trøllbundin
Faun: Hymn to Pan
FC Kahuna: Hayling
Gabrielle Roth: The Calling; Raven; Mother Night; Rest Your Tears Here
Gary Numan: Ghost Nation; My Name is Ruin; The Angel Wars; Hybrid; Petals; I Am Dust; Everything Comes Down To This; When the Sky Bleeds, He Will Come
John Fogerty: The Old Man Down the Road
Led Zeppelin: Ramble On; Immigrant Song
Lorde: Yellow Flicker Beat; Royals
Low with Tom and Andy: Half Light
King Black Acid: Rolling Under
Marconi Union: First Light; Alone Together; Flying (In Crimson Skies); Time Lapse; On Reflection; Broken Colours; We Travel; Weightless; Weightless,

Pt. 2; Weightless, Pt. 3; Weightless, Pt. 4; Weightless, Pt. 5; Weightless, Pt. 6

Metallica: Enter Sandman

Nirvana: You Know You're Right; Come As You Are; Lake of Fire; Something in the Way; Heart Shaped Box; Plateau

The Notwist: Hands on Us

Orgy: Social Enemies; Blue Monday

A Pale Horse Named Death: Meet the Wolf

R.E.M.: Drive

S. J. Tucker: Hymn to Herne

Saliva: Ladies and Gentlemen

Seether: Remedy

Shriekback: Over the Wire; Night Town; Dust and a Shadow; Underwaterboys; This Big Hush; Now These Days Are Gone; The King in the Tree; And the Rain

Shovelhead: Wriggle and Drone

Spiral Dance: Boys of Bedlam; Burning Times; Rise Up; Asgard's Chase

Tom Petty: Mary Jane's Last Dance

Tori Amos: Caught a Lite Sneeze; Blood Roses; Mohammad My Friend

Traffic: Rainmaker; The Low Spark of High Heeled Boys

Tuatha Dea: The Landing/Tuatha De Danaan; Wisp of A Thing (Part 1); The Hum and the Shiver; Long Black Curl

Warchild: Ash

Wendy Rule: Let the Wind Blow; Elemental Chant; The Circle Song

Woodland: Blood of the Moon; The Grove; Witch's Cross; First Melt; The Dragon; Secrets Told

Zero 7: In the Waiting Line

Biography

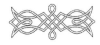

New York Times, Publishers Weekly, and *USA Today* bestselling author Yasmine Galenorn writes urban fantasy and paranormal romance, and is the author of over sixty books, including the Wild Hunt Series, the Fury Unbound Series, the Bewitching Bedlam Series, the Indigo Court Series, and the Otherworld Series, among others. She's also written nonfiction metaphysical books. She is the 2011 Career Achievement Award Winner in Urban Fantasy, given by RT Magazine. Yasmine has been in the Craft since 1980, is a shamanic witch and High Priestess. She describes her life as a blend of teacups and tattoos. She lives in Kirkland, WA, with her husband Samwise and their cats. Yasmine can be reached via her website at Galenorn.com.

Indie Releases Currently Available:

The Wild Hunt Series:
The Silver Stag
Oak & Thorns
Iron Bones
A Shadow of Crows

Bewitching Bedlam Series:
Bewitching Bedlam

Maudlin's Mayhem
Siren's Song
Witches Wild
Casting Curses
Blood Music
Blood Vengeance
Tiger Tails

Fury Unbound Series:
Fury Rising
Fury's Magic
Fury Awakened
Fury Calling
Fury's Mantle

Indigo Court Series:
Night Myst
Night Veil
Night Seeker
Night Vision
Night's End
Night Shivers

Otherworld Series:
Moon Shimmers
Harvest Song
Earthbound
Knight Magic
Otherworld Tales: Volume One
Tales From Otherworld: Collection One
Men of Otherworld: Collection One
Men of Otherworld: Collection Two
Moon Swept: Otherworld Tales of First Love
For the rest of the Otherworld Series, see Website

Chintz 'n China Series:
Ghost of a Chance
Legend of the Jade Dragon
Murder Under a Mystic Moon
A Harvest of Bones
One Hex of a Wedding
Holiday Spirits

Bath and Body Series (originally under the name India Ink):
Scent to Her Grave
A Blush With Death
Glossed and Found

Misc. Short Stories/Anthologies:
Mist and Shadows: Short Tales From Dark Haunts
Once Upon a Kiss (short story: Princess Charming)
Once Upon a Curse (short story: Bones)

Magickal Nonfiction:
Embracing the Moon
Tarot Journeys

For all other series, as well as upcoming work, see Galenorn.com

Made in the USA
Middletown, DE
10 November 2018